Minnie's

Antique and Curiosity Shoppe

☎ ☎ ☎

Lucinda Stein

Printed in Columbia, SC

ISBN-13: 978-1979935029

ISBN-10: 1979935025

☎ ☎ ☎

Other Books by Lucinda Stein

Dry Run, Oklahoma
2018 Oklahoma Book Award finalist

Jadeite's Journey
A young adult novel by Inkspell Publishing

Sanctuary: Family, Friends & Strangers
2015 Colorado Book Award finalist

Spiral of Darkness

Tattered Covers

Three Threads Woven
2010 WILLA finalist

Maggie's Way: The Story of a Defiant Pioneer Woman
Western Reflections Publishing

For my sister, Linda—
my favorite treasure hunter.

Breakout

-1985-

To my horror, my graduation reception was advertised to the public in my mother's storefront window. I hated living in the back of the store, a secondhand store no less. Sometimes a confused customer would wander through my bedroom like it was a showroom. More than once, my personal items were brought to the front register.

The day after my high school graduation, I packed the rest of my life into a tattered suitcase. Goodbye Watertown High School Class of '85. Goodbye stockroom bedroom. Goodbye taunts of Secondhand Rose. Three days later, I slid into the passenger seat of Billy's car ready to trade my hometown in South Dakota for the big city.

Billy glanced over, his grin filling the rearview mirror that tilted at an odd angle. "Ready to blow this town?"

I nodded, my face flush with a mix of excitement and last minute doubt. The engine backfired like a canon explosion, adding a measure of uncertainty to whether we'd make our destination. Billy and I had been friends since 7th grade. We were good buddies off on a quest. Contrary to rumors nothing romantic transpired between us. Truth was, I clung to Billy simply for the courage to leave home. I didn't care whether we lived in Minneapolis or its twin sibling, St. Paul, as long as my phone number was listed with a residential address in the telephone directory.

The needle of Billy's compass pointed to his direction in life. He was officially enrolled in culinary school in Minneapolis. With sun streaming through the windshield, we drove off in his rusted Pinto to a place where all our dreams promised to come true, my dream still to be determined. Bruce Springsteen's song, "Pink Cadillac," blared from the car speakers. Minnie, my mother, stood on the curb outside the store. She waved a scarlet and purple flag she'd made from old curtains for the express purpose of sending us off on our great adventure. I sank low in the seat. With my face hot with embarrassment, I swore I'd never return.

Abrupt Homecoming

-1990-

With a suitcase in each hand, I stood on Kemp Avenue and stared at the expansive display window that touted *Minnie's Antique and Curiosity Shoppe* in a decorative script font. I took a deep breath and entered. The sleigh bells on the door announced my untimely arrival.

Minnie lifted her gaze from a stack of paperwork, her dishwater-blonde hair caught in a loose bun and tied with a magenta scarf that hung to the middle of her back. Streaks of gray laced the tight hair at her temples. Even at 44, she was an attractive woman. She rushed from behind the counter as I set down my suitcases, the same two I'd taken on my great getaway from home five years earlier.

"Liza!" She enveloped me in her arms, hopping up and down all the while. Holding me by both shoulders, she kissed me on the forehead, chin, and both cheeks. I was either being blessed or in need of grave protection. A revenant could not have received a wilder welcome.

"Oh, baby, I'm so glad to see you." Minnie glanced behind me. "Where's Taylor? Guess he's parking the car."

"He didn't come." I held up a hand in warning. "Don't ask." The last thing I wanted to discuss was my divorce.

My mother studied me for a moment but refrained from asking any further questions. "I bet you're tired." She grabbed my luggage, and I automatically followed. I noted the building's odor. Antique stores possess their own unique elixir, a combination of must, dust, and old wood.

While I was living in Minneapolis, she'd sold the secondhand store and acquired the old JCPenney building on Kemp. The longtime staple of the Watertown business community had moved to the mall at the south end of town. Progress had afforded Minnie a good deal on the two-story building with a finished basement. Once again, I lived in a store.

This time I was officially one of the curiosities.

Once the site of JCPenney women's department, the balcony had become Minnie's private living space. My mother unhooked a heavy chain at the bottom of the wide linoleum stairway that led to the second floor. A laminated sign strung on the middle of the chain announced: PRIVATE RESIDENCE.

I followed her up the thirteen stairs and one landing that led to the balcony. Spacious, I could say that about the strange living arrangement. Near the center of the balcony, a loveseat faced two wicker chairs. A pair of mismatched end tables held turquoise Art Deco lamps. Seated, a person couldn't view the activity below on the main floor, but I'm sure curious customers would spot the tops of our heads if we used the area during business hours. I made a note to avoid that scenario.

My mother couldn't restrain herself and hugged me again. "I'm so glad you're back."

But was I?

Two beds stood at opposite ends of the balcony, each with secondhand dressers. Apparently, my mother had long anticipated my visit. An old-fashioned folding screen in the middle of the room gave an illusion of privacy once the beds were occupied. That didn't bother me. I'd sworn off men for a long time.

I glanced around the balcony. "Is there a bathroom up here?" After my four-hour drive, I needed one.

"Take the staircase to the main floor," Minnie said. "Head east, turn right, descend the stairway to the basement and make a left." She gave me everything but a roadmap.

I looked at her blankly.

"Stairs are great for the heart," she said.

I hurried down the first set of stairs leading from the balcony.

"Look at it as your daily workout." Her voice trailed above me. "Business, home, and personal gym, what more could a gal ask for?"

I made the main floor in record time and navigated the eighteen shallow steps to the basement. The brass railing slid through my hand. My desperate search was on for the much needed restroom. I located the room just in time, hidden in a back corner. Minnie had added a shower to the closet-size bathroom that originally contained only a stool and sink.

I had to give my mother credit. Not once did she press me for what went wrong with my marriage. Minnie never interrogated me. Perhaps she thought in time, I'd pour out my heart. But that wasn't happening.

In the looks department, I was the pepper to my mother's salt. I might have been adopted with my olive skin and dark hair in contrast to my fair-skinned, blonde mother. Minnie Murphy never once said I took after my father. She never spoke of him at all.

Once when I was eight, I had asked why she never mentioned him.

"You're *my* daughter, aren't you?" she said with that no-nonsense tone she used when irritated. "What more do you need to know?"

Up to the age of twelve, I convinced myself I was a product of immaculate conception. But in Junior High biology, Mr. Purdue made the case for reality with his graphic lesson on reproduction. Daydreams of my anonymous father included a con artist, a traveling salesman, a Catholic priest gone off the wagon so to speak, a doctor with a malpractice suit, a convict, a professional cat burglar, and a stoned hippie. The latter was probably my best bet.

The dresser's empty drawers gaped like hungry mouths. I unlatched my suitcase and dumped the contents on my bed. Minnie's last three letters fluttered to the floor.

In the apartment lobby in Minneapolis, my mother's letters had appeared weekly in the mailbox. Onion, basil, or mint often lifted from the stationary, whatever she might be working with in the kitchen. Her tomes ranged from five pages to fifteen, depending on her mood. I skipped over stories about customers unless a particularly intriguing account surfaced. She wrote about the weather (did she think I was in Florida?) her latest acquisitions for the store along with the bargain prices she'd paid, all the latest on the new mayor and the no-good city council member jailed for drunk driving Saturday night, the pitiful kid she'd caught shoplifting and was now trying to rehabilitate, the handsome stranger who browsed one day never to return, which bridge player considered leaving her husband, and the elderly church members who had passed away, promptly announced each morning at 9:30 a.m. on KWAT.

I skimmed her letters in the space of three minutes, penned a half page in return with mindless anecdotes about my job, and turned back to the television and my husband—if he had arrived home before midnight.

I retrieved the envelopes from the floor and slumped on the edge of the bed. At twenty-three, I had returned full circle.

Anyone in their right mind might wonder why I didn't stay in Minneapolis. Devastated after my divorce, I didn't feel I had a reason to live, let alone take advantage of what the city had to offer a single woman. My decision to move home was probably a form of self-punishment. Though Taylor was responsible for our breakup, somewhere deep inside I blamed myself for falling for him.

I recalled a folktale from a picture book I loved as a child. The strange lady who lived in the shoe had nothing on my mother. What better sentence but to boot myself back home?

The Barter Queen

Part of my penance included working at my mother's store. I unpacked a box from an estate sale and set the knickknacks on the counter. A variety of novelty salt and pepper shakers went to one side of the counter and nativity figurines to the other. At the bottom, I hit pay dirt. Vintage steel toys filled the bottom of the container: cars, tractors, and a red fire engine.

"I had to buy the whole box to get those," Minnie said. "By the way, what would you like to have for dinner tonight?"

"You know what I'm really hungry for?" I said. My mother was a great cook when she took the time to do it. "Your meatloaf special and green-bean casserole."

"That does sound good. Meatloaf it is." She dusted the tin toys with a cloth.

When your life falls apart, what's familiar turns to comfort. Minnie fixed my favorite foods and told me I could borrow her rundown pickup anytime she wasn't chasing an estate sale. Knowing Minnie, she must have warned everyone in town—I shiver at the thought—against inquiring, consoling, or referring to my divorce because no one ever did.

My mother's given name was actually Margaret, but after a youthful stint in California in the mid-sixties, she changed her name to *Min nee*, the Dakota Sioux word for water. The Pacific Ocean impressed Margaret, and somewhere along the line, she acquired a romantic passion for anything Native American. Water symbolized life, and to my mother, the new name represented the new Margaret. After renaming her father's business, Min nee's Secondhand Store, locals figured the wayward young woman had a spelling handicap and assumed the sign should read Minnie. And so it stuck to this day.

About a year after I returned, I quit mooning over my failed marriage, but I couldn't say I was happy. Resigned to my fate, but not content. I couldn't find a job that compared to the one I'd left behind—a receptionist at a legal office—so to my chagrin, I continued to work for my mother.

One afternoon Elmer Peterson approached the counter where Minnie tallied sales for the month.

I glanced up from straightening the end display across from the register. All the vintage bottle openers displayed on the top shelf were now organized exclusively by wood, Bakelite, and metal style. Old pop caps filled baskets on the second shelf. I hadn't made it to the third and fourth shelf, which were cluttered with an unlikely assortment of odd Frankoma mugs and Fiesta cups, some in pristine condition, and some with slight chips at the edges.

Elmer swept isolated strands of hair across his balding crown and set his jaw. "Let's make a deal."

My mother raised one eyebrow and waited for Elmer's offer.

A short man, Elmer raised his chin to meet Mother's eyes. "The Ten Star GT."

"Speak English, Elmer." Minnie narrowed her eyes.

"The amber Lucite bowling ball, the one with the Elk Lodge logo inside. What kind of deal will you do on that?" His clenched jaw meant business.

"Adding to your collection?"

I could hear the gears spinning in my mother's head. She was the queen of barter. Elmer had once confided he owned a collection of forty bowling balls which he kept in the basement of the local bowling alley, unbeknownst to his wife, Agnes. He needed another bowling ball like I needed another mother, but like all vintage connoisseurs, collecting becomes a lovely obsession. It was all about the thrill of the hunt.

"Hmm," Minnie murmured and placed her index finger against her lips. "That's a rare one, Elmer. Came from an estate sale. They found it in the attic."

"Uh huh." He shifted his weight and maintained his stare.

"You still have those chickens?" She knew for a fact that Elmer kept chickens on his farm three miles from town.

"Sure do." He frowned, probably wondering what she was up to.

"Liza and I enjoy a good egg or two in the morning. Would sure like to know we have a year's supply of breakfast eggs and a chicken once a month for frying." Minnie stepped back from the counter and waited, all part of the barter dance.

Elmer pursed his lips and stared at the tin ceiling, probably deliberating on whether the trade would go unnoticed by Agnes.

He extended his hand over the counter. "It's a deal."

"I prefer brown eggs." Minnie pumped his hand.

Elmer left to gather his prize from the middle of the store.

Mother glanced at me and smiled. "Now that's how it's done."

I nodded and turned back to the shelf. Barter was not my thing. My idea of a good deal consisted of offering the customer a 10% discount for cash. I suppose that made me the cash and carry queen.

"Just look at all these recipes for eggs." Minnie flipped through a vintage Betty Crocker cookbook she kept behind the counter for times when business was slow. "Twenty ways to Sunday. Omelets, soufflés, casseroles, *woo wee*, we're going to eat good."

I had to admit her bartering served a purpose. The antique trade didn't render a huge profit and after overhead costs, bartering brought us practical things we needed to live. Besides food, it might be mechanic repair, fixing the old boiler, or for my mother, even her weekly manicure. Minnie had learned the art of bartering in her father's secondhand store. Even as a teenager, she was a pro.

Minnie asked me what I wanted for my twenty-fourth birthday.

"Oil paint and an easel." I had my eyes on the vintage oak easel that came in earlier in the week.

"Pursuing your creative urges. How wonderful!" Minnie danced a jig before the storefront window, twirling her full ankle-length skirt and flailing her arms in the air. In my mother's way of looking at life, she saw an opportunity for her daughter to explore her artsy, loosey-goosey, inner soul.

In fact, we were a study in contrast. Typically, the daughter tests the limits of the parent. But in our case, I proved to be the conservative one, and she filled the role of wild child.

The world of art had been introduced to me in high school through Watertown's infamous art instructor, Frances Brank. One day Miss Brank took me aside after class.

"You have natural talent," she whispered, not wanting to cause jealousy among the students who stayed after school and worked on projects. "But you have to devote time and energy to art if you want to succeed."

I nodded, surprised at the unexpected compliment. "Yes, ma'am," I said for the sake of manners.

But I hadn't taken her advice and chose to use my class time to do easy projects like covering Tommy Jensen in a full-body cast with strips of plaster. Miss Brank stepped in to ensure I left adequate holes for his eyes and nose. I don't recall if we painted the hardened cast. But the girls in my class dripped with envy. Who wouldn't want to apply and smooth plaster strips over the buff body of the Watertown Arrows quarterback?

I requested the easel and paint out of boredom. I'd come home with the proverbial "tail between my legs" and was in need of a diversion. I checked out books on painting techniques from the Watertown Regional Library, and true to Miss Brank's advice, soon improved my artistic skill with hours of practice. One early evening after the store had closed, Minnie caught me painting under the natural light from the storefront window.

I paused. She cocked her head and stared at my rendition of Lake Kampeska at sunset. I'd discovered an old postcard in the ephemera section of the store and used it as my inspiration.

"You don't like it?" I asked.

"Oh, it's very realistic," she said as she narrowed her eyes.

"And?" I braced myself.

She squinted at my canvas. "We have cameras for realistic images. Wouldn't you rather put your own impression on it?" She studied my face. "Don't you ever want to cut loose?"

My chin jutted out; I could feel it. "Paint your own pictures, and I'll paint mine my way."

"Touché," she said and walked away, singing, "*I'll do it my way.*"

There were times I wanted to strangle my mother.

Minnie rushed up to me as I dusted a collection of ironstone. "He's here. That good-looking cowboy I wrote you about."

I replaced the white pitcher on the shelf. It took me a moment to recall a passing reference to a handsome stranger in one of her many letters. "That's nice, Mother." At twenty-four, I was repulsed by my mother's interest in the opposite sex. Like most adult children, I preferred to remain ignorant that such things existed in my mother's world.

"Come on." She tugged at my sleeve. "You have to see him. He looks like the Marlboro man."

Reluctantly, I tossed my dusting cloth on the shelf and followed. Minnie paused in the middle of the aisle and nudged me forward. "There, in the western artifacts." She twirled around and strode to the back of the store. I strolled over to the western memorabilia aisle. "Good afternoon," I said, cheerfully. "Anything I can help you with?"

The tall cowboy glanced up and smiled. His white Stetson definitely made an impression, his silver hair remarkably thick, the western-yoked shirt bright blue and tidy, and I have to admit, his boots shone like the sun over Lake Kampeska on a summer day.

"Just browsing," he said politely and returned to perusing the aisle.

My mind recalculated the total package. Without the Stetson, he might reach 5'10" in his western boots. A gap stood in for an eyetooth, and his wrinkles radiated from his eyes like a starburst. His weak chin and pale skin didn't exactly make him into the Marlboro man in the cigarette ads.

14

Later, Minnie caught up with me. "So, what did you think?" Her eyes widened in anticipation of my reaction.

"Truthfully, Mother," I began, "he's just an old cowpoke with a narrow ass."

She shook her head. "He's good looking in a rugged sense of the word." That faraway look she often got took over her face. "Bet he's up at dawn and riding the range under a beautiful sunrise. The stories that man could tell."

"Did you forget this side of the state is *farm* country?"

She fluttered a hand in the air like a parade queen. "He might be visiting from west of the Missouri. That's ranch country through and through."

I conceded with a nod. Better to drop the subject than listen to an ongoing diatribe. Minnie straightened her denim skirt, and retreated in her knee-high moccasins, presumably to interview the man on that very point.

A dreamer and non-conformist in a variety of ways, my mother retained many of the Midwestern values of her childhood. Every Sunday morning, Minnie could be found in the front pew of St. Martin's Church. Once a month, she played bridge with the minister's wife and other women from the Ladies' Club. I often wondered if she offered the ladies regular opportunities to practice the Christian virtues of patience and forgiveness.

My mother also took front row seat at the Farmer's Bar and Grill on Saturday nights.

"A bar is like a church," she was fond of saying, "they're both filled with sinners who celebrate the life God gave them, sometimes fall asleep in their seat, and start the next week with the best intentions."

That was only one of Minnie's unique philosophies. Many newfound friends from the bar materialized at our place Sunday

15

morning. Those stray cats, as I liked to call them, were given a place to sleep and breakfast the next day. One morning, I discovered Jay Taylor, a recently fired janitorial assistant, asleep in the vintage blanket section. The overpowering stench of alcohol threatened to taint the camp blanket beneath him. I literally ran to find Minnie.

"You can't bring drunk men home!" I stood arms akimbo.

"Just until tomorrow," she said. "I called his cousin, Henry, from Clear Lake. He'll pick him up tomorrow morning."

"Thank goodness." I walked off in a huff.

A month later, I found a young runaway sharing coffee with Minnie over the breakfast table. "Good morning, dear. This is Abbie," my mother said. "Abbie, this is my daughter, Liza."

Because I was no hypocrite, I refused to say "nice to meet you."

"Morning," I said at last. I scarfed down breakfast and excused myself—Minnie had taught me manners. With coffee cup in hand, I retreated to the front of the store. Twenty minutes later, my mother joined me at the counter.

She held up one hand while the words still formed in my mouth. "Her stepfather beat her. I think Ruth will take the girl in until she can find a job and get on her feet."

I remained mute. I couldn't bear the thought of a young woman being abused. Thank the Lord for Ruth Hopkins. The local spinster, we still used that word in the privacy of our homes, was a woman with a heart of gold. Rumor had it that Ruth had a rough life living with her bachelor brother until he died from alcoholism nine years earlier. Minnie firmly believed a person's calling arose from what they suffered.

I cornered other strays that year when Minnie wasn't around and warned them they'd have to find other accommodations within 24 hours. "We're running a business here, after all," I'd say. "I know Minnie means well, but truth is, the city would sue us if they discovered we took in boarders." I had no idea whether any such city ordinances existed. If the latest unexpected resident looked skeptical, I'd whisper, "Minnie's been having some mental problems lately, and I'm afraid I have my hands full." That last part always worked. Evidently, it wasn't a big leap to imagine my mother with something wrong with her head.

Paul Bunyan and Other Tall Tales

Holly Jones plunked the 1930 Remington typewriter before me, the carriage-return lever pointing at my mother's picture beneath the glass counter. The photo highlighted Minnie in a tie-dye sundress holding me at three-months-old. I had never seen a photograph of my father, never heard his name, and would go to my grave wondering about my genetic benefactor.

"It's a beauty," I said. A bargain at sixty-five dollars, the Remington would bring an easy hundred in the Twin Cities.

Holly whispered, "I fell in love with it at first sight." She glanced up and looked me straight in the eyes. "It's a little pricey, though."

The prices we set at Minnie's Antique and Curiosity Shoppe didn't allow a lot of haggling. Ten percent was the maximum we'd dicker. Because I was saving to buy my own house, I didn't budge on the price. "In Minneapolis, it might go for a hundred and twenty."

She stood her ground. "This isn't the Cities."

"You're right. In Watertown, we sell lower but we also have a slimmer profit margin."

She thought about that for a moment, her jaw jutting in indecision. Her thick single braid hung below her waist, silver winding through her brown hair like the fabric of a tweed coat. She was my age, twenty-four, but her premature gray hair and austere hairdo made her look older.

Holly and I had more in common than I cared to admit. Outside of church services, I never wore anything but Levi's or sweatpants. Some days I left my long hair loose. On rare occasions I used a curling iron to style my black locks. But more often than not, the ease of pulling my hair into a ponytail won out over fashion.

Holly drew out a change purse and unfolded her bills. Once again I was reminded how much Holly acted like a little old lady. To be expected, I suppose, for someone raised by elderly parents. The first time I met them I assumed they were her grandparents, but Holly quickly corrected me. I had always envied Holly, despite the age of her parents. She had what I wanted: two biological parents living in a traditional two-story house, a mother who dressed matronly, and a father so jolly it made me want to crawl in his lap like a child.

Holly counted out three twenties and one five, even-steven. At the antique store, we figured tax into the price to keep everything in even amounts. That method eliminated the need for coins in making change.

Holly leaned in and confided, "This typewriter wouldn't have lasted long in your store."

I raised my eyebrows emphatically. "The time to buy…"

Holly joined in and we sang in singsong unison, "is-when-you-first-see-it." Any antique aficionado will attest to treasure regret, returning later only to find that special item has been sold.

Holly's obsession with vintage typewriters was understandable. She was a writer. Short stories, free verse, and a few ambitious starts at novels made up her literary repertoire. Refusing word processing, Holly insisted on pounding her work out on an old Smith-Corona. An editor's jaw would drop at the sight of her antiquated method of submission, not to mention a shake of the head at the impossibility of timely revisions, but thankfully, that problem never arose. Holly never submitted her work. She never finished a piece. "Needs more revising," she'd say if pressed.

I handed her a handwritten receipt. "Thanks, Holly. Say hi to your folks."

"Call me if you get anymore in."

"I'll keep an eye out."

We were grateful for our regulars. They kept us in business along with the seasonal customers from out of town—the out-of-state relatives who penciled in an annual visit to our shop and those wise pheasant hunters who rewarded their wives' patience with gifts upon return from a warrior weekend.

With her prized possession clutched in both hands, Holly departed, a ring visible on her back jean pocket where a chewing-tobacco can had etched a circle over time.

Neither of us had dated in high school, another thing we had in common. My mother claimed I was a late bloomer. Not until after graduation did people call me pretty. Holly, bless her heart, was nice but as plain as unbuttered Wonder Bread. In another way, Holly and I proved polar opposites. She had never married. I had—but rued the day it happened.

Monday mornings didn't bring in much of a crowd. I sipped lukewarm coffee and studied a second photograph preserved beneath the glass counter. My mother's sun-bleached hair swirled in soft blonde curls halfway to her waist. She wore an embroidered peasant blouse that revealed a butterfly tattoo flitting on her bare shoulder. A live parrot perched on the other shoulder. The year was 1965. Need I say more? My mother was definitely a product of the hippie era. Though born and raised in a small town, Minnie had managed a temporary reprieve from South Dakota when she met up with the peace and love crowd in San Francisco for a year. In 1966, she returned to her hometown with a different perspective on life and a babe in tow. The mysterious father never materialized. That baby, of course, was me.

The bell on the front door jingled. I glanced up from arranging a window display and found Raymond Standing Rock looking in on me.

"Hi, Ray." He made a definite impression in his fringed leather jacket, alligator-skin boots, and black cowboy hat. He held a leather bag at his side.

"Good morning, Liza. How's it going with Grandma's dusty relics?"

"The middle-aged keep buying what their mothers threw out," I retorted.

"Hal-loo!" Minnie hurried over to greet Ray. She never lost her fascination with all things Native American, and Ray, being a Dakota Sioux from the Sisseton area, fit that fixation. Every few months, he'd bring in beadwork for Minnie's perusal. My mother had purchased Indian crafts from him since the days of the secondhand store, even though, looking back, that didn't seem like a great fit. Curious, I followed the pair to the counter where Ray laid out his latest merchandise.

"How've you been, Minnie?" he asked.

"You know me, always busy." She lowered her face slightly and looked up with a demure smile. Minnie always flirted with Ray. The man had a strong face and broad shoulders, and with Minnie's obsession with anything Indian, I could understand the attraction.

They got down to business, and Minnie examined the objects before her, five pair of colorful earrings, a beaded bolero and matching key fob, and three pair of baby moccasins. My taste leaned toward the tiny leather booties decorated with bright beads.

Minnie studied the middle pair of moccasins. A slight crinkle appeared between her brows as she glanced up at Ray. He gave a knowing look, though I can't say his expression changed any. She picked up one of the moccasins and turned it gently in her hands. At last, she placed it down with another look at Ray. "I'll take it all."

"Two fifty."

My mother opened the register. Like most things in the store, the register was vintage, an ornate Seymour Detroit Brass. She placed three fifties and five twenties in his palm, counting it out like a bank teller.

"See you in a few months, Minnie. You, too, Liza."

"See ya, Ray," we said in unison. I hated it when we did that. The bells rang as Ray left the store, his long braid trailing down his leather jacket.

Minnie picked up the same little moccasin she'd examined earlier. "Look at this."

I examined the shoe. "It appears worn." It wasn't the usual newly-made moccasins that our local Indians crafted by hand.

"You're right." She pointed at the beadwork near the toe. "See these mustard-colored beads?"

I looked closer and nodded.

"They're called greasy-yellow beads. They're very old."

My first thought was my mother had pulled a fast one. I considered why Ray wouldn't have known their value, and then I recalled the look he gave Mother. "Do you think he knew?"

She shrugged and looked away.

"You could get a lot of money for those." I had another thought. "Maybe they belong in a museum."

"I'm keeping this pair for myself," she said and strode off to the rear of the store.

Years ago, my mother told me Ray was a medicine man, a respected person among his tribe. "He's a skillful horseman and rides like the wind across the *Coteau des Prairies*," she embellished. "Like in the days before white settlers arrived, he retains the ancient customs of the Sioux Indians. He sees great visions."

The fanciful story appealed to my childish imagination, but as I grew older, I recognized the tall tales my mother liked to invent. Minnie definitely had a strong imagination, and it never faded over the years. Just the week before, she came up with a new story after she returned from playing bridge with the ladies.

"That June Johansson is quite the card shark," she'd said, removing her coat. "Fingers, I call her. You know, she once worked in Vegas back when she was young and quite a looker." Minnie slipped off her shoes. "When her skill at cards became apparent to the management, they promoted her to dealer. Between her sharp mind and nimble fingers, she soon gained the attention of the casino owner. He eventually asked her to marry him. That's when she decided to buy a bus ticket and roll home to South Dakota."

June was married to George Johansson, a quiet man who ran a local dry cleaners. I took the bait. "Why didn't she marry the casino owner? She would have been a rich woman."

Minnie tossed a conspiratorial wink. "Because he was connected to the *Mafia*."

I guess that made George attractive in a safe, conservative way if one believed my mother's tale.

My mother brimmed and overflowed with such stories. She wasn't a gossip because I never heard her repeat these stories to anyone else. Maybe it helped her pass the time or added a dimension of excitement lacking in her life, I'll probably never know. But Minnie wove stories as a spinner weaves cloth.

"Looks like you found something," I said with a smile.

The teenage girl set a candle on the counter, along with a Ball canning jar full of peppermint tea.

"That will be six dollars."

"What about tax?" the girl said. Her shoulder-length hair had been teased into that big-hair look, her bangs feathered.

"It's all included."

"I like that." She left humming Phil Collins's "Another Day in Paradise."

Minnie strolled down the main aisle of the store. "I told you they buy my things."

In the front corner of the store, my mother displayed some of her own handiwork. She made tie-dyed t-shirts and homemade candles. Minnie also had an entire line of bandana scarf creations: handmade pillows, block quilts with up to five different bandana colors, and bandana "napkins" tucked into Levi pockets cut from jeans. She included an extensive line of organic tea sold from clear glass canisters. Local gossip circulated that marijuana filled some of the jars. Watertown was a small conservative town and my mother the closest living-breathing connection to the hippie era—though long passed—many of them would ever know.

A young man in his early twenties entered the store and strode straight to the 25' glass display case that lined the east wall. Minnie's Antique and Curiosity Shoppe stayed true to its name with a special section of the macabre and the just plain weird. I considered the case a waste of floor space since customers rarely purchased these items. Minnie claimed the display drew in business, but I never saw any sales connected to those curious lookie-loos.

The collection included things that gave me the creeps when I thought about their former use, like ankle shackles and antique scalpels. The Jackalope, a legendary bunny with antlers, was a common South Dakota joke that tourists actually believed. On the other hand, I thought both the mummified cat along with the taxidermy version that Minnie purchased at an estate sale just plain gross. Old Mrs. Fellers had commissioned Albert Haining to eternally preserve her beloved cat, Tiger.

I begged my mother to get rid of the bone trumpet made from a human thigh bone, but she refused. The seller—that perpetuator of nightmares—had actually demonstrated its use by blowing until he sounded a precise note. That item allegedly came from Africa, but I feared it may have come from a mass murderer, who was, perhaps, the seller himself.

KELO television from Sioux Falls featured our curiosity aisle in a three-minute filler piece on the ten o'clock news. Minnie insisted it was only time before *60 Minutes* would appear on our doorstep. A few minutes later, the young man captivated with the oddities walked out without making a purchase, just as I predicted.

The exercise-wear fashion trend fit my sensibilities like Katharine Hepburn's rubber bathing cap in *Philadelphia Story*. (Minnie exposed me to movies of all eras, believing it gave a rounded cultural experience.) I was comfortable in sports bras, hoodies, and sweatpants found at Saturday morning garage sales. My other go-to clothes consisted of jeans, baggy flannel shirts, and boxy oversized t-shirts, my long hair, more often than not, caught up in a big scrunchie.

"Why do you hide that cute figure of yours?" Minnie often lamented. "You might as well wear a gunny sack."

"It's the style, Mother."

"You could at least tuck in your shirt so it looks like you have a waistline. Men appreciate a gal's figure, you know."

"Not looking for a guy. I've told you that a million times."

Minnie's own fashion style ran as eclectic as her personality. She wore long, hippie-style skirts and peasant blouses when she could find them in the secondhand stores, jeans but always with a low-cut blouse to show off her womanly figure; vintage dresses from the 50s through the 70s; and an occasional black cocktail dress on the weekend. A person might assume with Minnie's penchant for the bar life on Saturday night that she was on the "prowl," but other than an occasional dinner out with a gentleman friend, *her* emphasis on friend, she never brought anyone home, never spent the night away, and to my knowledge, never had a real date.

That made two of us with the exception of the disaster she fixed me up with the next day. What girl in her twenties wanted her mother to arrange a date? What girl of any age, for that matter? At the front counter, I had just wrapped a gold-rimmed Rockingham serving plate for Mrs. Butler. I was admiring the green and white Spode china, decorated with an exotic bird set in the midst of flowers and scrolls, when a tall man approached the counter.

"Liza?" The guy possessed a solid masculine face that was far too solemn. His arms hung limp at his sides as if he didn't quite know what to do with them. He looked to be in his late twenties.

He knew my name? "May I help you?"

"I'm Paul Bunyan."

"You're kidding, right? You're not that tall." I smirked.

A hint of annoyance swept across his face. "Yeah, I get that all the time."

"Sorry. Are you looking for something in particular?"

He produced a hesitant smile. "Our mothers know each other. From high school, I guess. Your mother said stop in anytime. Liza would love to have coffee with you."

Inwardly, I seethed. *She did, did she*? Before I could think of a reason to disappear, he asked, "Would this afternoon work? I'm in town just for the day."

"Well…" I stalled for what to say next, never equipped for spur of the moment situations.

"Hello, Paul." Minnie spun up at that opportune moment. "I see you've met Liza."

"I was just asking her—"

Minnie stepped behind the counter. "I'll take over, Liza. Go ahead."

I glared at my mother, but she averted her eyes.

"Great," Paul said. "Shall we?"

"Where's your blue o—"

"Beautiful blue sky," Minnie interjected and saved me from my smart mouth and a reference to a specific kind of bovine. "Beautiful day, isn't it, Liza?"

"Oh, yes. It certainly is." Turned sideways to Mr. Bunyan, I tossed a look that conveyed my true feelings to my mother.

We walked three blocks to the Sioux River Café where Paul ordered two coffees and apple pies ala mode without bothering to ask if I drank coffee or whether I wanted a slice of pie. I soon learned Paul was an insurance salesman from Mitchell.

"I have my own office," he said with a thrust of his chest.

"How nice." That prideful announcement poked at my weak spot for having accomplished nothing in my life, and like a zoo tiger getting prodded, I nearly growled, "That's wonderful."

"You and your mother are great businesswomen," he said before I could come up with an excuse to get back to the store. "Minnie's is famous all the way to Mitchell."

"Famous?" I said with a note of sarcasm.

"Well, with antique lovers, that is." He blushed slightly. He might have been attractive if he wasn't so bipolar—one minute full of himself, the next insecure.

I came from a family of business people, though their ventures never proved lucrative. My grandfather had run Murphy's Secondhand Store a block off Kemp, the chief business district in Watertown at that time. My mother, twenty-years-old, found him limp on the receiving-room floor one afternoon. His sudden death left her in charge of the hobbling business. Minnie soon discovered Elizabeth Murphy's job as dental assistant had kept the finances intact up to the time her mother had passed away five years earlier. The bookkeeping said it all.

"I really need to get back." I glanced at my wrist. The watch displayed the wrong time as I knew it would. The piece was a store item in need of repair that I'd put on purely for its jewelry appeal. I loved the turquoise and silver band.

"Would you like to go out for a movie sometime?" He looked almost fearful.

I leaned in and lowered my voice. "I'm sorry, but I have a boyfriend."

"But your mother said—"

"My mother doesn't know about him. You see, he's, uh, older and I'm afraid she'd disapprove."

"Oh, I didn't know. I'm...I'm sorry to have bothered you. I certainly didn't know." His face reddened to a bright beet hue.

I patted his hand. "It's okay. Mothers get things wrong sometimes, don't they?"

Like a gentleman, he walked me back to the store, but maybe it was only because his vehicle was parked nearby. We didn't talk. Crestfallen, he said goodbye outside the storefront windows, and I marched into the store on a mission to find Minnie.

I found her in the radio and clock aisle, humming. She glanced up, "How was th—"

"Don't ever fix me up with a date again."

"I thought you'd like him. He's conservative like you and he has a career. Paul doesn't drink."

I'd given up men—and wine—ever since my return home. "I prefer to choose my own men, thank you, and if you ever try to set me up again, I'll join a convent."

"We're Lutheran, Liza."

I could feel my pinched lips tightening over my eyeteeth.

"I just want you to be happy."

She meant what she said, but with Minnie, I had learned to stand my ground or suffer unwanted consequences. "You're perfectly happy without a man in *your* life." At the look on her face, I instantly regretted my words. My mother had never looked so sad. Or was it something else that clouded her face?

In regards to my own life, dating would only dust off the sorry mess of my divorce and reveal what I wanted to forget. That August Susan Hendrickson discovered three jaw bones of a dinosaur jutting from a cliff near Faith, South Dakota. Archeologists dubbed the 65 million-year-old specimen Sue after its discoverer. The newspapers reported the fossil turned out to be the largest T-Rex ever unearthed. Unlike Sue, the jaw bones of my unsuccessful marriage would be best left unexcavated.

Burgers and Brews

Holly Jones strode into the store, wearing her signature faded jeans and flannel shirt, no makeup. Bare blonde eyelashes gave her a slightly alien appearance. Though we'd been classmates, I wouldn't say we had been the best of friends, but we made small talk in the classes we shared and occasionally went to a movie Saturday night. Back then, we were both shy, neither with a date on the horizon.

"Hey, Holly," I said. "How's the writing going?"

"Working on a short story." She fidgeted with her hands.

I assumed as a writer she read a lot. "We have a big book collection." Since my divorce, I'd taken up reading some of the titles in our vintage book section. Television bored me, especially on our 24" set.

"Mother has lots of books." Holly dismissed my suggestion with a wave of the wrist. "I heard you're a painter now."

With Minnie as my mother, there were few secrets allotted me. "I'm trying."

"I'm looking for another typewriter, but it has to work," Holly said.

One thing you could say about Holly, hers was a functional obsession.

"Let's take a look," I said. Minnie continually added to our inventory, attending yard sales and estate sales on a weekly basis. Holly followed me down the aisle and nearly ran into me when I stopped short at the display of typewriters.

"I want it for my writing," she said, looking longingly at the old machines.

"You should get a computer. It's so easy to correct mistakes in word processing. With a typewriter you have to retype—"

She set her jaw. "I want to do it like the classic authors."

"Okie dokie." I knew when to quit. "This old Smith Corona still works. Minnie used it a while back."

"Ooh, look at the keys." She fingered them like fine china. "They're the old black-and-white keys with chrome rims. I'll take it."

"Good choice." I lugged it to the front.

"Hey, you wanna get a burger and beer tonight?" Holly said as she dug folded bills from her jean's pocket. She never carried a purse.

"Ah, okay. A burger would be good." I wasn't exactly sure what we had to talk about since we were only acquaintances and from so long ago. But what could it hurt? I'd been living pretty reclusive up to that point.

"Meet you at Maeve's Burger and Brew up the street. Say six?"

"Sure. See you at six."

Was that protrusion below her lip a wad of tobacco? Holly smiled and carted off her treasure. I studied the Copenhagen circle on her back pocket. At least I wouldn't have to endure a bunch of girlie frou-frou nonsense. Although I used blush and gloss and occasionally styled my hair, I didn't want to talk about dating or anything remotely connected to guys. Holly and I had the arts in common. That would have to do.

In Watertown, bars had the corner on the best burgers, fries, and onion rings. That evening I beat Holly to Maeve's, so I quickly found an inconspicuous table to the side. I ordered a Coke and waited. Although the bar had few customers at that hour, the scent of hops and fermented grains hung on the air, a permanent odor leached into the walls. A few minutes later, a fit-looking guy strolled through the bar and nodded as he headed to the pool table. I smiled politely and looked away. Holly rushed in at ten after six and gushed in apology.

"Had a new client call. Sorry, I'm late." Holly wore the same faded jeans but with a different plaid shirt, red this time. We could have been twins. My worn jeans had a rip at the knee, and I also sported an extra-large red plaid shirt.

The barmaid took Holly's order for a Budweiser on tap, and we ordered cheeseburgers and fries. Holly requested her fries extra crispy.

"Client?"

"I have a cleaning service." She took a swig of beer. "Mostly business offices. I work evenings and have the days off for my writing."

This girl was serious about her writing. "Wow, I'm impressed, Hol."

"It's not on the same level as your store, but it pays the bills." Holly set her mug on the coaster. "Still living with your mother?"

Ouch. In that moment I saw myself as a loser. No longer the girl who lived in a store, I had progressed to a grown woman dependent on her mother. The thought plunged to the cellar of my stomach. I didn't correct her on the ownership of the antique store. I was a mere peon worker for my mother, but that was too depressing to admit. "Where do you live, Holly?"

"I have a small Craftsman in the northwest part of town. There's a big yard and I plant a garden every summer." A wistful look took over Holly's face. "One of my favorite things is the open porch where I like to write in warm weather."

Our burgers and fries arrived. The barmaid slapped a bottle of ketchup on the table.

"Anything else I can bring you, ladies?"

"Mustard?" Holly looked at me.

I shook my head.

"Guess not. Thanks, Jean."

"Your house—that's great, Holly." I played with the Budweiser napkin beneath my Coke. "Wish I had my own place."

"You could save up for a down payment. It took me several years, but I did it."

"That's my plan but I should look for a second job or my nest egg will never amount to anything."

"You can do it, Liza. You just have to be disciplined."

Was I disciplined? Seemed like I followed whims that never seemed to go anywhere. I had never planned for anything in my life. I looked across the table and watched Holly bite into her burger. Maybe I could learn something from her. She made plans and followed through with them.

"Aren't you glad we're not in high school anymore?" Holly said, wiping ketchup from her mouth with a Michelob napkin.

I laughed. "More than I can say."

"Being in high school is like an actor off stage, you're just waiting for the real thing to start."

"Hmm." I nodded and thought about that. Unfortunately, that still described me.

* * *

The next week, I browsed the local want ads and found no listings for receptionists of any kind. I refused to be a waitress. Didn't have the patience to deal with people's demanding palates. Housecleaning, nope, not for me. Not enough patience for tidiness, either. So irony stepped in when I was hired at JCPenney at the mall. Now I'd work in the new JCP and sleep in the old. Transportation would be an issue. Days when Minnie needed the '55 Ford pickup, I'd be forced to bicycle to work or catch a ride with another employee. I informed Minnie I'd still work at the antique store on my days off.

"Happiness walks on busy feet," Minnie responded to my news. My mother had little quotes for everything.

"I'm saving up for a house." There it was out in the open. Maybe saying it would reinforce my determination.

She looked a little taken back but soon recovered. "Good for you, honey."

Surely she knew that was a long way off in the future.

"The starting point of all achievement is desire. Napoleon Hill said that." Minnie waltzed off to greet one of the ladies from her bridge group. I suspected she had a book of quotes hidden somewhere, but I never found it. Knowing Minnie, she probably had them all committed to memory.

What I liked most about working in the department store was that all the merchandise was new, brand spanking new. No former owners. No moldy odor carried from dusty attics and dim garages. Clean, spotless, and never used goods, clothes smelling of freshly dyed fabric. I even enjoyed the price tags and unpacked boxes. Everything was sparkling new. For the first six weeks in the women's department, I worked on a natural high. All of my life, I'd been around previously used merchandise. Officially part of the United States of America consumer-oriented society, I relished my new position. I was in heaven.

I tugged one arm into my jean jacket and peered out the glass door of JCPenney, regretting Minnie's trip to an estate sale that day. The late October wind gusted across the mall parking lot, leaves and fast-food wrappers airborne in the blustery gale. An empty pop can rolled under a sedan. As the bruised sky warned of heavy rain to come, I stared at my bike locked in the nearby rack. If I pedaled very fast...

Laura Ferguson from women's lingerie joined me at the door. "We're in for a storm, that's for sure."

I glanced over and nodded. A regular fixture of the place, Laura had worked at Penneys for over twenty-five years, including the old store on Kemp. Her silver hair was lacquered stiffly in place.

"Did you ride your bike today?" she asked.

"Afraid so." The wind was spitting moisture and working itself up for a bigger show.

Ellen Johnson and Faye Anderson joined our weather appraisal. Both women worked in the shoe department and had the same shift that week as mine. Faye wore a cashmere-looking sweater over a shape-skimming dress that aptly showed off her legs. I preferred dress pants, a giant step up for me. Faye had been the talk of the employee lounge since her engagement two weeks ago. She looked about twenty. Laura took one look at the sky and dug in her purse for her hairdo protector. "Heard we're in for a few inches of rain." She deftly unfolded the clear plastic, canopied her hair, and secured it with a quick tie under the chin. Faye glanced at me. "You didn't ride your bike today, did you?"

"I think I can ride it out. I'm in pretty good shape."

"Nonsense, I'll give you a ride home."

"I'd appreciate it if you could drop me off at my mother's store."

"Minnie's Antique and Curiosity Shoppe on Kemp," Laura said. "Liza lives there with her mother."

I cringed. That was something I really didn't want Faye to know.

In grade school, we lived in a corner of the freight receiving area of the inherited secondhand store that bordered the alley. The space was partitioned off to make a one-room apartment with a tiny kitchen, a cozy sitting room that served a dual purpose with a hide-a-bed that made out each evening for our bed, and a shower and toilet literally in the supply closet. As a young child, I never thought about it as a deficit. I spent most of my time in the main store. The latest displays, the new acquisitions, and the colorful characters we called customers, along with my mother's skill at bartering and bullshit kept my childhood interesting.

But the secondhand store became a thing of resentment as I grew older. By the time high school arrived, I was known as the girl who lived in a store. Boys called me Secondhand Rose.

I sheepishly shrugged my shoulders at Faye's wide-eyed look.

Faye recovered. "Let's head out to the car before it gets any worse."

I obediently slogged to Faye's car and avoided a glance at Laura for fear of sticking out my tongue at her.

Apparently I couldn't escape being cast as the girl who lived in the store.

Clothespins and Pinheads

S aturday was one of the store's busiest days, and I was even more determined to save every last cent my mother paid me. At the mall, my days off changed every month, our manager insisting everyone rotate weekends and night shifts. I carried my coffee to the front counter where Minnie filled a glass canister with wooden clothespins. "Whatcha doing?"

"Don't they look nice in this jar?" Minnie wore a jade satin blouse with an Oriental print. "Grace Humphrey brought these in from her grandmother's house. They're moving Rosemary into town next week."

The clothespins were the older type without springs, carved round knobs at the top of each pin.

"Look at this." Minnie held one up for me to examine.

"What am I looking for?" I yawned. After working the evening shift the previous night, I couldn't fall asleep for hours afterwards. The robust vapors of Folgers beckoned, and I took another sip.

"Look closer. See the name written in pencil?"

It said Shirley. Minnie held up another that read Ruth.

"The clothespins came from the days before Grace's grandmother married. Rosemary shared an apartment in St. Paul with two other young women, and they wrote their names on the pins to keep them separate."

I sat on the stool behind the counter and finished my coffee.

"I guess one of the women robbed a drugstore." Minnie glanced over and raised her eyebrow. "Can you believe it?"

Of course I didn't. Still sleepy, I nodded encouragement of the coming tale.

"She served a little time. They were more lenient with women back then." Minnie lovingly filled the canister with more clothespins. She screwed the lid on and set the jar to the side of the counter.

"Later that same woman married a pharmacist. Strange twist of irony, wouldn't you say?"

"Definitely."

"A few years into the marriage, she stole some pharmaceuticals and he divorced her."

"As well he should." Sometimes out of boredom, I played her game. Anticipating another adage I guessed, "Actions speak louder than words?"

"He married her sister." Minnie smiled. "If things are not as you wish, wish them as they are."

"Chinese proverb?" I yawned again.

"Yiddish." As part of her daily routine, Minnie opened the register to make sure we had enough cash on hand.

It was too early in the morning to understand Minnie's logic. The bells on the door announced the first customer of the day. A blonde browsed the jewelry featured in a display case across from the door. The woman's unbuttoned coat revealed a black blouse tucked into a short jean skirt. She turned from the jewelry display. "Liza, is that you?"

"Julie?" I walked around from behind the counter. "Julie Morrison. I almost didn't recognize you." She gave me a hearty hug. We went back to the days of confirmation class. More than once we got in trouble for giggling during the lesson. Once we hit high school, we gravitated to different groups of friends. I remember thinking she was everything I wasn't: blonde, perky, and popular.

"How are you?" she said. "Last I heard you were in Minneapolis."

"I was for a few years." I quickly diverted to another subject. "What are you doing these days?"

"I married Jim Bailey. We have two children, Annie and Jimmy, Jr."

"Two kids. Wow. How old are they?"

"Two and four. They keep me busy."

"I'm sure." Two kids hadn't marred her figure one bit. "I wouldn't have pegged you for an antique lover."

"It's a secret obsession." Her laughter brought back memories of singing hymns in the basement of St. Martin's Lutheran Church.

"Can I help you find something?"

"Just browsing today. Jim is giving me a break. You know, Mommy's time away."

I nodded as if I understood. "Well, enjoy."

Julie zipped her purse open and pulled out a pen and sticky note. "Here's my number. Call me next week. I want you to meet the kids. Anytime works for me."

"Okay."

"I mean it. If I don't hear from you, I'll send Jim after you. He works for the police department, you know." A hint of Cinnabar perfume drifted back as Julie strolled toward the center of the main floor. A middle-age woman with a red plaid scarf entered the store followed by a young couple.

"That's nice," Minnie said as I walked back to the counter. "You need to socialize more."

That was Minnie code for *I hope she fixes you up with someone*. I ignored her and unpacked a box of vintage jewelry my mother had purchased recently at an auction. I'd had a crush on Jim my entire freshmen year. Fortunately, I never told anyone, most notably not Julie. Throughout high school Jim had gone steady with a redhead named Jill. I was curious to know how Julie and Jim had gotten together. Guess that warranted a visit to Julie's house.

The red-scarf customer hefted a wooden box to the counter.

"Nice pick," Minnie said. "The graphics make it, don't they?"

The vintage box on the counter read "Atwood and Company, Palace Brand Roasted Coffee, Minneapolis" in black lettering.

"We live in Minneapolis," she said. "How crazy that we had to come to South Dakota to find this."

The woman was around my mother's age and wore her hair in short layers that feathered around her face. She wore an L.L.Bean sweater over jeans ironed with a front crease. I would have traded the vintage box straight up for her leather boots. I stepped up. "We have an Atwood coffee tin if you're interested."

"Really?" The woman's face lit up. "Wouldn't that be nice sitting on top of the box?"

"Let me go get it for you."

I returned with the corresponding coffee tin.

"Oh, yes," she said. "I'll definitely take that."

Minnie winked at me and rang her up. The lady's husband rounded the corner outside, and the woman waved him into the store. They left, he carrying the box and she the tin. "See you next time we come through town," she said over her shoulder.

"Bye now," Minnie said. The bells on the door rang again as the couple left. "Nice job, kiddo."

"Perfect fit, huh?"

"You've become quite an asset here. I think I'll give you a little bonus." Minnie swept her loose hair off her neck and flopped it like a fan. The heater behind the counter sometimes worked too effectively. She pushed a "no sale" key and reached into the register. "Here's a fifty for your house fund."

"You don't have to," I protested.

"I insist."

"Thanks, Mother. Maybe by the time I'm your age I'll be able to buy a house." Inwardly, I cringed. How insensitive that sounded. Minnie would never be able to buy a house. "Sorry, didn't mean it to come out like that."

Minnie threw her arms around me. "I know, honey. No offense taken." She squeezed me in a big bear hug.

"I'll add this to my house kitty." I folded the bill and tucked it in the pocket of my Levi's. Times like that made me appreciate Minnie. As quirky as my mother was, at her core she had a heart of gold.

I drove to Julie Morrison's house, Julie Bailey now. The house was in the northwest part of the city. Established trees lined both sides of the street, one advantage of older neighborhoods, lots of shade and big yards. Pots of wilted geraniums perched on the front steps leading to the modest one-story dwelling. Dry leaves had been raked into a pile at one side of the walk, and a white picket fence partitioned off the backyard. The house appeared so comfy and welcoming, tears came to my eyes. I blinked several times at my own sentimental envy and rang the doorbell.

"Come in and meet the kids." Julie's hair would have met our old Home Ec teacher's expectations: hair pulled back when cooking, not a hair out of place when entertaining. Two little kids giggled behind her. "This is Annie and this fine gentleman is Jimmy."

I stooped to their eyelevel. "I'm your Mom's old friend from school. My name's Liza."

Little Annie clung to her mother's leg and smiled. Jimmy beamed and stuck out his hand for a shake. "Nice to meet you, Jimmy."

"It's nap time for you two." Julie took their hands. "Be back in a moment."

The kids seemed well behaved for such young children. They didn't balk at taking a nap despite the fact there was a new person visiting. I was impressed. I spotted a wedding photo in a big 8" x 10" frame on the top of a glass-fronted bookcase. Julie and Jim looked as I remembered them both in high school, so young and happy as they posed for the camera.

Julie returned. "Thanks for waiting. I like to keep them on schedule. Naptime is my time." She motioned with a sweep of her hand. "Let's go into the dining room. There's a carafe of fresh coffee waiting for us. I'm sorry. I should have asked. Do you drink coffee? I can bring you something else."

"Coffee's fine."

Julie opened the French doors to the dining room. Though cramped with a table and six chairs, the room was cozy cute. Envy filled me to the pit of my stomach. "Nice house, Julie."

"It's comfortable. Someday we'll buy a larger house when the kids get bigger."

We sat across from each other at the table. In the background, "Proud Mary" by Creedence Clearwater Revival played on the radio. At that moment, I would have moved in with them if asked.

"You're looking good, Liza," Julie said. "You always were so pretty."

"The boys back in high school didn't think so," I said. "You were the one they all wanted to go out with."

"Oh, that was just because I was such a goofy thing. I talked way too much back then."

"So did you two marry right after high school?"

"Oh, no. Jim was dating Jill Peterson back then, remember? They broke up a year after graduation." Julie rolled her eyes. "She cheated on him with his best friend. That was the end of two relationships. The ironic thing was Jill and Ted broke up a year later."

That answered that question. "Lucky for you," I said.

We talked about our old teachers, the jocks and the cliques, and moved on to how Watertown had changed since graduation. I didn't mention the advantages Minneapolis had to offer. I'd wait until she asked. A door shut in the distance. Heavy footsteps tramped through the house.

"Well, look who's here," Jim said. "Little Liza Murphy from the class of '85."

"How are you?" I said. Jim Bailey stood there resplendent in his police officer's uniform. Instantly I remembered why I had that crush on him so many years ago. Brown eyes, tall, good-looking.

"On the other side of the law these days." He laughed at his joke and turned to kiss Julie on the cheek. "Broke my sunglasses. Came back for my other pair."

"On top of the bedroom bureau."

"You girls have fun. See ya, Liza."

I smiled. "Later, Jim."

Julie talked about the kids, her parents on the other side of town, her younger sister who moved to Texas, and her brother who farmed ten miles out of town. I told her about my job at

JCPenney and my budding artwork. I didn't have as much to say, my life significantly small compared to hers. After an hour, I announced I had to get back to the antique store. Minnie had an estate sale at four.

"It was so good to see you again." Julie surprised me with a hug.

"Good catching up."

Julie stood in the doorway. "Let's do this again."

"Thanks for the coffee." Julie was a kind person.

She waved from the front steps as I opened the truck door. I waved back. After she went inside, I drove away faster than advisable in a residential part of town. My hands clenched the steering wheel. Seeing Jim Bailey again had hit me like a tornado. He was even better looking than in high school. He'd filled out and had the physique of a man now. And that uniform didn't help any. I pounded the steering wheel and inwardly bludgeoned myself—I still had a crush on him.

Bubblegum Dreams

In Riverside Park, cottonwoods blazed under the sunlight. The warm days of Indian summer offered no excuses for staying indoors, and for once, I chose to take a day off from working at Minnie's. At a nearby picnic table, Holly's head hunkered over her notebook as she struggled to come up with the perfect word for her poem. I sat on a plaid stadium blanket with my watercolor brushes and paints surrounding me. I was determined to capture the old stone-arch bridge that crossed the Big Sioux River.

Painting the river would be the tricky part. I squinted and scanned for darks and lights in the water. I wet the river section with clear water and applied a light coat of ultramarine blue. Painting *plein air* was difficult since it was hard to control the drying time of watercolors—usually too fast. The best tactic was to layer increasingly darker shades of color, which meant I had to wait for each layer to dry before attempting the next. I set the watercolor pad in the sun to dry and strolled over to the picnic table.

"How's it going, Hol?"

She raised her head, her big-brimmed hat making her look like something out of the Old West. Holly tried to prevent sunburn at all costs. Her fair skin held blotches of pink pigment surrounded by blue veins. I'm sure she'd fry like an onion ring if she spent much time in full sunlight.

"The words are eluding me today." She sighed and leaned back with her hands on the edge of the bench. "How do I capture the sense of wellbeing this beautiful day brings?"

"Start with little things," I suggested. "You're always talking about using the five senses. Start with that."

"You're right, I should have thought of that." She narrowed her eyes. "Are you sure you're not a writer?"

"Not me." I laughed. "I prefer a brush to a pen, thank you."

"How was your coffee with Julie?" Holly reached for the thermos and poured lemonade into two paper cups.

"She lives in a cute little house and has two adorable kids." The lemonade was fresh squeezed, leave it to Holly. "Great lemonade. Do you ever wish you had children?"

She pursed her lips. "That's not for me. It's not that I don't like kids, but I never saw myself as a mother. How about you?"

Good question. Like Holly, I'd never really considered it, not even when I was married to Taylor. Probably because we were so young, the subject never came up. Thank goodness for birth control, or I'd be a struggling single mother, something I'd never considered before this moment. "Julie's kids are so sweet. I don't know, with the right guy it might be nice." An image of Jim appeared like a movie billboard. Who wouldn't want to be the mother of that gene pool?

"I can't see it," Holly said. "You as a mother." She turned to a fresh page in her notebook.

I felt like I'd been slapped. Was I devoid of nurturing or something? Did she think I didn't have it in me? Apparently.

Holly's pen was racing wildly, and I moved back to my art materials. As hard as I tried, I couldn't get the river to look right. After several attempts, I finally gave up and slid my palette knife between the top sheet of paper and the next on the watercolor pad.

I tore up the river attempt and turned to something easier, a big cottonwood at the edge of the park. The old tree produced leaves only at the top. By the time I finished painting, the tree looked like something out of Hansel and Gretel's forest, dark branches reaching out insidiously to grab any child who might venture beneath its grasp.

Maybe Holly was right, I'd make a rotten mother.

I worked at the antique store on Wednesday as JCPenney had claimed the coming weekend. The dark sky out the plate-glass windows agreed with the local radio pronouncement of rain that afternoon. I flounced the glass jewelry counter with the feather duster, forced to stop and move various knickknacks displayed on top. The bells on the door jingled and I glanced up. My heart flipped and I nearly dropped the duster.

"Hi there, Liza." Jim Bailey strode through the door, impressive in his police uniform. "How's it going?"

"Going good." I worked double time at acting casual. "And you?"

"Not bad." He glanced around the shop. He checked out my t-shirt, which I should have changed when I realized that Minnie had shrunk another of my shirts.

"Hey, just wanted to warn you," he said, "that there's some counterfeit bills floating around."

"Oh, yeah?" More casual acting. His brown eyes looked like pools of chocolate.

"Hundred dollar bills, so you shouldn't get many of those. Just check them closely, and if you have any questions, give us a call."

"Sure." I dusted around a figurine.

"Glad you're back in town, Liza," Jim said with a wink. "Hope we'll see more of you."

"Bye, Jim." My face warmed as he left the store. Was it my imagination or was that wink suggestive? Even worse, was I nursing an old crush? The phone behind the register rang.

"Minnie's Antique and Curiosity Shoppe."

"Oh, Liza, just the person I wanted." Julie's happy voice chirped into the receiver. "Do you want to go out for breakfast tomorrow morning? My cousin's staying a couple of days and she's willing to give me a little break from the kids."

"Tomorrow? Sure, it's my day off. What time?"

"Eight at the Wheel Inn. I can pick you up."

"Great. See you then." I hung up and slumped on the stool. I was a regular heel. A pure unadulterated heel.

Holly's face lit with anticipation like a child on Christmas morning.

"I think you're going to like this." I retrieved the machine from behind the counter.

"Ooh, it's beautiful." Holly stroked the bubblegum-pink portable Royal typewriter.

"I researched it." I stood back proudly. "The serial number dates it to 1957. See?" I pointed to a silver plaque at the top of the case. "Quiet De Luxe model. They designed this model to eliminate the clackety-clack of the keys. It bears a couple of small dings, but the color is rare. That pink makes it a real collector's item."

Holly looked up with raised brows. "Does it work?"

50

"I tried it out and all the keys work. Carriage bar, too. Nothing sticks."

"Thanks for saving this for me. You're a real pal."

Strike while the iron is hot. Even my thoughts sounded like my mother. "I have something else." I lugged a black number up next.

Holly's mouth hung open. "You're killing me."

"A circa 1917 Underwood No. 5." Minnie gave me a commission on everything I sold now. She considered it only fair because I'd turned into such a good saleswoman. I saw right through her; she wanted to contribute to my house kitty. Beneath all that eccentricity, my mother wasn't so bad.

"Will you take a check?"

"What do you think, Holly? Of course."

"Thanks." She pulled her plastic bank-issue checkbook from her back pocket like a guy.

"I know where you live, you know."

She looked up, apprehensive.

"Gosh, Holly, just jerking your chain."

She smiled halfheartedly. It was no wonder Holly had been shunned by not only the popular cliques in high school but pretty much by even the outcast crowd. But I envied her. She had her writing and her typewriters. She was content to be single. I needed to spend more time with her. Maybe that contentment would rub off on me.

"Hey, Hol," I said. "Minnie has a subscription to Reader's Digest, and I happened to leaf through an issue the other day. There's a short story contest you might be interested in. Maybe you should enter."

She pursed her lips and frowned slightly. "I have too much revision to do. Revision is the real art of writing, you know."

"But if you don't try—"

"What about you?" Her jaw tightened. "Don't see you entering any painting contests."

"You got me there." I handed her the receipt. "Enjoy."

Holly dropped her attitude and returned to the thrill of her treasures. I carried the Underwood to her car, and she cradled the bubble-gum delight. Back inside, I leaned over and picked up a box from Minnie's latest estate sale. She wanted me to sort through the miscellaneous items and price them. With a humph, I set the box on the counter only to be met by those brown eyes again.

"You're not off the hook," Jim Bailey said. This time he was in civilian clothes and to no surprise, he looked just as handsome in jeans and a t-shirt.

"Oh, hi, Jim," I said. "Didn't see you come in."

"You were busy carting Holly's typewriter outside."

"You're not off the hook," he repeated and leaned over the counter. "Julie told me you couldn't make it to our dinner party."

"Oh?" I played dumb.

"Minnie and I have worked out everything. She called her friend at Penneys, and Laura will switch shifts with you."

I wanted to strangle my mother. When would she ever quit? "Well, I guess then…"

Jim reached out and covered my hand resting on the counter. "It'll be fun. Glad you're coming."

I pulled back my hand and recouped my moxie. "Say hi to your wife."

Undeterred he winked and walked out the door.

My attraction for Jim was quickly evaporating, but something new stirred. I felt so sorry for Julie.

I didn't know how to dress for Julie's dinner party. We weren't in New York, so the occasion wouldn't be formal. On the other hand, I didn't want to be the only woman in Levi's. I hit the secondhand shop down the street and found some dress slacks and a satin blouse.

My worst fears were realized when I arrived to find I was the only single person there that night. The party consisted of three couples, including Jim and Julie. The husband of one of the couples worked with Jim on the force. I vaguely knew the wife of the other couple. Gail had been a few years ahead of me in school, but I didn't know her husband.

I followed Julie to the kitchen and whispered, "Why would you want a single girl at your dinner party?"

She smiled at me brightly. "Relax. Single people need to get out and socialize, too. Jim thought it would be good for you."

I tried to smile back at her. Jim was beginning to look like a fox.

Julie had set the table with her wedding china on a white tablecloth. Jim lit two tall tapers. Throughout the dinner, Jim and Julie went out of their way to include me in the conversation.

"Liza's an artist," Julie said. "I wish I had her talent."

Julie was sweet. She might have said I lived with my mother in an antique store.

"She was such a shy thing in high school," Jim added. "Not anymore." He winked.

With her attention drawn to me, Julie missed the wink.

The other two couples had a baby and two toddlers between them. I felt like the only Pentecostal in a group of Quakers. I longed to escape, but politeness required me to stay for after-dinner cocktails. As the ultimate hostess, Julie had made homemade Sangria. I fought yawns for the next hour as the conversation altered between confrontations on the beat and more baby stories. Finally, the couple from the tiny town of Henry said they had to be going. I stood up at the same time.

"Me, too. I have to work early tomorrow." Julie went for our coats.

Jim smiled at me. "Leaving so soon?"

"Happiness walks on busy feet." I *was* becoming my mother, and at the moment, I could care less.

Julie handed me my coat and gave me a squeeze. "Thanks for coming. Let's do coffee soon." She moved to Gail. "We'll have to get the kids together next week."

I stepped into the enclosed porch. Jim followed. "Glad you made it tonight, Liza." His hand drifted to my lower back and slid to my bikini pantie line. I twirled around. "Glad you're back in town," he said. "See you soon." He pivoted and returned inside the house.

I practically ran to Minnie's truck. Poor Julie. I didn't want to lose her friendship, but I had to avoid Jim. At my law firm Christmas party, a coworker had tried to tell me Taylor was flirting with other women. I didn't talk to her after that, not even when my divorce was imminent. It never went well when a person was told their life was falling apart.

Repurposed

I plugged the cord into the outlet, and lamplight blossomed over the red tablecloth. Someone had repurposed a vintage candlestick telephone into a lamp, a unique find from an estate sale in Minnesota. As Agnes Peterson watched, I demonstrated how the repurposed lamp worked. "You pick up the handset and the light turns on. Place it back in the cradle and the lamp turns off."

"How clever." Agnes had long ago discovered Elmer's deal with Minnie. Now she delivered the weekly eggs herself and in the process, became a regular customer. Agnes developed the habit of browsing through the store on delivery days, and collecting vintage telephones became her vice.

"You have to admit it's a conversation piece," I said.

"I'd prefer a candlestick phone in its original condition."

I agreed with her but said nothing. My job was to sell merchandise. "I'll let you browse. Nice to see you, Agnes." I returned to the front register where Ray finished his business with Minnie. For years she had purchased everything from beadwork to buckskin from Ray. They both looked sad. By the time I approached Minnie, he was halfway out the door.

"Transaction gone bad?" I asked.

Minnie dabbed at her eyes with a Kleenex. "He just lost his wife."

"What happened?"

"She had an aneurysm. Hit the floor and never felt a thing."

"That's terrible," I said.

Minnie nodded and headed to the back room. "Guess if you have to go…"

The register dinged as I checked for fives and tens. Minnie always said the death of a spouse came hardest for a man. I questioned her wisdom since she had never experienced marriage firsthand. But poor Ray. He was a nice guy.

Scattered snow flurries filled the air, and a squall was expected by evening. Three weeks before Christmas and already the temperatures had plummeted to 10° below zero with wind chill factor of 30° below. Whenever Julie called to get together, I suggested we meet at a coffee shop or café. "Give you a break from the kids," I'd say. Her folks lived in town and loved to watch the kids for her. Of course, I was avoiding the slightest chance of running into Jim.

That Wednesday morning Jim watched the kids on his day off, and we met at Ragels' Bagels on Broadway.

"I recommend the Everything Bagel," Rick, the owner, said. "Gives you a little taste of onion, garlic, sesame, and sunflower seeds." His brown crewcut was blond at the top, evidence of Rick's changing sense of style. "It's just what its name suggests."

"Make that two and we'll both have French vanilla coffee," I said. At Ragels' Bagels, they served the best coffee in town made from freshly ground beans.

Rick beamed. "Coming right up."

"I'll land us a table," Julie said.

"How's it going at the shop?" Rick asked. He was one of the friendliest guys in town. Always had a ready smile and a good word for everyone. If you were having a bad day, Ragels' Bagels was the place to go.

"A little slow this time of year," I said.

"This is a busy time for me—everybody wants hot coffee and warm bagels." Rick lifted his index finger, and for a moment the coffee grinder drowned out all sound in the room. "Summer slows down a bit, but overall, I do pretty good business year round. Everyone likes a morning bagel with a cup of Joe."

Julie waited at a table against the brick wall. "How are the kids?" I forced the next words out. "And Jim."

"Yesterday Annie tried dressing the cat in doll's clothes. Needless to say, she suffered a few ugly scratches."

"I can imagine."

"Jim's up for a promotion." Julie's eyes lit up. "But you can't tell anyone until it's final."

At that opportune moment, Rick delivered a pot of French press coffee and two mugs. "Your bagels will be up in a moment, ladies."

Julie's friendship meant a lot to me and, according to Minnie, had lifted me from the rank of antisocial hermit. Since the dinner party, however, I found our get-togethers slightly uncomfortable. I was on edge whenever she brought up Jim but had to act as if nothing was the matter. Even in normal conversation, my thoughts diverted to feeling sorry for Julie and debating—for the hundredth time—whether I should say anything about that night. I always talked myself out of it. Maybe the touch had been a slip of the hand. Maybe he'd come to his senses. Was that why I ran to the back room whenever he entered the store? If I spotted him in public, I'd cross the street or flee the grocery empty handed.

"We're having another party," Julie said.

I stopped breathing.

"But I know you aren't comfortable being the only single person, so you're off the hook."

Was I?

Minnie had left for a farm auction, leaving me to man the store. I rang up Elvira Anderson's purchase of Bakelite silverware. We seldom found entire sets of one pattern, but most people preferred a concoction of different types and colors. The blue-gray tint in Elvira's hair shone under the fluorescent light, the color popular with ladies of her generation. I figured she was close to eighty-five.

"You picked a nice one there," I said. "The chevron pattern is hard to find anymore." I wrapped the table knife in tissue paper.

"And I like the bullet handle on this spoon." Elvira caressed the red ribbed handle. She had worked across the street when Woolworth occupied the building, a claim to fame she announced upon every visit to our store. Elvira was a cutie. Petite at 4'5" in her practical rubber-soled laced shoes. She never left the house without makeup and freshly styled hair. She looked like a little porcelain doll. I always felt compelled to hug her before she left.

In the middle of our embrace, the bells on the door rang. *Jim Bailey*. With Minnie out, I had no choice but to maintain my station. I looked down and glanced back. If it weren't for the customers walking in behind Jim, I may have rushed to the back room and hid anyway.

"Hi, beautiful." Jim was working, evident by his uniform.

"How are you? Working the beat, I guess." The customers behind Jim wandered down the aisle to browse.

Jim leaned against the counter in that relaxed, macho way men communicate confidence—or their virility—while I shuffled nervously through some estate papers.

"I remember sitting behind you in algebra. You were shy back then. You didn't have a clue how cute you were." He produced that suave smile of his.

"Yeah? Being *cute* didn't get me any dates back then." I inserted a pencil into a little plastic sharpener. The point didn't need sharpening, and the lead promptly broke.

"That was because your shyness gave off a certain aura."

"How's that?"

"People misread it. Thought you were standoffish."

He placed his hand over mine and kept it there. "I'm glad you're back in town."

My hand felt like a captured bird, vulnerable and powerless. I swept my hand from the counter. "I enjoyed having breakfast with Julie the other morning."

"She's a great gal," he said, unperturbed.

This guy was unbelievable.

"Bet you get kind of lonely living in the old hometown," he said. "Not a lot of fish in the pond here. He tossed me a seductive smile and leaned closer.

"I'm doing just fine, and if I was into fishing, I'd find a man with a cottage on Lake Kampeska and a membership at the country club."

Jim's eyes widened as he drew back. Guess he hadn't expected that out of me. At that moment, my liberator blew in. Looking flushed, Minnie scurried up to the counter. "Hi, Jim," she said and then looked at me. "Honey, would you open the back door for the freight truck parked in the alley?"

I was off at a run.

"Thank you, dear," came Minnie's voice from behind. "How's Julie and the kids?"

My mother never hired freight trucks. A quick glance at the alley and I knew Minnie had created a timely diversion. I made a cup of tea in the back room and gave myself plenty of time to empty the cup. Half an hour later I returned to the counter. Minnie said, "Jim has sure been coming around a lot lately."

"Momma, I think he's a big fat cheater. He's been coming on to me, and the man knows I'm friends with Julie."

"That's what I thought. Why do they always go for a woman's friends? Handy, I guess."

"Do you think I should tell Julie?"

Minnie narrowed her eyes. "We seldom know what's cooking until it boils over."

"Italian proverb?"

"Amish," Minnie said. "You won't jeopardize your friendship with Julie by cheating with her husband. Besides, she won't believe that about her husband until he's caught in the act. There's too much at stake for her."

"I feel so sorry for Julie and the kids."

"As much as I want grandkids, I'm glad you didn't have any with Taylor."

That was the first I'd ever heard Minnie talk about grandchildren. "So am I."

"The kids are always the ones who suffer the most."

I stared at my mother, wondering if another layer of meaning hovered there, but she was busy clearing the counter, and our eyes never met. With a deep sigh, I expelled a blast of air, and the ashes of my failed marriage rained around me.

The next morning I opened the store. Minnie had chased down yet another estate sale. Seemed the cold temperatures were playing havoc on our elderly. I twisted the deadbolt, looked up, and gasped. With that captivating smile and dimple, he stood shivering in the South Dakota cold. The repurposed candlestick phone came to mind. That phone would make a good club, I thought, as I opened the door to my ex-husband.

African Proverb

Minnie swooped in on a gust of wind, looked up, and froze.

"Mother, this is Taylor."

By the look on Minnie's face, I could tell she was torn between being friendly or protective. I struggled to smile, and she took my cue. How ironic that five years after our wedding (and divorce) they would finally meet.

"Glad to meet you, Taylor." She held out her hand. "May I offer you some tea or coffee?"

Taylor sat on the extra stool at the counter. "No, thanks, Mrs. Murphy."

"Please excuse me," Minnie said. "I have some inventory to work on."

From the corner of my eye, I noticed Minnie headed to the balcony. Was she going to spy on us? I couldn't blame her, Taylor's sudden appearance was pretty outrageous.

"I'm staying at my uncle's place in Hayti."

If I remembered right, he had spent summers there as a child. I recalled Taylor said he never liked the man. Guess people changed as they grew older.

My mind struggled to catch up with reality. Finally, I said, "So, what are you doing in this neck of the woods?" I cringed at another of Minnie's clichés springing from my lips. Besides, he had already told me he was visiting relatives.

"Taking some time off from work."

"Oh." I could barely carry on a conversation. My ex-husband appearing on my doorstep was not something I had anticipated. "That's nice."

"So you work here, I guess."

His blue Scandinavian eyes bore into mine, the same eyes that made me fall for him.

"I also work at JCPenney in the mall."

"You always were a hard worker." He smiled, and I looked away. I was over him, after all.

"How's life?" I said.

"Same ol' same ol'," he said with a grin.

I summoned the courage to state the obvious. "You're here, why?"

"Thought we could have a cup of coffee, for old time's sake," he said. "We're still friends, aren't we?"

I was about to decline the offer when in strode my nemesis in full uniform. Jim smiled as he approached the counter, his eyes widening as he caught sight of Taylor on the stool. "Hey, Liza," Jim said. "How's it going?" Despite the fact that another good-looking man sat next to me, Jim leaned over the glass countertop and smiled.

"Taylor, this is Jim Bailey. Jim, this is Taylor," I said. "My ex-husband."

"You don't say." Jim studied Taylor. "We have laws against things like that in this town."

Taylor flinched and threw a worried look my way. I smiled and shrugged.

His face lightened when he realized Jim was joshing. "Oh, good one."

"We were just leaving." I grabbed Taylor's hand and turned toward the balcony. "Hey, Minnie! We're going out for a cup of Joe." Jim glared at Taylor like a jealous husband.

Minnie appeared at the balcony railing. "Have a good time, you two." Her vigilant eyes shone like silver dollars.

She'd heard every word. "See ya, Jim, Say hi to Julie and the kids." At times Minnie's nosiness came in handy. Taylor followed on my heels. Jeez. From the proverbial frying pan into the fire.

At Mabel's Diner, I studied Taylor as he stirred sugar into his coffee. Your typical blond Swede, he was light-skinned, tall, and handsome. My dark complexion had infatuated him when we first met. Ironically, his mistress was as blonde as a Barbie doll.

"Took time off from the soda plant?" I asked.

"Had a few days coming. Thought I'd use them."

Outside the window snow flurries fell, big and airy, the kind where you stick out your tongue and the flakes melt like powdered sugar. Soft fluffy snow that fell straight down was a special treat with our Dakota propensity for blustery winters. For a moment, I thought of Christmas carols and families around the fireplace drinking eggnog and what our children might have looked like. I bit my tongue and blamed the holiday music playing in the background.

"Did you ever wish we had kids?" Taylor said.

That made it official. I'd been sucked into a Sci-Fi flick, one with a creature that could read my mind. I shook my head and glanced out the window. The flurries had lessened. The music changed to *Frosty the Snowman*.

The nostalgia disappeared and my wit returned. "Good thing we didn't, considering you might have had kids from two mothers."

"Yeah, I was a real jerk then."

"Like you've changed in twelve months?"

"I was a fool." He glanced down at the table. "I threw away a good thing."

Hard to believe this was the same disarming Swede I'd fallen in love with. "How's life in the big city?" I blurted, anything to change the subject and get this unexpected reunion over with.

"Aw, you know. It gets old after a while."

"Lot of things to do there compared to this place." I swung my arm toward the window where a lone car drove past.

"It's no fun without someone to share things with." He turned his puppy dog eyes on me.

Exactly why I left. Everything was about fun for Taylor. "You'd be bored stiff in this little town."

"People change, Liza," he looked into my eyes. "I've grown up in the last year."

The music shifted to a sentimental tune. I stood. "I need to get back." With a wave of my hand, I rushed from the café and zigzagged home, turning the walk from four blocks to seven, just in case he tried to follow.

I welcomed the end to the strange reunion with my ex, but three days later, Taylor walked into the women's department of JCPenney with an elderly gentleman.

"Hey, Liza," Taylor said. "I'd like you to meet my uncle Prewitt from Hayti."

A frumpy little man, Uncle Prewitt wore bib overalls and a flannel shirt. In South Dakota that was a sure sign of a retired farmer. "Glad to meet you."

66

"We were at the mall today, and I figured we'd stop in and say hello."

Having Taylor show up in the aisle that divided women's casual wear and lacey lingerie created a surreal sensation. Somehow he'd grown even better looking since our impromptu coffee break. I refolded a perfectly folded pair of women's jeans on the end display, a great sale if you were petite and size four. I restacked another tidy pile of jeans.

Taylor's mouth drooped. "Guess we'll be going then."

"Nice to meet you," I said to Uncle Prewitt, who was gazing into space.

He drew his head back and held out his thick hand. "Come and see us anytime."

"Say, that's a great idea," Taylor said. "I can drive you out to see his place. It's a pretty farm."

"Oh?" Stalling. What to say?

"When's your next day off?"

"Tomorrow, but—"

"Great. I'll pick you up at eleven tomorrow morning." Taylor nudged his uncle's arm, and they walked toward the mall concourse. As they left the ladies section and exited through the men's department, Taylor looked over his shoulder. "It'll be a nice, relaxing drive." He winked and left me frozen in place, wondering how I got myself into these situations. The uncle was obviously not a fabricated story as I had first thought, but people didn't really change for the better, did they?

Shifting from foot to foot, I waited at the front counter of the antique store, regretting my agreement to visit Taylor's relatives. The time had come. I needed to talk to Taylor and make it clear that we couldn't keep seeing each other. But plans had been made, and his relatives were expecting us. I had to go through with the visit, but I would make my feelings known.

"Regrets?" Minnie said as she grabbed a rag from beneath the counter. Her bright orange dress wrapped around her hips like a sarong from India.

"This will be the last time we get together." I was practicing my spiel already.

Minnie dusted a wooden African mask. "Only a fool tests the depth of the water with both feet."

I glared at my mother.

"African proverb," she said and went back to dusting.

"Life is either a daring adventure or nothing," I retorted. "Helen Keller."

"Hmm." Minnie muttered.

I changed the subject. "What are your plans for today?" This time of the year we were always closed on Sundays.

"Pickle Party at Evelyn's this afternoon."

"Oh?" I watched for Taylor's car out the front display window.

"Such a variety. Dill, sweet pickles, candied apple, pickled asparagus, beets, and my favorite, watermelon pickles."

I puckered my lips at the last. I had tasted Evelyn's pickles made from watermelon rinds. Far too sweet for my taste. "And what exactly do you do at a pickle party besides eat pickles?" With no interest whatsoever, I fought to think of anything but the coming drive to Hayti with my ex-husband. A nervous quiver shot through my stomach.

"You should come sometime." Minnie's eyes lit up. "We try different pickles with a variety of crackers and cheeses. We vote on our favorite pickles and on our favorite combinations. And we always have a theme. This year, I suggested the 1920s era. We all dress in Twenties attire, and Evelyn will play music from that time period. It'll be a real hoot."

Taylor's old blue Corvette pulled up at the curb. A horn tooted from outside. I cringed.

68

Minnie tossed me a dark look. She didn't have to say a word. She considered it rude for a gentleman to honk for his date instead of coming to the door. Maybe it came from my mother, but I'd always been irritated by that same gesture when I was married to Taylor. "Have fun at your speakeasy," I said as I rushed out the door. There was more to the Pickle Party than what Minnie let on. I knew the ladies always served wine.

Taylor made an exception to his old ways and opened the car door for me. I settled in the vintage Corvette to the aroma of Taylor's cologne exuding throughout the vehicle. I had always liked the smell of Brut, and his close masculine presence brought back our first year of dating. Everything rose so familiar and yet troubling at the same time. We turned onto 5th Avenue to Bryan Adams singing "Everything I do, I do it for you" on the radio. That song would melt a nun's heart.

"Aunt Louise will have a big spread for us at dinner." Taylor glanced over. "She's looking forward to meeting you."

"Hmm." I nodded. As Taylor turned back to the road, I did a quick study of my ex-husband: strong jaw, that thick hair I had always liked to rake my fingers through, and his signature worn-leather jacket. Faint expression lines etched around his eyes— Taylor was five years older than me—but it certainly didn't detract from his good looks. That was when I knew. I should have gone to the Pickle Party.

Dark treebanks delineated farms scattered across the snow-covered countryside. The blast of warm air shooting into Taylor's car betrayed the cold outside. A few miles south of Watertown, we passed a round barn with a polygonal cupola. I'd always loved that white barn.

"What a crazy-looking building," Taylor said. "Why would they make round barns?"

"It's the safest place in South Dakota."

Taylor glanced across the seat. "How's that?"

"Pennsylvania Shakers believe the devil likes to hide in square corners." Minnie told me that when I was ten. "So if you're running from the devil, it's a good place to be." I tossed a pointed look his way.

"I'll keep that in mind." He stared out at the straight line of asphalt stretching into the distance.

"Farmers considered the design more practical," I continued. "All the cows faced the middle, and the farmer would drop hay through the center of the loft." I fought back a smile.

Taylor's right dimple deepened, and he flashed that old familiar grin.

A few minutes later, he turned right onto a gravel road. "Another three miles and we'll be there."

We pulled into the drive of a foursquare farmhouse—a square two-story building—with a barn looming a hundred feet behind it. The structure was the traditional red rectangular barn seen in pastoral paintings. Chickens pecked dirt at windblown spots of ground. Free-range eggs came to mind, much coveted by big-city customers. We walked to the farmhouse where the front screen door opened before we made it to the porch.

"This must be Liza." The top of the woman's head rose just over halfway up the door. Her friendly smile put me at ease and relieved some of the tension I carried. Uncle Prewitt leaned around his stout wife and smiled.

"This is my aunt Louise." Taylor gave the woman a big bear hug. This was a side of Taylor I'd never seen. Like me, he didn't have family in Minneapolis. His mother had died when Taylor was a boy, and after Taylor's graduation, his father had moved back East. I'd never met the man.

I waited until Taylor made himself comfortable on the burgundy sofa, before I claimed the other end. Louise and Prewitt sat opposite us in their matching easy chairs. Red and

70

green lights blinked on a tabletop Christmas tree adorned with little plastic snowmen.

"Supposed to be a big 'un coming," Uncle Prewitt said. "Up to a foot of snow on Tuesday."

"Do you play canasta?" Louise asked.

"Just hearts and crazy eights, I'm afraid." I hoped she wasn't about to teach me.

"I just love canasta. Prewitt and I have passed many a long winter's night playing cards."

"I'm sure it helps pass the time," I said.

"Oh, that it does, dear." Louise's hands clasped together in her lap.

"Liza's an artist," Taylor interjected. I had mentioned I was attempting watercolors.

"What do you paint, dear?"

"Landscapes mostly," I said. "Sometimes a still life."

"How nice," Louise said.

I didn't think of myself as a full-fledged artist, but it felt good Taylor saw me that way. But then I considered whether he only said it to make points with me. After a few minutes of chit chat, Louise invited everyone into the dining room for dinner. She had prepared a traditional roast beef dinner complete with mashed potatoes, cooked carrots, and lots of onions swamping the prime South Dakota beef.

After dessert, I feared we'd be corralled into a game of canasta, so I was proactive and asked Uncle Prewitt to give us a tour of the barn after dinner. Louise told us to go along without her.

Since I was a little girl, I'd been fascinated with barns. The animals held part of the appeal: the wide faces of cows with their moony eyes, the velvet-soft noses of horses, and the furry tabbies who earned their bowls of cream by chasing mice. But it was more than the farm animals. The building itself fascinated

71

me from its wide barn doors, the head stalls for milking cows, the milk room, to the most captivating of all, the hayloft.

"Uncle Prewitt, would you care if I climb up the loft?" I asked.

"Beware of the hatches. We throw hay down to the cattle through the holes in the floor. Don't fall through."

"I'll watch out for her," Taylor said.

I climbed the wooden slats nailed onto the wall and boosted myself into the loft. Taylor emerged behind me. I passed a gaping hole large enough to swallow a person. Below, a pile of hay mounded over the ground-level floor.

"Watch your step," Prewitt yelled from below.

Dust motes danced in the air as I craned my neck back and studied the high beams. "What's that over there?" I walked farther back into the loft. Someone had tucked three trunks beneath the low angle of the roof.

"Careful," Taylor yelled. "Watch for holes."

I lifted the lid of a camelback chest. For its age, the interior was in good shape, even better than the exterior. The smaller metal trunk held an array of nicks and dents. The lid of the flat-topped wooden trunk had broken slats.

With hands at his waist and elbows flared, Taylor stared out the loft window. "It might be nice to live on a farm."

I hadn't expected that of Taylor. "I always wished I'd grown up in the country," I said. It beat living in the back of a store.

"Maybe a hobby farm." Taylor turned to me. "Some people work in town and live in the country."

"You could raise a few cows for your own meat." I surveyed the expansive loft. At one end, hay bales stacked high against the open studs. I got caught up in his daydreaming. "Chickens, too. You'd always have fresh eggs."

Taylor placed an arm over my shoulder. "Fresh eggs and smoked pork. Can't beat that."

I slipped from beneath his arm. "Suppose we should head down." We descended the ladder where Uncle Prewitt stood waiting. I asked if he was interested in selling the largest trunk.

"Louise made me store them up there. She doesn't want anything dated in the house. Make me an offer."

"Fifty?"

Prewitt rubbed his chin for a moment before he grinned. "I'll take forty."

Using a barn pulley, Taylor tied two ropes to the chest and lowered it through the loft door at the gable end of the barn.

"Careful," I yelled from outside as the trunk swayed precariously back and forth. Taylor didn't look overjoyed at his unanticipated task.

I'd been in the antique business for too long. Like Minnie, I'd grown an eye for the vintage, antique, and collectible. I suppose it couldn't be helped.

On the drive home, I was cognizant of the ease I felt sitting next to Taylor—like we'd never parted. As if we were still married. Caught up with the pastoral scene and the warm sense of family, I didn't spill my practiced speech. Seasonal songs on the radio didn't help. I imagined a horse-drawn sleigh as "Jingle Bells" danced over the radio. Call me a coward, but I'd wait for a phone call from Taylor to tell him it was over between us.

Pieville

I took slow, deep breaths and after a few moments, tried lying on my side. I fluffed my pillow and rolled onto my other side. No matter what I did, sleep wouldn't come. I slipped into my fleece-lined moccasins and crept downstairs. Under the glow of the floor lamp Minnie used for a security light, I stared out the display window. Streetlights lit up the gently falling snow. It was a magical thing when we received snow without winds gusting and snowdrifts up to three feet.

Taylor had left three messages in the last two days. His persistence throbbed like an abscessed tooth. Like putting off a tooth extraction, the pulsating reminder wouldn't go away.

The boiler in the basement rattled and chugged, breaking the melancholy stillness. In the musty aroma pervasive from everything vintage, I turned on a table lamp, and the amber glow draped a beautiful cherrywood desk I'd discovered a few months ago.

In mid-October as I rode my bicycle to the mall, I had spotted a yard sale on 5th Street. I braked at the sight of wooden furniture scattered across the lawn. Minnie always needed antique furniture for the store, and the vintage desk appeared in good shape. I paid for it and hurried on to work. My mother picked up the desk later with the truck. I had never gotten around to taking a good look at it until tonight.

The 19th Century relic had survived with only a few minor scratches. The slant-top desk opened to pigeon holes and small drawers that, upon closer investigation, were made with dovetail construction. Out of curiosity, I pulled out all the drawers and felt inside. Behind a column, I felt something protruding in the wood and pressed. A hidden drawer popped out. Aha. A place to conceal valuable documents, a changed will perhaps?

I turned the drawer around and discovered a false back. Upon opening it, I found a yellowed envelope with a postmark of 1917. Over the years, the glue on the back had dried and detached the seal, making it easy to satisfy my curiosity. Delicately, I unfolded the stationary.

May 6. 1917

Dearest Ruth,

I am doing well. Basic training is grueling at times but necessary. I miss you terribly and often wish we had married before war was declared on Germany. Now, however, I believe we should wait until this blasted conflict is over. Your picture warms my heart whenever I gaze on it, which is often I must say. Though your beauty can not be denied, it is your sweet, kind heart that I miss the most.

Yours forever,
Anthony

I never had that kind of love with Taylor. After a week without contact, I believed it was finally over. But his phone calls started up again two days after Christmas. The next call, I promised myself. I'll tell him it's over the next time we speak.

"I saw you the other day with someone." Julie smiled coyly. "He was quite handsome."

I studied Pieville's tin ceiling, which dated back to the building's origin. We sat in a red booth that mimicked an old Chevy car seat from the 50s. I studied the black and white squares on the linoleum floor. "That was Taylor, my ex-husband."

"You're kidding!"

The waitress arrived with two cobalt mugs of hazelnut coffee.

"Thank you, Norma." I turned back to Julie. "It's a long story."

She shot me a wry look. "I have time for a soap opera."

"He's in the area visiting relatives." Norma returned with two slices of pie, my Dutch apple ala mode and Julie's pecan. Pieville had twenty types of pies on their menu, all handmade with the best crust in town. Norma used her mother's recipe for the crust. Hazel's secret piecrust recipe was touted in bold letters across the menu.

Julie held a forkful of pecan pie midair. "And he just happened to look you up after a year?"

"Mm-hmm." The vanilla ice cream melted over the crumb topping. "He took me out to his uncle's farm. His aunt made dinner for us."

"Cozy." Julie lifted one eyebrow and smiled.

"I'm not going to see him anymore." I wrapped both hands around my cup.

"I've heard of couples getting back together," Julie said.

"Yeah, but if it didn't work out the first time…"

Julie shrugged. I had hoped for her agreement.

I drew in a breath and released it. "How are the kids?"

Julie rambled on about their latest antics. Annie had snuck into Julie's cosmetics and performed a makeover on her brother. "Ruined my lipstick, needless to say. I had to pluck chunks from the carpet." Julie grimaced. "On a brighter note, Jim officially got his promotion."

"That's great," I said. Talk about makeovers. That man needed a total character upgrade.

After our coffee, I walked back to the antique store and shoveled snow into the gutter. I was determined to avoid any further meetings with Taylor, if for no other reason than I was tired of my emotions shifting back and forth like a child on a swing.

Taylor asked me to ring in the New Year with him. I sidestepped the invitation by suggesting coffee on Saturday. I prepared for the heart-to-heart talk that had long been brewing and ironically found myself thinking of Taylor while dusting antiques, at work in the mall, and when I lay in bed at night. Detoured by memories, I recalled those happy days of dating. A great dancer, Taylor took me dancing every weekend before we married, and we continued the routine for the first two years. I felt so loved in his arms, but slowly we abandoned the dancing for movie nights spent in front of the television. Then Taylor began going out with the guys on Friday nights. I don't know when hanging out with the guys crossed over into hitching up with other women, but by the time I realized what was happening it was too late. I discovered the affair had been going on for at least a year, and I couldn't live with that.

So why was I seeing Taylor now?

Two days before the dawn of the new year, Taylor's aunt found me in the women's department of Penney's and gave me a warm hug.

"Isn't this a nice place to work," Louise said, looking around at the reduced-price Christmas sweaters and flannel pajamas.

"Doing a little shopping today?"

"I need a new pair of dress shoes, and I know Penney's always has the style I like." Louise opened her purse and pulled out a coupon clipped from the newspaper. "And a free coffee at the food court."

"That's nice," I said.

"You know Prewitt and I like you very much. Don't know why you two ever broke up. You make such a cute couple. And Taylor's been miserable after that gal in Minneapolis left him."

"Is that right?" I kept my face expressionless as my blood pressure rose. "She dumped him, did she?"

"Vanessa didn't even give him a warning." Louise tsked. "He came home one day, and she was gone. Television, too. Not even a note."

"Aww." I feigned sympathy. "How long ago did that happen?"

"Oh, let me think." Louise looked heavenward. "Just the week before Taylor called and asked if he could come visit."

If blood could boil, mine was boiling over. A sudden visit to the uncle that Taylor told me he didn't like. Relatives that just happened to live near Watertown.

"So sad." I put on my best empathetic face. "Had they been together long?"

"Oh my, yes." Louise's brows dipped in concern. "Two years. Can you imagine? They'd lived together for two years, and she just up and leaves him."

"Must be rough to have a loved one betray him like that." My jaw tightened down to the molars. I glanced at my watch. "I need to meet with my manager. It was good seeing you again, Louise."

Louise smiled broadly, proof she hadn't caught my sarcasm. "Come and visit us anytime."

I hightailed it to the restroom at the back of the store. Locked in the stall, I pressed the back of my head against the door. Two years. Vanessa had to be the woman with whom he cheated on me. She must have moved in half an hour after my shoes left the premises.

So his paramour leaves, and Taylor hunts me up. I banged my head against metal. How could I be so naïve? Though I never had true peace about it, I'd toyed with the idea of a second try. I flushed the toilet and returned to work. I checked the dressing rooms for rejected clothing and abandoned hangers. My armful of hangers plummeted into an empty box with a clatter.

And, unlike Taylor, I had genuinely liked Uncle Prewitt and Aunt Louise.

I stormed to the office and ordered Veronica to refuse all calls for me unless it was my mother. She did me one better by promising to inform any male callers that I no longer worked there. That evening I confessed the mess to Minnie.

She wrapped her arms around me. "Everything will be okay. I promise." She swept a strand of errant hair away from my eye. "Tomorrow is a new day," my mother cooed. Somehow her trite saying brought me a measure of comfort.

The next morning I tagged new merchandise at the antique store. "I'm avoiding the phone today, Mother."

"No problem. If it's customers, they'll call back." Minnie opened a small 1940s suitcase. "Look what I found at the auction."

I peered at a picnic set of red Bakelite silverware with matching plastic plates.

"That's cute."

"I thought so." The phone rang, and I let my mother answer it. "Minnie's Antique and Curiosities," she said. Her expression tightened, nostrils flared. After a moment, she spoke. "A house divided against itself cannot stand." She paused. "And you should know I keep a shotgun behind the counter." She slammed down the receiver.

"Taylor?"

Minnie nodded. "Did you see the matching thermos with this set?"

I grinned. "The shotgun was a nice touch, Mother."

Minnie looked up and smiled.

The next evening the phone rang after store hours. Minnie answered the extension in our living quarters. "Hello?" She listened for a moment. "As Albert Camus once said, 'Life is a sum of all your choices.' My daughter does not wish to see or speak with you again, and if you come on the premises, I will call the police or use the shotgun, not necessarily in that order." The phone thudded into the receiver. "That's that."

"Thanks. I think that will do it." That night, I slept like a baby.

The traffic south of town melted the inch of snow that fell on the road the previous evening. The sun danced in and out of fast-moving clouds as I made a surprise visit to Prewitt and Louise. This wouldn't be easy. I knew they'd welcome me into their home, and I would have to forego their hospitality for a private talk with Taylor.

Between Minnie's responses and the failed attempts at calling me at the mall, Taylor surely had gotten the message by now. But I didn't feel right letting Minnie do what I should have done from the beginning. Taylor's pitiful rebound still infuriated me, but he deserved to hear *adios, adieu, arrivederci,* goodbye from me. After all, I had encouraged him by meeting him for coffee and visiting his relatives. Turning off the highway, I practiced my speech as tires rumbled over gravel. Half a mile farther, I turned into the drive to the farmhouse.

I braced myself. Taylor's car was parked out front. Prewitt's old pickup stood nearby. A Toyota sedan appeared at the side of the house, presumably Louise's preferred mode of transportation. After a deep breath, I walked to the front stoop and knocked. Louise answered the door. "Oh…what a nice surprise." She glanced nervously behind her. I followed her gaze to the sofa where Taylor sat.

Louise lowered her voice. "Honey, she arrived this morning."

I peered around Louise's head. Taylor's arm draped over a cute blonde.

"Vanessa, I presume?"

"Frankly, we wish it would have worked out between you two."

I touched her arm. "It's okay, Louise. It would never have worked out for us. Stop and see me next time you're at the mall."

"I definitely will, dear." Red ringed Louise's eyes, but I didn't know if it was for me or herself.

Prewitt's voice rumbled from the end of the living room. "Who's there, Louise?"

I shook my head and Louise called over her shoulder, "Just someone needing directions."

I rushed to the car and placed it in reverse. My pulse raced as I drove too fast down the gravel road to the pinging sound of my mind bouncing between anger and embarrassment. Incensed that he'd cheated me out of breaking up with him. Humiliated for believing I was doing the right thing. Add a pickup load of self-loathing that I'd ever thought it could work between us again. In the end, I was left a sniveling fool.

One of Minnie's sayings came to mind. *Doing the right thing won't always make things right, but it'll help you sleep at night.* This time the quote was directly attributed to Minnie Murphy. I recalled Vanessa's cotton-candy face and felt like a fool all over again.

I turned onto the highway with another saying spinning in my head. *You deserve better.* New quote by Liza Murphy, reformed dreamer.

Retro 1965

Evidence of another estate sale piled up behind the counter. "That's an unusual ironing board." I leaned over and examined it. The wooden piece had slats on one side.

"It's a rare piece." Cinched with a western belt, Minnie's black wool cape was saved from mediocrity with bright red and yellow chevron stripes. A silver rodeo buckle shone at her waist, a denim skirt brushing cherry-red cowboy boots. She manipulated the hinged sections and the ironing board transformed into a step stool.

"How clever," I said.

"It was innovative for its time." Minnie stood back with hands at her hips. "Multipurpose at its best." She narrowed her eyes and studied me. "You okay?"

"As you might say, Mother, let bygones be bygones."

Minnie offered a quick hug as the bells on the door announced a morning customer. I looked up to see Raymond

Standing Rock trying to catch Minnie's eye. I glanced at my mother and found her avoiding eye contact with him.

"Hi, Ray," I said.

"Aren't you growing into a pretty young woman." Ray glanced at Minnie. "You take after your mother."

Minnie tossed a determined look at her recent receipts. Why was she so rude? I left the counter and forced Minnie to acknowledge the poor man. Over a shelf of white stoneware pitchers two aisles away, I spied on them.

Ray placed his bag of Native crafts on the counter. "I like your outfit, Minnie."

"Thank you," my mother said. "How are you, Ray?"

"Needed a little trip out of town to ease the winter doldrums."

Ray had been a familiar face in our store for years. Was it my imagination or was he watching my mother with a smitten look? The widower must be lonely after the death of his wife. Just when I was thinking they might make a good couple, I heard my mother's all-business voice. "What do you have for me today?"

Beads tinkled over the glass counter.

"I'll take the necklaces."

"They're yours," Ray said.

My mother wrote out a receipt.

"Care to join me for dinner tonight?" he asked.

With a jerk, my mother raised her head. "Sorry, I'm afraid I have plans." She counted out the appropriate bills for the purchase and handed Ray the cash.

"A good steak doesn't catch your interest?"

Like me, Ray saw straight through my mother's excuse. *What would it hurt, Mother?*

"Sorry, already made plans." Minnie needlessly shuffled paperwork.

"Another time then." Ray retreated in defeat. The sleigh bells jangled.

I whisked back to the counter. "Ray's a nice guy. Why wouldn't you have dinner with him?"

"He has too many women around him as it is."

Before I could question her further, Minnie retreated to the back of the store.

After the episode with Taylor, I was driven to fill my life with something positive. I enrolled in an adult-ed class held at the high school. For the next eight weeks and two nights a week, I'd explore the techniques of oil painting. Self-instruction via library books could teach me the basics, but an actual art instructor would provide me with more in-depth lessons in technique. I was hyped. Upon purchase of the materials from the supply list, I felt like a serious student of the arts.

On Tuesday night I walked into the high school classroom with my tote bag of supplies. I had imagined my high-school art teacher's surprise to find me taking art seriously at last. I practiced a little speech, thanking Miss Brank for her advice several years ago. Some of us are slow learners, I'd quip with a smile.

To my great surprise, a man with chestnut hair sat on the edge of the teacher's desk talking to another student. I looked around. No Miss Brank. With disappointment, I chose a table in the middle of the room and slumped onto a stool. Ten adults had signed up for the painting class. Across the room, I recognized Sally Sanders who worked at the bakery and acknowledged her with a wave. Four senior citizens—one our token male, and three women in their mid-forties sat at the table ahead of me. Two young women, who looked barely out of high school, sat upfront as close as possible to the instructor. The reason for that was obvious.

The instructor would draw any woman's appreciation. With that face, he rivaled a soap opera star. Though closer to my age, he was hot enough to appeal to a teenager. His green eyes accented thick wavy hair. With broad shoulders and the trim waist of a Calvin Klein model, he had the kind of slim build that made him appear younger.

"Welcome, everyone." He stood to gain our attention. "I'm Beau Bartlett and I'll be your partner in creativity for the next eight weeks."

I dug in my bag for the class syllabus and unfolded the paper. Sure enough, I had missed the name of the instructor printed three lines from the top. I had been in a hurry that day to register for the class before I headed to the mall. I glanced toward the front of the classroom. He was definitely a Beau.

The girls smiled coquettishly at our handsome instructor. They were cute and skinny, that age where they obsessed about the opposite sex. In our small town, young women were always on the lookout for a new arrival.

"I studied art at SDSU." His smile came warm and sincere. He appeared to lack the inflated male ego that good looking guys usually clutch like a royal scepter. One of the young women flipped her blonde hair and beamed. The other girl stared up at the instructor with moon eyes. Their fawning was beginning to grate on my nerves.

"I grew up in St. Paul," he continued, "but my maternal grandparents lived in Watertown, thus my decision to attend college nearby in Brookings. I worked in the art department after receiving my master's degree." He leaned against the edge of Miss Brank's desk. "I've been a full professor for several years and am currently on a sabbatical. I've always liked Watertown and *voilà*, here I am, ready to help you explore the beauty of painting."

I mused about that old stereotype of artists: impetuous and moody. This guy appeared mellow and comfortable with himself.

"Tonight we'll start with a classic still life. All the basic skills of painting can be honed in a simple composition of fruit." He performed a Vanna White wave before an arrangement of pears and grapes set in a blue pottery bowl and flipped on a spotlight over the table. "Your first assignment is to sketch the composition with a charcoal pencil on the 8 x 10 canvas from your supply list. You'll find the easels along the back wall. I have a few stretched canvases if anyone had trouble obtaining one."

The blonde in front raised her hand. I half rose from my stool and spotted several canvasses below her table. She beamed at the instructor as he approached.

I retrieved an easel and set up my canvas. Ignoring the twittering young women, I planned to take full advantage of instruction from a bona-fide college professor. After my terrible Taylor escapade, my desire to develop my painting skills had intensified. I was resolved to be an artist.

"Determination is 90% of success," Minnie always said. "Many talented people have given up their dream because it didn't come easily. Only those determined to go the long haul will find success."

I don't know where Minnie found her wisdom. She wasn't a professional woman. Granted, she was a businesswoman, but I wasn't sure running a secondhand store and bartering antiques qualified her to counsel me on a career. Still, as much as my mother's idiosyncrasies embarrassed me, I usually respected her advice.

The instructor walked around the room as we sketched the still life. I looked up as he passed.

He nodded at my canvas. "Nice sketch."

The professor walked down a row of tables. A pair of Levi's never looked so good. If he had been my instructor back in high school, I might have applied myself.

The next week, Minnie surprised me with her purchase of a real collector's item. She opened the back delivery door to a two-tone Corvair van, green and white. "Isn't she a beauty?"

The van appeared to be in good condition, the paint slightly oxidized but no rust. No missing paint. I stared back at my mother. Was she going through a midlife crisis? Men her age would opt for a sports car, the powerful engine substituting for their lessened prowess. After I thought about it, the van made sense. Minnie was reliving her short stint as a hippie.

"Planning a trip to San Francisco?"

"Of course not, silly." Minnie pointed to the roof. "It opens. Almost as good as a convertible."

I stared at the largest antique she'd bought yet. "Are we in the vintage auto market now?"

"I'm keeping this sweetheart for myself," Minnie said. "It's a 1965 Greenbrier van. I got a sweet deal from an elderly man in Henry. His kids weren't interested in the vehicle, and he wanted to clear out his garage for a new Honda."

She opened the doors for my inspection. The vinyl seats remained intact though permanently soiled. Was Watertown ready for Minnie's retro jaunts across town? I could see her in a purple tie-dye t-shirt and wire-rim sunglasses with pink lenses driving down Kemp and honking just for the attention. The van turned out to be a portent.

The next week, Minnie began dating. To my knowledge, my mother had never dated since I was born. And this proved not to be an isolated event. Within the month, she dated a half dozen different suitors. My head spun at the whirlwind of men that blew into Minnie's life.

Dr. LeGear

B illy Barber rubbed his chin before the 25" long thermometer. "I like this one."

Dr. LeGear's
Prescriptions
for
Livestock
Poultry
Dogs

Dr. LeGear
The Pioneer

Satisfaction
Guaranteed

"It's an eye catcher, for sure," I said. The thermometer retained its original yellow and red colors. Advertising thermometers were highly collectible, especially large pieces that made great wall decor.

"How old do you think it is?" he said.

The light shone off Billy's smooth scalp, his baldness made more evident since he stood shorter in shoes than my 5'6" in bare feet.

"Minnie would know. Let me get her over here."

I found my mother dressing a porcelain doll. "Billy has a question for you." Minnie set the doll in a sitting position on the shelf and followed me to the display. Billy studied the manufacturer's fine print on the reverse side with his pocket magnifying glass.

At the moment, we stocked quite a variety of old thermometers. A 29" tin Dad's Root Beer hung between a Bubble Up model and a Royal Crown Cola with a bold upward arrow. Gasoline advertising thermometers were the most sought after, and we had only one left, a Texaco Motor Oil.

"I believe the Dr. LeGear dates from the early 1900s," Minnie said. She pointed out a 1940s Marvels thermometer that announced the advertising slogan: "the cigarette of quality." Below the red rooster the cheeky wording read "worth crowing about." Nearby, a John Deere thermometer advertised Moose Lake Implement.

"How's business at the bowling alley?" Minnie asked.

"We have more leagues going this year." Billy smiled up at Minnie, who also stood taller than our local pin operator at Tommy's Lanes and Lounge. Billy reset the pins, waxed the alleys, and organized the bowling leagues.

"I bet you keep busy," Minnie said.

Was it my imagination or was she actually batting her eyelashes at the man? Billy was a nice man, but he lived at home with his aging mother and spent all his time at the bowling alley even after working hours.

"Guess we have that in common, Minnie," Billy said with a silly grin on his face. "We're both hard workers, ain't we?"

Minnie touched his hand lightly. "That we are." She winked.

With my back turned, I pressed my fist against my mouth. I'd never seen my mother flirt with anyone. And with Billy of all people? Their conversation remained in earshot as I walked away.

"Care to go to dinner with me Saturday night?"

I froze in my tracks.

"I'd love to, Billy."

I couldn't believe my ears. What was she doing?

After Billy paid for his Dr. LeGear's veterinary thermometer, I turned to Minnie. "Did Raymond bring these in?" I fingered the beaded key fobs.

"He brought them in yesterday. Something new they're making."

"They're pretty. I might buy one for myself." I placed the three-tone blue fob to the side. "Have a date with Billy, do we?"

Minnie maintained her gaze on the counter. "Is that a problem?"

"Never known you to date." I busied myself with some old skeleton keys in a bowl.

"Maybe it's time."

I looked at her then. She met my eyes. "Billy Barber. Really, Mother?"

"He's a nice man." Minnie lifted a broom from against the wall and hurried toward the rear of the store.

I shook my head. *Billy Barber?*

The date with Billy was not a fluke. The following week, I caught Minnie at lunch with the vice president of Farmers and

Merchants Bank. I had run into the Drake Restaurant to pick up an order to go when I spotted them at a corner table. A definite step up from Billy, Frank Jensen looked sharp in his three-piece suit and carefully groomed hair. As a recently divorced man in our small community, there would be wagging tongues, insinuating that my mother caused the breakup. I couldn't believe she would put herself in that position, not to mention lend herself to a rebound relationship. A familiar sensation rose as my stomach tensed. All the years of being embarrassed by my mother flooded back, and for the millionth time, I second-guessed my decision to move home.

Saturday morning, Minnie needed to deliver a vintage teapot to Kreiser's Drug.

"The drug store?" I said.

"The Blue Willow is for Emily Jones," Minnie said. "You know the pharmacist, Jerry Jones? Emily is his mother. Emily and her daughter, June, love fine china. Like mother, like daughter."

"I'll take it." I whipped around the counter. My mother was driving me crazy with her continual platitudes, and I needed a break.

I bowed my head to the blustery wind and crossed to the opposite side of the street. The drug store on the corner was in the historic Goss building dating back to 1889. The Kemp side of the three-story block building held three store fronts and the Maple side four.

Halfway to the pharmacy counter, I ran into Emily's husband, Joe. "Hi, Joe. Perfect timing. I have a package for your wife."

"More china, I'm sure," he said. "But I shouldn't complain. There's worse compulsions in this world."

I nodded and handed him the box.

94

"I heard you were back in town," Joe said. "Welcome home."

His son, Jerry, strode up to us in a white lab coat. "Hello, Liza. Welcome back. I'm headed to the post office. I'll take that to your car, Dad."

"Thanks, son." Joe turned back to me. "Did you know there's an opera house above us?"

"In this building? I never knew Watertown had an opera house."

"And you should see what we found. I have some things you might be interested in."

I followed Joe's slow pace to a door that opened onto a dark hallway, the only light came from the door ajar to the drugstore. We walked for a few yards until we came to a wooden staircase. He turned and the silhouette of Joe's slouched figure stood eerily in the musty air. He picked up a flashlight and led the way. "I have to take it slow, so be patient."

"No problem, Joe. I'm in no hurry." Between the deep shadows and squeaky stairs, I felt like Indiana Jones.

The aging stairs were comprised of raw wood. We arrived on the second floor, and the beam of the flashlight swept across the massive room.

"We're standing on the main floor of the opera." Joe aimed the flashlight past rows of theater seats to a wide stage with faded designs painted around the border. He directed the light to the high ceiling.

The enormous opera house was almost terrifying in the dark. A shiver skittered down my neck as *The Phantom of the Opera* came to mind. In the darkness, Joe's shadowy figure might have been the criminally insane phantom from the book. After a moment we returned to the hall outside the opera, and Joe handed me the flashlight.

"Go up one flight of stairs and take a gander at the opera boxes. My old legs can't take more steps. I'll wait here."

"But you'll be in pitch blackness."

"I'm not afraid of the dark. Go."

I thought what a great place this would be for art exhibits. *If* there was light. Maybe Beau could use his influence as a university professor to prod the city council. If they donated funds to add electricity, the theater could be used for multiple purposes.

I found the next stairway. In dim light, the aging centenarian was scarier than any horror movie I'd ever watched. Each stair creaked as I climbed to the third story. I half expected the phantom to step into the beam of the flashlight. Through a doorway, the flashlight revealed the balcony. With no idea of the sturdiness after all these years, I chose to observe from the hall. Joe told me to look at the opera boxes, so I continued and made a sharp turn.

A series of arched openings lined this part of the hall. The flashlight beam struck a railing, and in a wave of dizziness, I watched the beam plunge through the deep expanse of space to the floor below. I entered one of the opera boxes, floor creaking beneath my feet, and shone the light around the private room. The outer wall cracked, and I jumped. I took a breath and assured myself the old building was settling. Faded floral paper peeled at points from the walls. So this was where the well-heeled sat. From the floor below, opera goers would gaze up at the wealthy, whose status in society was figuratively and literally far above the average citizen.

My meandering thoughts turned to Joe. Poor guy— lingering in the dark. I hurried back to the second floor. Even though I knew he waited there, I flinched when light hit the form of his body. The image jarred a childhood nightmare I used to have: the stranger who was my father standing ghostly in the shadows.

"What did you think?" Joe asked.

"Magnificent. Thanks for showing me this. Minnie will be green with envy." I hooked my arm in his, worried that descending the stairs might prove hazardous for the elderly man.

When we arrived back on the first floor, Joe shined the flashlight on a wooden table. "Look what we discovered up there. I'd be willing to sell them if you're interested."

The light shone on a pair of ornate silver opera binoculars, the remains of an old banjo, and several skeleton keys of varying sizes.

"Takes you back, doesn't it?" Joe said.

"I feel like I've time traveled today. I'll let Minnie know about the items."

As Joe opened the door to the brightly lit drug store, I was temporarily blinded.

"Dad!" Jerry sounded alarmed. "Tell me you didn't climb those stairs again."

Joe turned to me and winked. "Just showing Liza the relics on the table."

I kissed Joe's cheek and hurried out the door. The wind had died down for the moment. I gazed up at the third story of the brick Goss building. Something white stirred at one window. Was it my imagination? The hair on the back of my neck prickled as I hurried back to Minnie's.

Later that week, a man called the store for Minnie. I figured he must be a customer until I heard her reply she'd meet him at the Wheel Inn at seven. Only one thing made sense. The proverbial midlife crisis had caught up with my mother. Heaven help us all.

I was not dating, but Minnie was on fire with a team of firefighters in hot pursuit. The irony of the situation was not lost on me. At my age I should be the one dating, but after the incident with Taylor, I had no inclination whatsoever for pursuing a relationship. Instead, I poured my energy into my painting classes.

I found it amazing how fast three hours could pass. Lost in the world of composition, contrast, and color, I basked in the smell of turpentine, the sweep of the paintbrush, and the amazing power of color. For three hours, longing for a normal life, my own mortgage, or a better job, and concerns about my crazy mother didn't exist. I was right where I wanted to be, doing what I wanted to do. Happiness filled those precious hours.

That night the young blonde dropped out of class.

"I have too many family obligations right now." She scribbled her phone number on a piece of paper. "But if you hold another class, you can give me a call."

I bit my tongue to keep from laughing. Family obligations, not likely considering her age and self-absorbed personality. From what I observed, she probably had become disillusioned with the fact that our handsome instructor continued to teach her painting techniques instead of exchanging phone numbers. The piece of paper was a last ditch effort to sway the instructor.

At last week's lesson, Bartlett had pointed out some tips to the young woman. "Keep in mind, contrast—light against dark—is more essential than color."

"But I love color." The blonde glanced up from lowered eyelashes.

"Contrast," he continued. "Light against dark." He moved on to the student behind her.

She shot a look back and narrowed her eyes.

During that same class, Professor Bartlett paused at my canvas. "Good composition. I can see you thought about the way the eye travels across the picture. Nice contrast but try to limit the number of colors. Choose two greens with varying degrees of light and dark."

I nodded. A person could get carried away with color. But unlike the flirty blonde, I was open to helpful criticism.

"Nice job," he said and walked on to the older gentleman behind me. A waft of his cologne had left me momentarily dazed.

At the beginning of each class, Bartlett gave thirty minutes of instruction in some aspect of painting, and I drank it all in. But I had to work at not staring as he looked out over the classroom with those green eyes or raked through the loose hair above his forehead. Handsome men were trouble, hadn't I learned that? Taylor and Jim proved my point. The male psyche couldn't handle all that female attention.

I was there to improve my artistic skill. I wanted to be a serious artist if it meant studying for the next twenty years. Beautiful canvases appeared in my mind as I stood in a big-city gallery, waiting for a patron to ask me about a painting. I might be hunched over and gray, but I saw myself as a true artist.

"Class, you have ten minutes to clean up."

I glanced up from my painting of Uncle Prewitt's barn. I'd taken a photo of the structure the day Taylor took me to visit his aunt and uncle. The lighting that evening made for great shadows. Contrast, as Beau Bartlett would pronounce the effect. I spun my brush in turpentine and pressed the bristles against the side of the jar. One more spin and I wiped the bristles with a thick cloth.

I packed up my tubes of oil paint and placed my brushes in an old tackle box.

Bartlett approached my easel. "Do you have time for a cup of coffee?"

I lifted my head to find only two older women and myself remaining in the classroom. "What?"

"I'd like to talk to you about your work." He looked at me as seriously as my Sunday school teacher when I was twelve.

"Oh…well…I suppose I have a little time." Would he tell me I had no artistic talent and should consider a class in black and white photography? Or was this a line?

"Let's meet at the bowling alley in ten minutes." He leapt up and turned to the woman across from me. "Here, let me help you with that canvas, Mrs. Franklin."

I walked out into the dark to Minnie's truck. At least, he hadn't suggested a bar. On second thought, they did serve beer at Tommy's. I clenched my jaw and caught myself grinding my teeth. If I detected the slightest hint of his coming on to me, I'd let him have it. I'd tell him I was in his class for one purpose and one purpose only. This time, I was making no mistakes.

Toil and Trouble

T he thud and ensuing whirr of balls rolling down the lanes provided the backdrop to our conversation. Beau Bartlett, beach-boy type turned professor, droned on about the magic of good composition and how light and dark could take the viewer into a picture and onto a well-planned journey. I sipped my cola and played with the ice as I watched strikes and spares appear across the alley. To be polite, I nodded and made occasional eye contact with my art instructor.

"I recognize raw talent when I see it," Beau said. "You just need to hone a few techniques."

I placed my glass down. "Is that a backhanded compliment?"

"I'm sorry," he said. "Sometimes I forget that the time and practice that goes into learning the craft can be daunting." He paused. "I see real talent in your work. It's obvious you're serious about learning."

Sitting there in the bowling alley, both of us in faded jeans and t-shirts, we might have been an ordinary couple on a date. I reminded myself that Beau Bartlett was a professor on leave and would return to the world of academia when his sabbatical ended.

"So, what brought you to Watertown," he asked.

"I grew up here. Nothing too exciting about me."

"You've never left?"

"I lived in the Cities for five years." I threw up my hands. "But here I am again, just a small town hick."

His mouth pursed in irritation. "Do you think I feel you're beneath me because you grew up in a small town?"

I'd insulted him. I was left speechless and bobbed an ice cube in my glass. "I never went to college."

"So you *do* believe I'm a pompous ass." He raised an eyebrow.

I studied his face and realized that was one thing the man wasn't despite his degrees. "Sorry, sometimes I wished I'd gone to college and studied art. Pardon my insecurity."

"Let's stick to what we both have in common." He smiled. "We both love art."

I raised my drink, and he clinked his bottle of Michelob against my glass.

"Bet you didn't know I used to shovel shit on my grandparents' farm."

"You're pulling my leg, now."

"Nope, spent summers as a kid on the farm. Shoveled manure in my grandpa's barn." He sat back and crossed his arms.

"Bet you didn't know my family home is an antique store. Literally. We live in the store." Really. Why did I admit that?

"I knew there was something unique about you."

My face bloomed with heat.

"Did you play with porcelain dolls and dress up in Victorian dresses?"

"Actually, I liked to play with the old metal tractors and trucks. When I dressed up, I put on vintage chaps and fringed vests. Sometimes when my mother wasn't looking, I'd try on the beaded breastplate of a Dakota Sioux chief."

"What I'd give to see a picture of that." Beau's smile turned down on one side. Something about that asymmetrical grin made him more human.

"I was given a tour of the Goss building on Kemp," I said. "There's a theater on the upper level. Might be a great place to display your paintings." In class, he had told us that he painted on a weekly basis. When questioned by one of the students, he revealed that his work was in several galleries across the country.

"That's a great idea. I'll have to check that out."

I told him to talk to Jerry Jones.

"You have a beautiful smile," he said. "I'd love to paint you sometime."

Warning flag. I frowned at the idea of modeling nude. Was that what this little get together was about—posing nude? I pushed my empty glass to the middle of the table and shoved back my chair.

"No, no." He held up both palms. "A portrait. I was thinking of a portrait. Jeez, you've been snake bit or something. My Catholic upbringing taught me to treat a lady like a lady."

"It's getting late." I stood. "I should be going."

Beau glanced at his watch. "Sorry. You probably have to get up early. No offense taken?"

"Nope, not me," I quipped.

"See you next week in class."

"See ya." In the parking lot, I drew my coat collar tight around my neck. He was right. I was definitely snake bit, but I wasn't taking anti-venom anytime soon.

* * *

The next morning Holly Jones leaned over the counter. "That's our new Methodist minister."

I looked over at the stocky man with silver sideburns milling around the vintage book section.

"I heard he's a widower." Holly looked as if she was interested in the man, who had to be at least twenty years older. Holly and a minister? I couldn't see it—Reverend Wright in his neatly pressed dress pants and Holly with her tobacco-can imprint on her rear pocket.

"Hello, Reverend," Holly said, her pale face turning pink. "I didn't know you liked antiques."

"I like to peruse antique shops. There's something about the past that's so fascinating, isn't there?"

"Oh, yes." She twisted her hands and smiled from ear to ear.

I'd never seen Holly interested in a man. She was definitely out of practice—if she'd ever had any.

"Reverend, this is Liza..." Holly paused as Minnie walked up to us. "And Minnie Murphy. They run the store."

"Actually," I said, "my mother owns it."

"Of course," Reverend Wright said. "Minnie's Antique and Curiosity Shoppe." He offered his hand to Minnie and then me. "Glad to meet you."

Minnie casually took his arm as if they were old friends and escorted him down the aisle. "I have something you must see."

Holly and I exchanged looks. Out of curiosity, I followed.

In a section with farm equipment signs, Minnie reached for an item hung on a pegboard. "Very apropos, don't you agree?"

She dipped her chin and glanced up through her eyelashes. What was going on with my mother lately?

I had to admit she had a knack for the humorous and matching an antique to a customer's personality. Minnie held up a vintage farm tool, a canvas bag attached to a metal top with a wooden handle on the side. The graphics on the bag read: Seed Sower. Touché, Mother.

A deep chuckle rose from the short man. "It's perfect. I must have that for my office."

Minnie tilted her face and winked. "I thought you'd like that."

"Say, I'm new in town and I'd love to have company for dinner. Care to join me?"

"And what makes you think I'm available?" Minnie smiled coquettishly.

Reverend Wright's neck blazed red. "I didn't see a wedding band and assumed—"

"You assumed right," she said. "I'd love to join you for dinner."

He blinked and recovered his composure. "Friday night, say seven?"

"Seven it is."

I walked away before I could be detected. The Reverend? The gossips would have a party with that one. I could hear it now—Jezebel!

That confirmed it. My mother was definitely caught in the throes of a midlife crisis.

My art class drew to an end. I had learned a lot from Beau Bartlett, and I remained more committed than ever to becoming a serious artist. The evening of our last session, Professor Bartlett announced he'd be offering another class the end of April. He encouraged everyone to consider registering for the second session and to tell any of our friends who might be interested. I was halfway out the door when he jogged up to me.

"I hope you're going to taking the next class." That smile alone could sell real estate in the Nevada desert.

"I'll think about it."

"You've grown a lot in this class. I see real talent in you."

"Thank you." I avoided those piercing eyes.

"Don't let it go to waste."

Miss Brank's speech came back to haunt me. "…you have to devote time and energy to art if you want to succeed."

"I've learned so much from you. I'll probably take the class."

"Great," he said. "See you in April."

I hitched my tote bag up my shoulder and headed down the hall. Relief swamped over me. He hadn't tried to ask me out, not even for coffee. I caught my reflection in the window and straightened my drooping shoulders. I raised my chin and walked faster.

On Saturday night at ten-thirty, the clack of the deadbolt on the delivery door told me Minnie had returned from her date with Myron, the widowed janitor at our church. Myron wore a perpetual scowl that came from a long refusal to wear eyeglasses. Minnie seemed to have no taste or discrimination when it came to men. And unbelievably, that week my mother had dates two nights in a row. Her dinner date with Reverend Wright had transpired the previous night. Lunch was on the agenda for Monday with someone named Timothy. I was keeping track.

I counted her footsteps up the wide stairway to the balcony and turned down the volume on *Knots Landing*, a spin off from *Dallas* but not as good. The only reason I watched the show was to see if Gary and Val would get back together, which they did. Even if those happy endings didn't often occur in real life, I enjoyed seeing it played out on television.

"How was the movie?" I looked up from my reclining position on the couch.

"Robin Williams was wonderful as Peter Pan." She tossed her wool cape over a chair. I was often the one to tidy up our living quarters. Minnie didn't have a problem leaving things right where she flung them.

"You watched a kid's film?" On second thought, that fit my mother only too well.

"Oh, you must see it." Minnie sat on the end of the couch near my feet and yanked off a bright red cowboy boot. "It's for all ages." With an extra heave, she removed the second boot. "Besides, we should never lose the child hidden in all of us."

The scent of buttered popcorn lifted from her clothes. Something stirred in me—that smell tapped a fuzzy memory. "I remember going to a movie when I was little." I turned off the television "I must have been three or four. Of course, I don't recall what the movie was, but I remember…there was someone else with us, and we shared a box of popcorn." I looked at Minnie. "A man. There was a man with us."

"That was so long ago." Minnie retrieved her coat and uncharacteristically placed it in the antique wardrobe we used for jackets and coats. "It could have been anyone. A neighbor, my cousin from Clear Lake, who knows?"

I dropped the subject. What I do remember was sitting between the two of them. I remember feeling warm, safe, and happy.

Julie and I squeezed into the middle row of seats, the theater packed for the showing of *Thelma and Louise*. Julie had ceased inviting me to couple's affairs. I was grateful on many levels. Lately, Julie didn't seem her carefree self. While we waited for the previews to start, I leaned over. "Is everything okay, Jules?"

"Of course, silly." She smiled but her mouth held a hint of tension.

My first guess was Jim. How long could a womanizer keep that kind of secret from his wife? Surely, it would show up as playful flirting with other wives at their frequent dinners with other couples. But I remembered how despondent I felt when I started to realize all was not right in paradise. I didn't want to be the one forever connected with revealing the ugly truth about Julie's husband. Jim hadn't made an outright play for me, though if I hadn't discouraged him and Taylor hadn't appeared when he did, he was certainly moving in that direction. My friendship with Julie meant too much to me. I was glad I didn't have to be put in that awkward situation.

I related to both characters in the movie: Louise, a diner waitress, whose musician boyfriend was always on the road (who knew what happened backstage with his groupies) and Thelma, whose good-old-boy husband wanted his wife to remain quietly in the background. I cheered their escape on a road trip together, but from there on it turned gloomy. Louise kills a man who tries to rape Thelma, which puts them on the run. The suicide ending made a dismal finale to the story.

The lights came on in the theater. "Promise me we'll never do the cliff scene, even if our lives get that bad," I quipped.

"I understand their despair. Sometimes life just gets too hard."

My obtuse attempt at humor had struck a sour chord. Julie grabbed her coat and made for the aisle.

"Sure there's not something you want to talk about?" I said softly.

"Nope," she said. "But let's pick a more upbeat movie next time."

"Of course." I shuffled behind her, wishing she'd talk to me, but I knew all too well that emotions stewing inside a woman had to come to a boil before any sense of things could be made.

Just like those lines in Macbeth:

> Double, double, toil and trouble;
> Fire burn, and cauldron bubble.

Macbeth Act 4, scene 1, 10–11

All Shades of Green

I dumped the contents of the clear plastic bag on the counter. Coins jangled and chimed as they fell over the accounting notebook (Minnie refused to come into the twentieth century and use a spreadsheet for the store). Sometimes customers bartered with Minnie. In the case of these coins, Emma Lou Reilly, a longtime family friend, had proposed a barter. Mrs. Reilly traded her old coins for a vintage christening gown for her grandniece.

I flipped a nickel, and the iconic buffalo appeared. The reverse side of a penny displayed an Indian head. I tossed one of the Morgan dollars in my palm, imagining an Old West gambler appreciating the solid feel of silver in his hand.

Minnie walked up behind me. "Purchased a 10 lb. sack of those once at an auction."

I glanced up. A leather belt with turquoise medallions circled her waist, cinching a denim skirt that brushed her black Tony Lama boots.

"The owners of a farm in Minnesota were preparing to lay a shed foundation and discovered them buried in the dirt floor."

"Crazy farmers." I tossed two Morgans just to hear the ring of silver.

"Not so crazy," my mother said. "It was probably hidden there during the Depression when no one trusted the banks."

"The Dirty Thirties?"

Parodying the show *Kung Fu,* Minnie kissed my cheek and said, "You are correct, grasshopper."

Minnie might be my mother, but she was not a great example of financial wisdom. She had never owned a house, and with all her bartering, I doubted she had a savings account. On the subject of treasures, my kitty for my future home amounted to $3,500. Once Minnie learned of my plan to buy a house, she refused my share of the rent. Still, I had a long way to go to obtain my dream of home ownership. Who was I fooling? Maybe I'd never own a house.

Sleigh bells announced the entrance of Raymond Standing Rock.

"Hey, Ray," I rang out. Minnie turned her back and fussed with a box of trinkets.

"Hello, Liza." He tilted his head. "Hello, Minnie."

"Oh hi, Raymond." My mother whisked out the feather duster and wiped a spotless Western Ho platter that had come in last week. "Have some wares with you today?" My mother kept her eyes on the platter.

"Not this time," he said. "Was wondering if you'd like to have dinner with me?"

She glanced up. "Sorry. I have another commitment tonight." Minnie picked up a lady's embroidered handkerchief and refolded it.

That was the first time in my life I'd heard Minnie fib, other than the story about the freight truck, but that was to protect me from Jim. Despite her merry-go-round of dating, I knew she didn't have an engagement that night. She had talked about watching a rerun episode of *Dallas,* one that she'd missed.

"Coffee then?" His brown eyes beseeched her but to no avail. Minnie shook her head, her eyes still on the handkerchief.

I couldn't take his hang-dog eyes any longer and blurted, "Hey, a cup of coffee sounds good."

Minnie's head flew up. She gave me a stern look.

"Why sure, Liza," Ray said, looking truly pleased. "I'd like that."

"Oh, I guess we're not that busy." Minnie threw the duster beneath the counter.

"We can't both leave the store," I said. "You go and I'll keep the store open." Though there were no customers in the store at the moment, midday proved to be the busiest part of the workday.

"What good is having your own business if you can't close when you want?" Minnie retrieved her tooled-leather purse from below the counter and headed for the door. She promptly flipped the sign to CLOSED. Ray and I looked at each other.

Minnie glanced back. "Come on. Let's go," she said.

Two slightly befuddled people—Ray and I—stood staring. After a moment, Ray cleared his throat, and I grabbed my jacket.

We headed to Ragels' Bagels. At that time of the day, the bagel business was slow. Ray shoveled spoonfuls of sugar into his coffee cup while Minnie stared.

"That's not good for you, you know." A slight frown rode her forehead.

"Is that so?" He smiled and added another teaspoon of sugar.

Minnie pursed her lips.

The song lyrics about sugar making the medicine go down skipped through my head. Was there some bad medicine

113

between the two? I did recall three sets of beadwork earrings once that Minnie decided were substandard after she'd purchased them. And one time she asked Ray if she could pay him the next day so the register wouldn't be short on cash. He'd refused. Stuck for ideas on conversation, I said, "So how's the town of Sisseton faring these days?" I sounded like some old farmer.

"They still roll up the street at six p.m." He glanced out the window. "I'm ready for spring, aren't you?"

Outside, the sun shone brightly in the late-March sky. Scoops of stale snow lay in the gutters and along sidewalks where the snowplow had built up ridges.

"I've been dreaming about spring," I said. Every year since I was ten, this occurred like clockwork.

"Always listen to your dreams," Ray said. "Let them speak to you."

I smiled politely. Ray was definitely talking like a medicine man. The only thing that dream told me was that South Dakota winters lasted too long. I wondered why Minnie thought this calm, kind man was a womanizer. Considering all the crazy dates my mother had gone on lately, a dinner date with Ray would be a move up. But what did I know? My record with men spoke for itself. Maybe womanizers learned to be sweet and kind in order to seduce women.

"How are your children, Ray?" Minnie spoke at last. I noticed her cup of Chai tea was half empty. Of course, she'd say half full.

"May just had her second baby, a boy this time. Star is getting married this summer to a nice Sioux man, and Pearl is expecting her first baby in June. Sunflower is still my baby, at least for another year. She's seventeen." Ray's face lit up when he talked about his children. He removed his billfold from his hip pocket and showed us pictures.

"That's nice, Raymond." Minnie's voice came softer this time. "You have a beautiful family."

Our coffee break dragged on with recurring periods of silence. Minnie knew him better than me, so why didn't she make more of an effort at conversation? Finally, their beleaguered tête-à-tête came to an end, and we walked back to the store. Three customers stood frowning at the sign on the door that displayed our business hours.

"Sorry, ladies." Minnie rushed to open the door. "Here you go." With a wide smile, she held the door for them. At the counter, I looked back at Ray, tipping his hat at Minnie. My mother lifted a hand and ducked inside the store. Outside the display windows, clouds overtook the sun. It would be a long time before spring officially arrived.

The first of April could be a schizophrenic time of the year. Cold one day, warm the next. In the Dakotas, forty-five degrees felt like a heat wave after a winter of 20° below zero.

Minnie mentioned we were growing short on change, and I jumped at the chance to do a bank run. The promise of spring hung on the air, and I drank it in. Sunny days held the fragrance of buds ready to burst and sprouting grass. The smell alone gave me spring fever, and I used every excuse to run errands in order to be outside.

Errand completed, I reluctantly returned to the store and found the counter unmanned and the phone ringing.

"Minnie's Antique and Curiosity Shoppe. Liza speaking."

"Can you come in tomorrow at ten?" a female voice said at the other end of the line.

Stay Alert and Doors Will Open. Minnie had quoted Jonathan Lockwood Huie last evening. I had been scanning want ads all winter, looking for a job that would be more lucrative than JCPenney. I had answered an ad for an office receptionist.

Three days earlier, I had picked up the application, and returned it promptly the following day.

I hung up the phone. A moment later, I hitched up the waist of my jeans, bent my knees, and pivoted behind the counter, doing the Urkel dance.

Next morning, I arrived at Swenson's Dentistry promptly at 9:50 a.m., wearing dress slacks and a blue blouse, the height of dressing up for me. Minnie cajoled me into wearing a string of fake pearls, which made me feel like I was fifty. She insisted a job in a dentist's office required more traditional attire. The young woman at the counter explained she was the dental assistant and couldn't wait until they hired a receptionist, so she could do the job she was hired to do. Amber, as her nametag announced, offered me a seat and said Dr. Swenson would be with me shortly.

With a mix of boredom and nerves, I flipped through a fashion magazine. I rarely wore dresses, but I assessed the short denim skirt on page seven modeled by a leggy blonde. The blue opaque tights made the skirt melt into a single piece of clothing. The Doc Martens boots were something I'd consider if I wasn't saving every penny for my dream house.

"He'll see you now." Amber gave a thumbs up.

For a moment, I imagined a dentist appointment rather than an interview and cringed inwardly at the thought of a metal pick probing my teeth. I followed Amber into a back office with a window overlooking Broadway. Wearing a white lab coat, the dentist glanced up as we entered the room.

"Dr. Swenson," Amber said. "This is Liza Murphy."

Dr. Swenson stood and shook my hand. "Nice to meet you, Liza."

Slim and tall, the man proved much younger than I'd have guessed, maybe thirty tops. His short trimmed hair looked more fitting for a drill sergeant than a dentist, but it was his

116

unassuming smile that impressed me the most. Kindness exuded from that face. Probably a patient man, a man accustomed to routine, required steps, and procedures. He would make a good boss.

"Have a seat, Liza." The scent of spearmint hung on the air. He returned to his chair and browsed my application form. "I see you've worked with the public." He glanced up and smiled. "That's always a plus." The dentist looked down again. "JCPenney. Good place. Great customer service." After a few minutes of awkward silence as he skimmed my references, he shoved the paper aside. His fingernails were immaculate, as well they should be. "So tell me, Liza, why do you want to be a receptionist at a dentist's office?"

Obvious question but I didn't see it coming. I cleared my thoughts and gave myself time to come up with a satisfactory answer. "The atmosphere is pleasant. I have a calm demeanor that will put patients at ease, and I know a lot of people in this town. I'm sure I know many of your patients by name. That can't hurt, can it?" Shouldn't have said that. My nervousness leaked out like a melting Popsicle. "And I won't have to do inventory." Wrong again. I shut up, afraid to further incriminate myself.

"Honesty, that's refreshing." He nodded as if to himself. "You're a hometown girl, so yes it helps that you know people." He pushed the chair back from the desk. "You're my last interview this week, and I've pretty much made up my mind."

I knew it. He'd made up his mind five interviews back. Probably some bubble-headed beach blonde. I rose from the chair. "Thank you for your time." Beneath the surface, I was fuming.

"Wait a minute," he said. "Don't you want to know who I hired?"

Did he assume I knew her, too?

I paused with my best blank face.

"You're hired, Miss Liza Murphy." He tilted his head and smiled.

I stood there for a moment before I fully comprehended his words. "Oh. Thank you. I promise I'll do a great job for you."

"Don't you want to know what I pay?" He wore an amused expression.

"Of course."

I left his office smiling. I was going to have a lot more pennies for my house kitty.

Minnie pushed a wooden factory cart down the store aisle. Piled high, wire baskets shivered and shook as she aimed the cart towards a booth I'd emptied earlier in the week.

"Egg baskets?" Some of the baskets had metal ribs rubber-coated in red, yellow, and black. "What are we going to do with that many egg baskets?"

"There's more in the back." Minnie careened the long cart around the corner and parked it halfway into the booth space. She brushed aside wisps of hair that had escaped her long braid. April had brought out one of Minnie's favorite wardrobe items: a peasant-style dress, this one in blue and purple paisley print. "Forty-seven to be exact. Elmer Peterson's grandparents were big egg producers in their day. He made me a good deal."

Not a big call for egg baskets these days, but I kept my silence.

"I know what you're thinking," Minnie said. "But I have some great display ideas." She winked. "You'll see."

Two days later, I checked on the booth. My mother had indeed come up with a plethora of uses for the baskets. She'd filled them with items suggestive of their use: balls of yarn in one, socks in another, flip flops, baseballs, gloves, paperback books, and as if a person had to be told, crumbled up sheets of paper in another. Artificial daisies filled two baskets lined with moss. Hooked from the ceiling by chains, several baskets hung upside down, their wire handle pointing to the floor with an Edison-style lightbulb inside.

Minnie looked over my shoulder. "What do you think?"

"I have to hand it to you," I said. "You thought of everything."

"I'll take that as a compliment."

I glanced back and saw another face peering over Minnie's shoulder. Lester Brown nodded his head. "Looks nice, Minnie."

Lester had retired from the Post Office years ago. He was often seen pushing a cart down the streets of Watertown, looking for pop cans to recycle. One might think that all that pushing had stooped his shoulders, but Lester's arched back originated from birth, an unfortunate congenital defect. I always wondered if he had chronic neck pain from looking up from such an odd angle. Poor guy.

"Lester," Minnie said. "How are you today?"

"Fine as frog's hair." He grinned as he peered up at her from his permanent stoop. "You're so inventive, Minnie. Nice use of egg baskets."

"Thank you," she said. "I thought it turned out pretty good myself."

I leaned around my mother. "Hi, Lester."

"Hey there, Liza. Saved me any pop cans?" Lester knew I indulged in Coca-Cola.

"Half a garbage sack. Let me go get them." I was barely in the aisle when Lester asked Minnie to dinner that night.

"Sure, Lester," she said. "I'd love to."

I decided Minnie must be on a charity mission for lonesome men. A lonely hearts club of sorts. How crazy and foolish. Why lead these guys on? But then word must surely have gotten around that Minnie was dating every single man over fifty. In a small town, news flew faster than geese on the day of opening season. Then it hit. An unexpected wave of self-pity washed over me. Pretty bad when my mother dated more than me.

Even Holly Jones, miracle of miracles, had started dating a widower who dabbled in writing fiction. She had come in the store five days earlier, and for a moment, I didn't recognize her. She'd cut her long hair to shoulder length and flipped the ends. Holly had even put a brown rinse in her premature gray locks, though the hair color looked faded. Was that a touch of blush on her cheeks? Holly looked fifteen years younger...and happier.

"He writes Sci-Fi," she said. "Isn't that cool?"

Holly dating? I never thought I'd see that in my lifetime. I had to ask. "How did you meet?"

"At the library," Holly said. "They started a writers' group on Wednesday nights." Holly blushed slightly. "He was running late and sat next to me. We've sat together every session since."

"So-o-o, you haven't actually gone on a date yet?" That made more sense.

"Let's see. We had dinner at the Drake, breakfast at the Wheel Inn, went bowling one night at Tommy's, and oh yeah, we went dancing Saturday night."

Holly dancing? I was speechless.

She leaned in closer. "Henry has two children, a son who farms with him near Clark and a daughter who lives in Estelline. They're very nice people. Of course, they're young adults, but it's like I have an instant family." She beamed.

Holly was moving too fast for me to keep up, not to mention herself. "You aren't already hitched?"

"Oh, silly." She threw a mock jab at me.

Obviously, the man had to be much older than Holly, but apparently he made her happy. I stared as Holly exited the store. To my amazement, she wore a new pair of colored jeans. The characteristic snuff can ring on the rear pocket had vanished.

First Minnie, now Holly. I reminded myself that unlike them, I had no desire to join the dating scene.

It's like I have an instant family. Geez, was she for real? Nerdy Holly Jones with her face buried in a book and her fingers glued to typewriter keys. An unsettled feeling wound around me, and my face warmed at the realization that I was lizard green with envy.

Sample Toothbrushes and Muscle Cars

Julie's dining table shone from light flooding through the French doors. Little Annie spun around for me, wearing a pink tutu and a tiara.

"You're so pretty," I gushed. Oblivious to the women in the room, her brother, Jimmy, played with a Tonka truck on the floor, revving the engine with gusto.

When I was a child, my mother told me a story about my birth. She whispered in my ear, "You were born a flower child, birthed beneath the shade of a tall palm tree. Himalayan magnolias bloomed around your sweet little face."

"What do magnolias smell like," I had asked.

"Roses and lemons all stirred together." Minnie rolled her eyes upward. "You took your first breath amid beauty and perfume."

Quite a story for a seven year old. I remember feeling special, like a beautiful princess, which I suppose was the desired result. Years later, I passed the story off as a hallucination from her hippie days. What had Minnie been smoking?

Ice cubes chimed against my glass as I stirred a teaspoon of sugar. "Great ice tea."

"Sun tea brewed on the back deck," Julie said, "infused with fresh strawberries." Annie danced off to her room, and the green Tonka trunk chased pink leotards.

"The kids are sure growing."

Julie stared at the grain in the maple table.

"Julie?"

"I think Jim is cheating on me."

My sharp intake of breath couldn't be taken back. "Oh, Julie." She searched my face. "I'm so sorry." Should I have said something earlier?

"Jim says it's my overactive imagination." She waited for something. Confirmation? Denial?

"Honey, that's crazy making."

"He says I need to tame my jealous streak."

My chin tightened. "Trust your instincts."

"What if I'm wrong?" Her eyes looked so pathetic.

"What does your gut tell you?"

"But how can I be sure?"

My mind spun. Do I tell her Jim flirted with me? But if they get back together, she'd never forgive me and our friendship would be over. Think. Think. "I know a guy who is a private investigator. Tell him I referred you, and he'll give you a discount. If nothing turns up, you can quit worrying." Actually, Minnie knew a guy, but that wasn't important at the moment. "I'll call you when I get home and give you his number."

Julie rose from her chair and hugged me. I fought tears for the outcome was almost guaranteed. Poor Julie. She didn't deserve this.

On the drive home, I broke down in sobs. Every woman in love desired to feel like a princess: special, adored, treasured. I dried my tears and considered a positive outcome. After the pain, after the heartache, Julie would be able to go on with her life. Weren't we all stronger than we knew? Life as a single parent had to be better than living a marriage with an unfaithful husband. I parked in the alley behind the antique store and pondered my own life. What if I had gone down the wrong road with Taylor? A second time, no less. I squeezed my eyes shut.

Nine to five, Monday through Friday were pretty sweet hours at Swenson's Dentistry. Framed photographs of ocean-side beaches adorned aqua walls. White wicker furniture with thick cushions further fostered the impression of being at the beach. A five-foot potted palm sat in the corner. I sat behind a white quartz counter and greeted patients as they checked in, made appointments over the phone, and managed payments and billing. Minnie started referring to me as "my daughter, the dental receptionist. After a few days of training with Amber, I worked happily on my own.

Between patients, Dr. Swenson would come out to the reception area, lean over the counter, and make small talk. Wasn't the sunshine wonderful, what movies had I seen lately, and what did I like in school? I figured dental exams and drilling for cavities had worn him down until I saw Amber waggle her eyebrows behind his back. I flicked my index finger with my thumb, hoping she'd get my meaning. Just in case she didn't, I spoke to her after she escorted a patient back to the reception room.

"Kent's nice, don't you think?" Amber smiled mischievously. "I think he likes you."

"I'm serious about this job," I said. "I'm not interested in men."

125

Amber's eyes widened and her hand flew to her mouth.

"Not that. I'm not interested right now. Too many bad experiences, you know?"

"I get it. We've all been there."

I wondered if she had. She was fresh out of dental school, maybe twenty tops. As I'd told, Dr. Swenson, I did know about three-fourths of his patients. Minnie constantly relayed the fact her friends had seen me at the dentist's office and how wonderful I'd gotten such a nice job or how I worked great with the public, so pleasant, so easy to deal with. That grew old fast. I would just nod, but I could tell Minnie was proud of me.

Minnie's dating extravaganza remained in full force. The night before, she attended bingo night at the Elks with Bertram Buttons, who owned the shoe store on the corner of Kemp and Maple. They'd gone to school together, so I didn't think much of that date. Tomorrow she had a dinner date at the Drake.

"Who's your dinner partner?" I asked.

"Dr. Ogden."

"*Doctor*?" Minnie was moving up in the world. "Is he new to town?"

"He's been here for a few years." Minnie polished the old register with a cloth.

"What type of doctor?"

"He's an optometrist."

I found myself slightly disappointed. I had geared up for a plastic surgeon. They made more money. "That's nice, Mother."

My letdown turned upbeat when the gentleman came to pick her up. The silver hair at Dr. Ogden's temples beautifully accented his thick, gray hair. Oh, he was handsome. Minnie laughed as they made their way out. I hoped this one would work out. Do you know what you've got there, Mother? Handsome, professional, and well to do. Something inside told me none of that made a difference to Minnie. She'd look at the inner soul as she always did.

If only she'd waited for someone like that years ago. I'd have a father, and we'd probably live in a big house with a veranda overlooking the lake. My easel would be set up with a perfect view of a sunset exploding on the horizon. I leaned over the counter with chin propped on my palms and allowed myself ten minutes of fantasy living.

One patient didn't show, and the last patient of the day canceled. At Swenson Dentistry, we worked hard to avoid empty slots. I mailed reminders a week prior to appointments. Part of every work day included calling patients two days before to remind them of their dental visit.

I relayed Mrs. Garret's apology to Dr. Swenson. "Her sister, Emily, was taken by ambulance a few minutes ago."

"I hope you told her it was no problem," he said. "Emergencies come up."

"They've lived together for the last twenty years. Mrs. Garret is a widow, and Emily never married. Mrs. Garret sounded pretty shook up."

"Poor dear." Dr. Swenson rubbed his chin. "Well, I suppose…say, would you mind helping me move some boxes from my home to the office? Nothing too heavy, I promise."

"I'm on the clock." I eagerly complied, curious to see where he lived. In the back parking lot, Dr. Swenson walked up to a bright red Corvette.

"Dr. Swenson, you do have a wild side after all," I said.

His face was hard to read, offense or embarrassment struggled behind his expression. Sometimes I needed a filter. Not everyone got my sense of humor. "Sorry, just surprised is all."

"It's not too much? The color, I mean. I debated over this and a black one."

"It's beautiful." He opened the door for me, and I slipped into the luscious smell of new leather.

"You don't think it's too flashy for a conservative community?" He looked at me for confirmation.

"No, no. If you've got it, flaunt it." I admired the control panel before I sensed a pregnant silence in the vehicle. I glanced over and caught him staring over the hood. Shoot.

"That's exactly the reaction I didn't want," he muttered.

"You'll have to excuse me, Dr. Swenson. Sometimes, I don't think before I speak. What I meant was if you're going to have a classic sports car, you want it to stand out, don't you?"

"Think I'll save the Corvette for day trips. Usually I drive my Suburban to work." He looked over with a sheepish look.

I nodded. Time to keep my mouth shut.

"We're not at the office. You can call me Kent."

I hoped Amber was wrong. This guy came off as a little too…unsure of himself. Dr. Swenson drove out of town, and I realized we were headed to Lake Kampeska. Why should I be surprised? He was a dentist, after all. He dialed the radio to an easy-listening channel, and it dawned on me the background music at the office proved more than a soothing measure for patients. We drove around the east side of the lake and passed two-story brick buildings built to impress. He pulled into the cement driveway of a one-story house with a grand double door that greeted the visitor with aplomb and dignity. Potted boxwoods stood as sentinels at each side of the door.

He pushed the remote and opened the double garage where his white Suburban offered a more conservative face to the community. "We'll take the Chevy. It has more room for the boxes."

Kent pointed to a stack of boxes that lined one side of the garage. He explained the dental supplies had been sent to his billing address rather than the shipping address. "I know it sounds crazy, but I prefer to do my own bookkeeping." We exited the car. "Would you like to see the place?"

"Sure." Like a kid at Christmas, I did. He held open the door that led from the garage. Had to give him credit for being a gentleman. After all, I was only an employee.

The door opened into a combination mud room/laundry area that led to a large kitchen with a cooking island, granite counters, and more cabinets than I could imagine filling. A built-in wine rack filled a wall next to the side-by-side refrigerator.

"Nice kitchen," I mumbled.

"Thanks." He waved me on to the great room. "This is my favorite room."

Through glass doors the lake sparkled under the clear sky, stretching to the far shore. My daydream the day before came back to me. It was *déjà vu*, either that or I had had some strange kind of ESP. "Beautiful." I approached the doors and saw a cobblestone veranda with a brick fire pit at the edge. Matching flower boxes lined the veranda and stairs that led down to the lawn. A cobblestone path continued through silver maples and ended at the dock.

"Very nice, Kent."

"Thank you. It's a great place to entertain though I don't tend to do much of that."

"You'll have to change that. This is too good to go to waste."

"Maybe this summer you can help me plan a little party."

He watched me, waiting for my reaction. I fumbled for a noncommittal answer. "We'll see."

He showed me the formal dining room and stopped at the den. I noted bronze sculptures among the bookshelves and original watercolors on the walls. Kent obviously appreciated art. I was relieved he didn't show me the bedrooms. Kent offered me a Coke, and we loaded the back of the Suburban. It was new, too.

On the return trip, Kent turned up the radio and forewent conversation. In my mind, I toured the lovely lake house again and dreamt I'd become a lady dentist and not a simple receptionist. I had mentally slighted Minnie for not holding out for a doctor, yet I wasn't much better when it came to life choices. Why hadn't I considered going back to school? Everyone had choices, but many of us never considered our options. I closed my eyes and drifted into the new car smell of leather and plastic.

We unloaded the boxes onto dollies and made two trips to the dentist office. Dr. Swenson bid Amber, who had stayed to clean up, and I a good weekend even though the clock read 4:35. I pulled into the back alley of the antique store and parked. Friday night, a delivery pizza, and a videotape movie sounded perfect to me.

It took a moment for my brain to register the scene before me. Minnie had said the old van needed new tires and a complete tune-up before she'd think of driving the vehicle. Damp earth from last night's rain revealed a telling dry rectangle on the ground. The green and white Greenbrier was gone.

Cavity-Ridden Notes

The lights were off in the stockroom. A note posted on the backdoor drew my attention. I double-checked my watch. It was only quarter to five. Minnie never closed before 5:30. I tore the envelope from the door and opened a lined sheet of paper, the left side shredded where it had been ripped from a spiral notebook.

Dear Liza,

Needed a break. Road trip. Don't worry about the store. If you want to open it on the weekend that's up to you. If not, put a note on the front door: Closed for Renovations.

Ha! Will call in a few days.

Love, Mother

In the twenty-four years I'd known my mother, she'd never taken off on a whim. The word, *vacation*, wasn't part of her vocabulary. A weekend expedition to hunt for antiques occurred once a year, but never a true vacation. I tried to reason it out.

Wasn't it about time she deserved a break? Yet, it wasn't like her not to tell me in person. And why the clandestine note?

My stomach twisted. I removed pizza from that night's agenda and ambled down the alley where a tin garbage can had tumbled over in back of the bakery. Empty flour bags had spilled out, dusting the ground with white powder. I found myself heading to the river, strolling through Riverside Park until the sky darkened, and the evening chill prodded me for my forgotten jacket. On my way back bruised clouds rolled up, and Watertown streetlights guided me home to an empty balcony in the old JCPenney building with its slight musty smell and a reminder that no one could ever truly understand another human being.

Out of a sense of duty, I opened the store Saturday morning. I was on my fifth cup of coffee—had slept like a lively night owl—when Georgia Brewer entered the store. Permanently plastered in place with Aqua Net, Georgia's bouffant hairdo remained in style for women of her generation. Twenty-five years older than my mother, Georgia stood 5' in heels. Her cheeks bloomed from powdered peach blush.

"Is Minnie around?" she asked. "She had some vintage hats she wanted me to see."

Georgia belonged to Minnie's bridge group. Obviously, my mother hadn't mentioned her impromptu trip to the ladies either. "She's not here at the moment. But I know she was saving a box of hats for someone. Let me get them for you."

"Thank you, dear."

Three hours later, Wilbur Hood, an old bachelor who frequented the Farmer's Bar and Grill stopped in and inquired about hood ornaments. He had a collection, he explained.

"I believe we have one or two in the display case." I paused. "Say, Wilbur. Has my mother talked about taking a trip?"

Wilbur screwed his lips sideways and glanced at the ceiling. "Can't say that ever came up in conversation."

"A vacation maybe? Tourist attractions. A visit to a friend?" I was desperate to find a lead.

"Sorry, Liza. Don't recall anything like that. Minnie always seems so happy right here in her own little world."

"Thanks anyway, Wilbur." I pointed. "Glass case by the door."

Pumped on caffeine, I still couldn't make sense of my mother leaving the way she did. It was so uncharacteristic of her. I worried that something was seriously wrong. Her health? She seemed as healthy as an ox, as she always claimed.

The doctor. The handsome optometrist. Maybe they had eloped. That didn't make sense either. They certainly wouldn't have taken a chugging old van that backfired. They'd have flown to Rio de Janeiro in a flourish of luxury and comfort.

Why, why, why, I asked myself incessantly. *Stop.* I slapped my forehead with the heel of my hand. My insatiable quest for an answer would drive me crazy.

"I've wanted a van ever since San Francisco."

My mother had told me that the day she'd driven the Greenbrier home. Had she headed to the West Coast? I could see her trying to relive her hippy days or at least the memory of them. But not telling me in person, that just didn't "ring true." Nothing fit. An ulcer would consume my stomach lining before Minnie got around to calling me.

Monday morning I reminded John Forrester of his appointment which had taken place three days earlier. I greeted Sarah Peterson as Sandra Pauls, her longtime nemesis. I drank too much coffee and twice spilled Coke over the day's printed schedule. But after Amber found me sleeping in a corner of the restroom, I knew I'd gone too far. Dr. Swenson called me into his office.

He sighed deeply and straightened some papers on his desk. I knew the job was too good to be true and waited for my official sacking.

"Is something wrong, Liza?" His quiet voice was reassuring. It would be a calm, almost comforting dismissal. I noted the glass jar with white sugarless mints. That's why his breath always oozed minty refreshment.

"It's my mother." I sighed, relieved to have my anxiety out in the open. "She's gone. Left me a note. Something about a road trip." Kent tilted his head and leaned forward, official body language for empathetic listening. I continued, "She said she'd call, but she hasn't yet." I was rambling but couldn't stop myself. "I know it's only been a couple of days, but it's not like her. First," I raised my index finger, "she never goes on vacations, and second," I lifted another finger, "she always tells me things in person. I mean, who leaves a cryptic note for their own daughter?" I caught sight of my wringing hands and separated them. I glanced down, feeling somehow both vulnerable and ridiculous.

"I'm sure you're worried about her," Kent said.

"I'm freaked out. When someone you love does something unexpected, so uncharacteristic, you don't know what to think." I realized the last time I felt like this was when I was married. Taylor hadn't come home for three days, without the courtesy of a verbal notice, written note, or phone call to explain his absence.

"Definitely." Kent's index fingers formed a triangle.

"I'm sorry it's affected my work. If you want me to leave today, I don't blame you."

Kent pushed back his chair from the desk. "Don't worry about that. But I do have one condition."

I waited.

"You have to talk to someone about your feelings. You can't let them build up. Amber or I would be more than willing to listen."

I gave a perfunctory nod though I wasn't a person who ordinarily liked to confide in acquaintances.

"Try to take comfort in the fact your mother said she'd call." Kent stood. "You know what I do when I can't sleep? I go for a walk, doesn't matter what the hour." He smiled warmly.

I nodded and didn't let on that I'd tried walking. Didn't worked. In desperation, I'd tried jogging, not effective either. Counting sheep was ridiculous. I even resorted to an inventory of the jewelry case one evening. Still wide awake for hours.

Kent placed a hand on my shoulder and escorted me from his office. I felt like an errant child. At least I still had my job.

I don't know if it was the fear of losing my job or the fact I'd finally confided in someone, but that evening I slept like a baby. The next afternoon, the phone rang as I came through the back door.

"Minnie's Antique and Curiosity Shoppe," I said breathlessly. "May I help—"

"Liza, there you are," Minnie's voice came over the landline.

Those should have been my words. "Mother, where are you?"

"Just have a minute. I'm double parked," she said. "How's the job going?"

"Fine," I lied. "Why didn't you tell me you were leaving?"

"Just needed a break. Came over me all at once. I was afraid if I hesitated, I'd never leave. Don't worry, honey. Everything's all right. Oh, no, there's a patrol car. Don't need a ticket. Call you next week."

The phone went dead. With the receiver still in hand, I realized I still didn't know where my mother was, where she might be heading, or why she needed a break. A break from all that dating? But that was easily resolved with a simple no. Disconnect beeping blared from the phone, and I slammed the receiver into place with a few choice words.

Everything's all right. I'd have to take her word for that. Anger quickly replaced my distress. She'd made me worry for days and still wasn't forthcoming with an explanation. My mother was exasperating sometimes.

The phone rang again. Minnie must have realized how curt she'd been.

"Yes, Mother."

"It's me...Julie." Her voice cracked. She sounded like she'd been crying. "Can you come over? I really need to talk to someone."

"Of course. I'm on my way."

I hugged Julie at the door. Disheveled hair and baggy sweatpants didn't do her any favors. Stains ran down the front of her gray t-shirt. How long had she been like this? We sat in the living room where she informed me the kids were staying with her mother. Julie had taken my advice and hired a private investigator. She handed me the glossy 8 x 10 black-and-white photographs. I winced. Jim checking into a motel with a clerk I recognized from the grocery store. Jim and a woman I *didn't* recognize having dinner in a dark corner of the Drake. The last photo showed him making out in a car with a girl who looked like a minor.

"Jeez, Julie," I said. "I'm so sorry." It was worse than I'd thought. One affair would have been trouble enough, but the man turned out to be a compulsive womanizer.

"I talked to a lawyer," Julie said. "I'm filing on Monday."

"More importantly, how are you dealing with all of this?" Stupid question as her physical appearance told it all.

"My first reaction—my life is over."

I could understand that emotion. Julie's marriage and family meant everything to her. She reached for her purse but instead of pulling out a tissue, she withdrew a breath mint. Considering her lack of personal grooming, she probably hadn't been brushing her teeth either.

Julie's jaw set. "But I decided I wouldn't give him the satisfaction of ruining me. I have two beautiful kids, and we're going to make our own life."

"I don't have kids, so I can't pretend to know the implications of a divorce with children involved, but I certainly know about a cheating husband. You're going to go through a roller coaster of emotions, Jules. Relief, fury, hope, despair. Allow yourself to feel everything. It's all part of the healing process."

"Yeah, I've already cycled through many peaks and plunges." Tears built in her eyes. "I just never expected this, Liza."

"No one ever does."

"I have a favor to ask of you."

"Anything."

"Help me repaint the house. I need a change—make it different, fresh, my own place. I want to paint every room a new color and then I'll redecorate."

Julie was going to be all right. "I'm great with edges," I said. "Smoothest lines you ever saw."

"Thanks. We'll work around your schedule."

"Seven in the evening works for me. Start picking out your colors."

Julie smiled and dug in her purse. She waved half a dozen paint swatches.

Painting became a way of life. I spent Monday, Wednesday, and Friday rolling paint on Julie's walls. Tuesdays and Thursdays found me back in Beau Bartlett's art class. He saluted when I entered the room. I smiled and chose a table. Half of the class members were new, and we had added two older men and one teenage boy. I had forgotten how good looking Professor B was but quickly shoved that thought aside.

Fifteen minutes later, Beau stood and introduced himself. "In this class, you'll do a landscape, a still life, and a portrait." A few older women exchanged worried looks. "I realize," he continued, "that some of you are comfortable in only one of those subject matters, but I believe it's good to push yourself and try something new. Even if you don't continue, let's say, with portraits, what you learn will carry over to everything you paint."

That night we sketched a still life he had set up before class: green wine bottle, a long-stemmed glass, and three pears. By the end of the class, most of us had begun painting. Beau walked up behind me.

"Feeling impressionistic, are we?"

Maybe it was what Julie was going through, perhaps it triggered too many past memories for me, but I had decided to forego a brush and paint with a palette knife. I loved the feeling of broad, three-dimensional strokes. "Mm-hmm," I muttered and continued to apply varying shades of yellow to the pear. I added blue-violet to the shadow side.

"Nice to see you again." He wandered over to the lavender-haired lady next to me, who applied paint with slow, tentative strokes.

As I cleaned my palette knife at the end of the session, Beau asked for a moment of my time after class. I must have given him a funny look because he added, "Won't keep you but a couple of minutes, I promise." He moved on and spoke to another student.

The last student was packing up her supplies in a canvas tote when Beau approached me.

"Since you're interested in impressionism, you might like to see the work of one of my students who's taking private lessons. He's very talented and producing some interesting paintings. Can you drop by my loft studio on Saturday?"

I pictured his studio on the top floor of one of the historic downtown buildings. That old line—want to come up to my place and see my etchings?—ran through my mind.

"Sean will be there if you're worried about being alone with me." His left eyebrow rose as he smiled.

"What would I be worried about?" I was quick to say. "Where's your studio located?"

"Remember I told you I worked summers for my grandparents?"

I nodded.

"I inherited my grandparents' farm five miles north of town. I lease the land, but I retain the old house. Made a studio in the upper level of the barn."

"In the *hayloft*?" That was all it took.

He laughed. "I'll give you the grand tour."

"Let me write down the directions." I fumbled through my purse for a piece of paper, gum wrapper, anything.

"It's easy to find. Take the highway north of town for three miles, turn right on the township road, and drive two more miles. You'll see a white foursquare with a red barn behind it."

"Got it. What time?"

"Any time between ten and noon, that's Sean's lesson time."

I hooked the tote strap over my shoulder. "See you Saturday."

"Saturday it is."

I felt his eyes on me as I exited the classroom. Why did that man make me feel so nervous?

Poor Investments

After work I ran into Reverend Wright at the grocery store.

"How are you, Liza?" Dignified from his gray hair to his creased Dockers, the man looked into my eyes as one familiar with searching souls. "How's your mother doing? I noticed the store's been closed for a week. Is everything all right?"

"Minnie's taking a little vacation," I said. "She's way overdue for one. Hey, I'm running late for a dinner engagement. I'll tell her I ran into you." I rushed from the aisle without my much needed two-percent milk, not wanting to be asked questions about my mother's imaginary vacation. I didn't like to fib. But was the fictional dinner engagement any better than making up a vacation destination?

On the way to the truck, I ran into Myron, clad in his nondescript but serviceable matching blue work pants and shirt. "Haven't seen your mother around for a while." He shifted his thick-soled boots. "Will you let her know I was asking about her?"

"Sure, Myron." I opened the driver's side door. "Sorry, I'm a bit rushed." I drove around the corner and pulled into the convenience store where I would pay twice as much for milk as I would have at the grocery. I was eager to get home and prop up my feet before joining Julie for another night of painting. Dusky amethyst for the living room was on the agenda that night. At the refrigerator cooler, I twirled around and nearly bumped into Billy Barber.

"Liza, good to see you."

I gazed down on his smiling face. "Hey, Billy." His stubbly chin needed a shave.

"I've been trying to get hold of your mother, but she doesn't return my calls." His grin sagged into a frown.

I'd put off listening to phone messages, partly because I didn't want any messages from Minnie. I deserved to talk to her voice to voice. "Minnie's been on vacation, traveling around a lot. Don't know where she is at the moment. I'll let her know you called."

Billie looked relieved as I spun to the checkout counter. I drove straight home to avoid any more encounters with Minnie's boyfriends.

A few days later, I drove north of town. Fields of oats and alfalfa had been planted, evident by neat rows of seedlings poking from the earth. High puffy clouds left plenty of blue sky and little chance of rain. I recalled visiting my great-grandparents' farm forty miles from Watertown when I was five. At that time, they were retired and leased the land, refusing to move to town despite their advanced age. I don't remember a lot about the visit, but certain things stuck out: vast open fields, the sweet smell of the wind, and a building that threatened to engulf me. Their massive white barn rose from the flat landscape like a fortress overlooking the entire world.

I guess barns still captured my imagination. I recognized Beau's black Jeep and pulled into the dirt drive. While debating whether to knock at the farmhouse door or head to the barn behind it, a figure appeared at the barn's loft doors.

"Up here," Beau yelled.

I climbed the slight incline to the barn. Once inside, it took a moment for my eyes to adjust and when they did, it was clear the bottom level retained its original form. Pitchforks and shovels hung on weathered wood, along with coiled lassos and leftover twine. Stalls lined one side of the barn and milking stations the other. The smell of old hay swam in the air, evidence that the barn hadn't fulfilled its purpose for years.

"Glad you made it." Beau met me near the stalls. "Haven't touched this part. Call me nostalgic."

Along with that faraway look in his eyes, a dimple rose on his cheek. He looked quite disarming.

"Follow me," he said.

We walked farther into the shadows. Beau flicked on a light and a chair lift appeared. A railing had been welded around the lift. "Cheaper than an elevator." He swung open the gate and motioned me forward. The space barely accommodated two people, and as we stood only inches apart, I could feel the heat from his body. My skin prickled. I hadn't been this close to a hot guy for a long time.

He activated the lift, and amid mechanical whirring, we rose to the upper floor of the barn. I stood amazed at the hayloft's transformation. A gentleman worked on a canvas at the far end of the loft, but for the moment, I was transfixed on the studio itself.

Slabs of oak flooring shone under skylights added between the roof's open beams. Creamy-white sheetrock ran halfway up two walls to where old barn wood continued to the rafters. Along with two barn pulleys with attached ropes, the exposed studs and beams of the structure insured the occupants never forgot the space's original purpose. Knotty pine covered two ends of the loft, again only halfway up. Behind the hayloft doors, a picture window had been installed with side windows that cranked open for fresh air. Paintings of all subjects and shapes lined the walls.

Three easels rose at different spots across the studio, and a counter with a sink lined the far wall. Adjustable spotlights hung throughout the space. In one corner, a platform held a chair, for life drawing models, I assumed. No doubt about it, Beau Bartlett was living my dream.

"It's wonderful." I couldn't have imagined a more perfect studio. I approached the window that looked down on the farmhouse and the field across from the gravel road. He'd been watching my reaction. "Glad you like it. It's pretty special to me." He glanced over at the painter. "There's someone I'd like you to meet."

As we approached the artist, I was captivated once again, this time with the canvas. An impressionist painting of a house overlooking a lake covered the canvas. I nearly salivated at the luxurious colors, shades of seafoam green, aquamarine, turquoise, and ultramarine blue.

I turned to the tanned gentleman, probably in his fifties. "Your painting is beautiful."

"Thank you." He glanced at Beau.

"George, this is Liza Murphy, a student from my community night class. Liza, this is George Fuller, a talented artist in his own right."

"Beau is too kind. He's taught me more than I ever hoped to accomplish. He's a great teacher."

"Liza is working on an impressionist piece, and I suggested a look at what you're doing."

I was so not on the level of this man's work. "I love your painting," I gushed. "Your brushstrokes give almost the same effect as a palette knife."

"Large brushes and a loose hand," George said. "That's the secret."

So fearful of making a mistake, I didn't have that kind of confidence. My every stroke was calculated.

"We'll let George get back to his painting," Beau said. "Care for a cup of coffee?"

"Sure." Anything to prolong my visit to the dream studio.

"Have a seat by the window, and I'll be just a moment."

A drafting table stood a few feet away, probably where Beau sketched his compositions. Two leather swivel chairs sat before the window, an end table positioned in between the chairs. I flipped through a book on Cezanne's paintings in between watching chickens peck around the farmyard and a border collie sniff around an outbuilding. Beau returned with two steaming mugs.

"George has quite a way with impressionism, doesn't he?" Beau set a carafe and two mugs on the table. I noted his masculine hands, yet his fingers reminded me of a pianist—long and sensitive. For a moment, I wondered how those hands would feel on my skin. I bit the inside of my lip. *Stop it, Liza.*

"So beautiful. I'm dripping with envy." The coffee tasted like Columbian but smoother, definitely not brewed by Mr. Coffee. "His work is intimidating. I'll never paint that well."

"Every artist has their own style and technique. It would be self-defeating to try to paint like someone else."

"The paintings on the walls," I asked, "yours?"

He nodded. "Some recent. Some dating back to my student days."

"You are so talented." The studio held portraits in smoky chiaroscuro, others in more contemporary styles, landscapes, cityscapes, seascapes, and still lifes. "If this is your Fortress of Solitude, it's working for you."

"You could call it my home away from home."

"Mm. Nice work if you can get it."

He refilled my cup. "Your part-time job must give you a lot of time to paint."

"I'm working fulltime now."

"Oh?"

"Receptionist at a dental office. Nine to five. Monday through Friday."

"Still leaves nights and weekends." He studied my face.

"Yeah, guess it does." Was he insinuating that if I was serious about becoming an artist, I'd use all my spare time? I shifted my feet. How dedicated was I to my dream? As Minnie would say, I put the shoe on the other foot. "How much time do *you* spend painting?"

"I assume you're referring to my fulltime position at the college." He stretched out his legs and crossed his feet. "Let's see. Four nights a week since on Wednesday evening I'm in charge of the student painting lab. Weekends, I devote either the morning or afternoon, depending on my mood."

So much for the proverbial other foot. "Guess all that painting pays off." I glanced at the nearest canvasses. I stood, feeling I'd overstayed my welcome. I didn't want to infringe on George's time. "Thank you for showing me your studio. And George's artwork. I appreciate it."

"Why off in such a hurry?" He set down his mug. "Let me show you the house. Since your family's in the antique business, I'd like to show you a few things." He glanced over his shoulder. "Be back in a few, George."

George waved a brush without looking back. "Take your time. I'm on a roll."

Outside, our footsteps crunched over gravel as we walked to the farmhouse.

"I'll warn you. I haven't done anything to the house," he said as he opened the back door. "Part of me likes it just the way Gramps and Gram left it. But sometimes I worry that it's a little strange to leave it as if they might walk in at any moment."

The roomy kitchen had glass cabinets that showcased old stoneware and china. The varnish on the oak table had darkened over the years, and the linoleum dated past attempts at "modern improvements."

"I love the apron-front sink," I said, careful to focus on the positive.

"If I knew there was good wood beneath the old flooring, I'd remove the linoleum in a minute."

"I'm sure there's wood beneath it considering the age of the house."

We entered the dining room with its dark china hutch and table for eight. Heavy maroon drapes blocked the sunlight. The brass chandelier was tarnished but nothing a good polishing couldn't fix. "Nice woodwork here, just needs a good sanding and varnishing."

"Hadn't thought of that. That china cupboard must be pretty old." He looked at me for confirmation.

"My mother would know more about that than me, but I'd say it's pretty old. Two hundred years or more. That means it came from Europe, probably handed down through the generations."

"Very likely." Beau pointed to a framed photograph on the wall. "That's my grandparents, Robert and Julia Bartlett."

Their round smiling faces projected a happy couple. For a moment, I imagined them as my parents—disregarding the obvious fact they had lived in an earlier generation—two loving parents, an honest but hard-working life on the farm, and peaceful evenings spent in the early twentieth-century farmhouse.

Beau moved on to the next room. We stepped into the parlor, a hideous rendition of the sixties: gold carpet and a floral print sofa in pea green and saffron.

"I like the bay window." Across the road, oats gleamed green under the sunlight, the crop still low to the ground. I could almost hear Julia calling me to dinner.

"Did you see this?" Beau pointed to the corner.

"What a sweet secretary." The upper glass cabinet held aged bindings and a few knickknacks. "May I?"

"Of course."

I opened the slanted top that revealed cubby holes for stationary, pencils, and ink wells. "Nice."

"I've always liked that piece even when I was a kid. I pictured myself writing the next *Treasure Island* on it."

"Instead, you became an artist."

He grinned. "Can't do everything."

I followed him up the open stairway, my favorite part of the house so far. I imagined living there, the entire house to myself. I'd tear out the linoleum and gold carpet, of course, but the structure had great bones. The house deserved to be loved again. The upstairs held four small bedrooms. Back then, size wasn't the premium it was today. I'd tear down a wall between two of the rooms and make a master bedroom. Instead of closets, each room possessed an antique wardrobe.

"Check this out." Beau motioned to the cozy bathroom with its claw-foot tub. A chain dangled from a water tank high above the stool.

"I love those old tubs." I imagined a long soak, suds up to my chin.

Back on the first floor, Beau asked me to join him on the clear plastic-wrapped sofa. It crinkled beneath our legs, and we both broke out laughing.

"So strange, it's funny, huh?" he said.

"Seriously though, it's a very nice house," I said. "It has a lot of potential."

"I figured you'd appreciate it." An uncomfortable silence filled the room. Then the cuckoo clock erupted, and we laughed again.

"I'd like to take you to dinner some time," he said.

"I guess that would be okay." Was it?

"You don't sound very enthused."

I shrugged. "I don't know if I'm ready for the dating scene."

"Bad experience?"

"Bad marriage."

"Only one way to find out." He threw a lighthearted look my way.

"One step at a time, okay?"

He held up one hand in a Boy Scout salute. "Baby steps, then. Coffee and dessert?"

I smiled and stood to leave.

"Should I call the store?" he asked.

I'd have to go through all those messages on the machine. "Sure."

Beau walked me to the pickup. "Thanks for stopping by." He opened the truck door for me.

"Thanks for the tour."

In the rearview mirror, I caught him watching as I drove away. In the fall, he'd return to his teaching position at the college, and I'd be left watching numbed jaws shuffle out of Swenson's Dentistry. Getting together with Beau didn't make for a wise investment of time. I stared straight ahead at the gravel road. Somehow, I wasn't feeling particularly wise.

New Inventory

The sign on the front window read Closed Monday through Friday. After two weeks people were starting to wonder about Minnie's Antique and Curiosity Shoppe. I kept the store open on the weekends just to keep my mother's business afloat.

Sally from the bakery three doors down, pounded on the door Saturday morning before I had a chance to open the store.

"Is your mother going out of business?" Sally loved to pass on the latest "community news."

"Oh, no." I hastily caught my hair in a ponytail and double wrapped the elastic band. "She's on vacation. And you know I work fulltime at Swenson's Dentistry."

"I knew that the day you were hired. Kent is my husband's second cousin."

"About time my mother took a vacation, don't you think?"

"You betcha. Don't work too hard, Liza."

Before the door had clicked shut, I pulled a marker and a large piece of paper from the chest of drawers behind the counter. In large capital letters, I scribbled: ON VACATION. CLOSED M-F OPEN SATURDAY AND SUNDAY. I posted the sign in the window in attempt to slow down gossip.

June Johansson aka Fingers popped in around noon and scooted straight to the counter. "Is she still gone?"

"Afraid so." I thought about her question. "She told you she was leaving?"

"Of course, dear," Fingers said. "She wouldn't leave the bridge group high and dry."

"Of course not." Beneath the surface, I fumed. She'd told June she was leaving but not me?

"Let her know we miss her," she said over her shoulder.

Midafternoon Agnes Peterson strolled in with a dozen eggs.

"Hi, Agnes," I said. "I'm afraid Minnie's not back from her journey."

"Oh, I know that. Minnie said to bring in a dozen every couple weeks for you."

"I see." I opened the register and checked for enough cash for the day. So Minnie had planned her trip quite well, it seemed. I was beginning to feel like Cinderella, the abused stepchild. "Did she happen to say when she'd be back?"

Her eyes widened like two eggs sunny-side up. "She didn't tell you?"

Humiliated, I fudged the truth. "Oh, roughly. Just don't remember the exact day."

Agnes eyed me for a moment and relaxed. "That sounds like your mother. A little impetuous, isn't she?"

"She can be." I produced a confident smile and shrugged. "You know Minnie."

Agnes returned my smile. "Yes, yes. We all know Minnie."

I decided then and there to make an appearance at the bar and grill that evening. I would pump Minnie's bar buddies for information and see if I could find out anything more. Although

Wilbur Hood had been clueless, he obviously wasn't interested in Minnie's travels. I could only hope some of her other acquaintances would know something.

At nine that night I joined the revelers at the Farmer's Bar and Grill. Not much had been done to the interior over the years. Decades of lounging forearms had worn the varnish from edges of the wooden bar. The vinyl-padded stools were now vintage 50s items that could easily be sold at Minnie's. Over time, smoke and beer had leached into the walls and wooden floorboards. My go-to jeans and flannel shirt felt right at home. For a festive touch, I had tied a red bandana around my ponytail.

I ordered a Bud Light at the bar and surveyed the early crowd. Wilbur Hood sat with a group at a long table along the wall. Bingo. I moseyed over like a regular. I recognized the other five ale drinkers: Maggie Wilson, a widow from church; John Letters, an appropriately named retired mailman; Angie Larson, Minnie's long-time buddy; Ben Waters, a retired loan officer from Farmers and Merchants Bank; and Lori Best, a veteran waitress at the Wheel Inn.

Ben shouted, "Hey, come join us, Liza."

Lori waved me over. "Here's an empty chair."

"So how's that mother of yours?" John asked.

"Same ol', same ol'." I sipped at my beer. Chilled mugs and the coldest beer in town made the bar and grill's reputation widespread.

"Bet Minnie's filling that old van to the gills," Angie said.

I choked on my sip of beer. "F-filling the van?"

"With antiques, of course," she said. "Rebuilding stock and finding curiosities. You know, what Minnie does best."

Hmm. If it was that simple, why hadn't she told *me*? But I played along, nodded knowingly, and took another sip of chilled Bud.

With her index finger, Maggie bobbed the green olives floating in her beer. "A little bit of vacation, too. Said she needed to get away." She leaned into the table and whispered, "When was the last time your mother went on a vacation?"

"I can't really remember," I shifted my eyes to the floor. "Never" was the correct answer.

"I'd say she deserves one," Ben said. "To Minnie." He raised his glass, and we all toasted my mother.

"When did you last hear from her?" Lori asked.

"Couple weeks ago." I chugged a long drink to avoid saying more.

"I wouldn't worry, Liza," Angie said. "She's probably keeping busy."

"And having a grand old time, too, I bet." John guffawed and raised his glass again. "To Minnie!"

After two more toasts to my mother but no further news garnered, I yawned. "This seven-day work week is catching up with me. I'll leave you youngsters for the night life." I got several chuckles from that one.

"Night, Liza," Lori said, waving her many silver-ringed fingers.

"Join us anytime," Angie added.

"See ya." I walked the three blocks back to the antique store. An occasional car drove down Kemp but no one I recognized. I hadn't learned much more than I knew before I joined the ranks of the Farmer's Bar and Grill regulars. I could only hope Minnie's next phone call would be more enlightening.

I slept in till ten. The hot shower did little to refresh me. Determined to open the store by noon, I skipped church services. I officially declared myself a workaholic. With a mug of strong coffee in one hand, I flipped the door sign to OPEN. I retrieved the Star Tribune from the sidewalk and returned to the counter for a leisurely read of the Sunday paper.

Over the next hour only a few stragglers wandered in: couples out for a Sunday walk, and a bicyclist or two enjoying the warm May afternoon. I waved to Mrs. Wiggins and her five-year-old grandson, Tyler, as they passed the storefront window. I was adding an antique Radio Flyer to the display. I met them out on the sidewalk. "Hi, Mrs. Wiggins. Enjoying the sunshine?" I knelt to Tyler's level and high-fived him. He had plump cheeks, big green eyes, and cinnamon-red hair. He was so cute. An older model Buick with a faded blue hood, pulled up to the curb as Tyler waved goodbye. I reentered the store, grinning like a besotted sweetheart.

While contemplating whether it was worth opening on Sundays, the sleigh bells clanged, and a pretty girl approached the counter. The Native American teen carried a box, and I knew without a doubt she had crafts for sale. A toddler trailed behind her.

"Morning," I said.

She glanced at me but didn't return my smile. "I have silver jewelry." She opened the lid and set the box on the counter.

"Any relation to Raymond?" I asked.

She gave a blank stare.

"Raymond Standing Rock?"

She shook her head. Her little sister looked up with big brown eyes, her tiny round face adorable. Long black braids framed her cheeks. "Hi, cutie."

The child stared back at me.

"That's okay." I winked at the toddler. "I wasn't too keen on strangers as a kid either."

I examined the objects in the box: various necklaces, rings, and bracelets with either turquoise or jade stones. Few people would pay for the expensive squash blossom necklace. The store already had several turquoise rings. I withdrew a cluster bracelet with two rows of oval stones. *Nice*. I examined another silver cuff with a row of three hand-cut turquoise cabochon and a nice flattened rope design on the silver. I checked both for a stamping of sterling silver. Neither had the marking, insuring each was a genuine vintage piece of jewelry. "How much for these two?"

The girl looked at me slyly. "A hundred each."

I shook my head. "Too much. We have to make a profit."

"Good pieces."

"I agree, but we need to add a markup."

"Give you both for a hundred eighty."

"I'll give you seventy-five for each. A hundred fifty for both."

She looked at me as if assessing my boundaries and nodded.

I counted out the bills, seven twenties and one ten.

"I'll be back in a couple of weeks. I'll show you more."

"All right." I doubted we'd be in the market for more jewelry, but sometimes customers asked us to be on the lookout for specific items.

She turned to leave and paused halfway to the door. "Be back in a few weeks."

I smiled and reexamined the bracelets. They were pretty pieces, and I debated if I wanted to buy one for myself. Undecided, I set the three-stone cuff in the safety deposit box below the cabinet. I grabbed a key and set the other bracelet in the glass case across from the front door. After I locked the cabinet, I admired my placement of the bracelet among the other turquoise pieces. I was about to return to the counter when a small head appeared on the other side of the case.

I glanced around for the teenager although I'd watched her leave the store. Or had I? I was busy admiring the bracelets. "Come here, honey. Take my hand."

The little girl somberly obeyed. I walked her to a wicker settee in the middle of the store. "You stay here for a moment." A china-faced doll stood on display nearby. It had a cracked face, so I didn't worry about further damage and set the doll next to her. "I'll be right back."

I scurried up and down the aisles and peered in displays. "Miss! Are you still in the store?" Ran down the basement stairs. No one there, either. I retraced my steps. With each empty row, fear clamped tighter over my chest. I covered the entire store in a few minutes, my eye muscles strained from scrutinizing every nick and cranny. Positive I hadn't missed an aisle, I jogged to the front door and looked up and down Kemp. Only one empty car was parked farther down the block, Sally's Camaro. My pulse beat in my throat as I raced to the door of the bakery. The handle resisted my grasp. The sign in the window had been flipped to CLOSED. Sally was probably mixing dough in the back room.

Gasping for breath, I ran back to Minnie's and found the little girl curled up asleep on the settee. Clutched beneath her chin, the doll was encircled within her arms.

I watched the clock. Fifteen minutes. Twenty. Surely, she'd realize the child was missing, turn around, and come looking for her. Thirty minutes. The teenager would be in deep trouble for not watching her little sister. Forty-five minutes. Maybe she got down the highway before she realized the toddler wasn't with her. After an hour and thirty minutes, it dawned on me the child had been left on purpose.

I dropped to the floor and leaned against the settee. Darn it, Minnie! Where the hell are you when I need you?

Lollipop and Crayons

The automatic coffee maker we kept behind the counter gurgled as I brewed a double-strength pot of coffee. The strong aroma didn't wake the child as I feared. I pushed the settee behind the front counter without waking the toddler. She was really out. I tipped back the stool and leaned against the wall, sipping the strong coffee as if a dose of mega-caffeine would force my brain into overtime and order my next step.

I picked up the phone. My first instinct was to call the police. Surely, they'd know what to do, what agency to call. My index finger aimed for the nine button and hovered in space. Ugh, that would be social services. They'd dump the poor child in a foster home. Something in me recoiled at the thought.

I'll be back. That's what the teenager had said.

My memory kicked into overdrive. The teen had paused halfway to the door. "I'll be back in a few weeks," she said. Did that hold a double meaning, a cryptic message that she'd return for the child?

159

Minnie always said Native American culture was unlike ours. They viewed time differently. Days passed with light and dark, not hours and minutes. Where we might think their kids were unsupervised, they allowed children to act like children. One fact stood out: native people adored their children.

If the teenager who sold me the bracelets returned and her little sister was in a foster home, social services might make it difficult to bring the two back together. But why had she abandoned the child? Perhaps a temporary problem had prevented the teenager from caring for her sister. Sick parent. Financial problems. Housing problems. I set down the second cup of black coffee and made myself stop. I was driving myself crazy.

My body tensed from my jaw to my chest. Minnie, why aren't you here? I clenched my fists, nails biting into my palms. At that moment, I'd never been so angry with my mother.

I could quit my job at Swenson's Dentistry. How stupid would that be? The best paying job I'd had so far in Watertown, and of course, there went the savings for my dream house. *Be practical, Liza. Be smart.*

The sleigh bells offered a temporary reprieve from my dilemma as they announced the arrival of customers. I didn't relish explaining the situation to our local patrons. To my relief, strangers appeared in the doorway.

"Good afternoon," I said.

The middle-age couple smiled warmly. "We were on our way back to Sioux Falls when we saw your hours in the antique listings." The woman held up the brochure. "Subject to season or whim," she read.

Minnie's sense of humor surfaced once again.

"Good excuse to stretch our legs," her husband added.

"Make sure you check out the basement level." I pointed to the wide stairway at the back.

The toddler chose that moment to awaken. She studied me like an archeologist at his dig but fortunately didn't panic.

"Oh, how darling," the woman peered over the counter. "What a precious daughter you have."

I began to protest. "Oh, she's—"

"She has your hair and your eyes." The woman began cooing. "Aren't you a cutie?"

"She's adorable." The husband made a silly face for the child. The toddler stared at the man and glanced over at me.

I gave up at that point. They were strangers after all.

The toddler slid off the settee and grabbed my leg. I didn't blame her. The man's "faces" were a little scary. I lifted her to my lap, and the child grasped my arm. "Let me know if you have any questions."

The couple headed down the left-hand side of the store.

"I don't even know your name," I whispered. "But you sure are pretty."

The child held my eyes for a moment and then popped a thumb in her mouth.

"What am I going to do with you?" I sighed. A wet diaper check came first on the agenda. Surprised to find little training panties, I discovered the kind that served double duty as diaper for accidents and underpants for potty training. I scooted to the restroom in the basement and held her on the toilet. I was amazed when tinkling sounded in the stool.

"Good girl." I pulled up the dry pants. Even I knew that was quite an accomplishment.

Twenty minutes later, the couple approached the cash register. The wife set a cherry-red Golden Wedding coffee can on the counter.

"Do you collect coffee cans?" I said to be polite. Minnie believed in talking to your customers. It was not only good public relations but often led to more sales once customers revealed their interests.

"Actually no, but my sister in Sioux City, Iowa does. She has a birthday coming up, and I know she's been hunting for this brand."

"It's the perfect gift then."

The woman glanced at the toddler. "Henry, isn't she adorable?"

"Can we wrap her up and take her home with us?" The man chuckled.

On the surface, I smiled, but inside I unsheathed a dagger and its steel blade sparkled. Though an innocent comment, the man's words triggered a conviction that waiting for the sister was the right decision.

After they pulled away from the curb, I flipped the sign in the window to CLOSED and grabbed a twenty from the register. We headed to the grocery where I purchased a dozen more training pants in the smallest size available, a gallon of milk, and a box of Cheerios. The rest of what a toddler might eat would have to wait until I did some research.

In the parking lot, the child lifted both hands. Oh, boy. I set down my packages, and positioned her on one hip. My other arm lugged the two grocery bags. Thank goodness, the antique store was only a block away.

The call I'd yearned to receive from Minnie never materialized. Monday morning, I swore off the phone as a coward's way to resign from my job and drove to Swenson's Dentistry, with my mystery child in the backseat. In the freight room of the store, I'd fished an old car seat from a pile of junk in the corner. Minnie had once purchased the contents of a storage shed sight unseen and a few baby items had come with

162

the package. I was relieved to find an old playpen, which would have to serve for a bed.

I entered the reception room, lights dim prior to official business hours. Amber traipsed in from the back room as I switched on the lights.

"Who do we have here?" she said.

"A friend's child." I aimed for a genuine smile but knew it fell short. Thankfully, Amber's attention was diverted. The toddler sat in a chair, tearing a page from the magazine I'd given her. I grabbed the magazine and handed her my shoe. Dumb reaction but the first thing that came to mind.

"What's her name?" Amber fingered one of the child's braids. "Aren't you a sweetie?"

"Sweetie," I blurted. "Her nickname's Sweetie."

"Her name is *Sweetie*?" Amber glanced up at me.

"Uh, it's her nickname." *Think quick.* "Her name's...Susannah."

"Why not Susie then?"

I shrugged. "Sometimes nicknames don't make sense, do they?"

Amber smiled at Sweetie. "Couldn't find a sitter, I bet."

"That's what I was going to talk to Dr. Swenson about."

"He's in his office. Aren't you a pretty little thing?"

I looked at Amber "Would you mind?"

"Go ahead. We'll have a good time."

I found Dr. Swenson deep in concentration over a file on his desk and knocked though the door was open.

"Come in, Liza," he said. "Just going over patient records."

"I'm afraid I...," I began. My hands shook. My stomach felt queasy. I couldn't believe I was going to ditch a good job. "I have a friend...who's out of town...I mean, the parent is out of town, and I really appreciate you giving me this job, but I'm afraid my mother is out of town too, and she can't…and someone has to…"

Dr. Swenson's expression went from quizzical to beaming. I glanced behind me. The toddler, now known as Sweetie, stood in the doorway with Amber standing behind her. "Sorry, she was bound and determined to follow you."

"Who is this little beauty?" Dr. Swenson rose from his chair. He grabbed a sugarless sucker from a cup on his desk. "Is she old enough?"

"Have to supervise it," Amber said. "Can't have the stick stuck in her throat."

"Liza?"

"Sure, I'll keep an eye out."

"She's adorable."

"A friend's daughter," Amber said. "They can't find a sitter."

This was a grateful exception to a trait I hated in women— quick to speak for another person.

"I don't have a problem, as long as she doesn't interfere with your work." Dr. Swenson spoke to Sweetie though his words were aimed at me.

"We'll give it a try," I said. "She's pretty quiet. Haven't heard her cry once." *So far*. Plans formulated in my mind. I'd pull one of the waiting room chairs behind the receptionist's counter. "Thank you, Dr. Swenson." Then I realized they both thought I meant one day. I was about to say something when I decided to see how things went. If Sweetie didn't turn into a problem, I'd reveal the extended nature of the situation later.

"No problem." He returned to his office.

"Watch that stick," Amber warned.

"Of course. I'll be a regular hound dog."

I'd averted the loss of my job for one day. What was that famous AA saying? I improvised and made *On the fly, one day at a time* my new motto.

The phone rang that evening at eight. In my hurry to answer it, I tripped on the area rug, scrambled up, and answered the telephone.

"Hello?"

"Hi, honey. How's everything?" Minnie's voice sounded relaxed and rejuvenated.

"Where are you? I need to talk to you—"

"How nice to be missed. Before I forget, would you pay the utility bill? I hope you're not trying to work fulltime and keep the store open weekends. I don't expect that of you."

My anger boiled. "Where *are* you, Mother?"

"I'll be back before you know it. Traveling like a regular gypsy." Her laughter rang like a soft chime over the phone. "What did you need to talk to me about?"

"What's your opinion of foster homes?"

"We've all heard the horrible stories of abuse, but I know there are many good ones out there, too. But even in the best ones, there's often several children. Not sure if the kids get the personal attention they need. Years ago I did know of a couple from church who couldn't have children, and they treated those kids as if they were their own." She paused. "Why are we talking about this, anyway?"

"I need you to come home, Mother."

"I'll be home soon. Don't worry, I'll be getting under your skin before you know it." A little laugh tailed her sentence. "Bye, honey. Take care." Click.

I hung up the receiver. She knew she got under my skin? I always thought I'd kept that well-hidden. My anger receded and turned into guilt. The rip of paper drew my attention. Sweetie was tearing a page from a vintage *Life* magazine. "Not that one, honey." I grabbed yesterday's *Watertown Public Opinion* and set it before her. The slash of newspaper zipped through the air.

The kid was a human paper shredder.

The next morning I settled Sweetie on the floor behind the office counter with an array of coloring books and crayons purchased at the grocery store. I glanced down and saw bright streaks of color on the linoleum. Footsteps approached from the back room, and I used the toe of my shoe to scatter books across the crayon marks.

Dr. Swenson's eyes widened when he caught sight of Sweetie behind the counter for the second day. I gulped. "Is it a problem?"

He smiled. "Not if she's as quiet as she was yesterday. If that changes, we'll need to talk."

Swenson was the best boss ever. "Thanks, I appreciate it." What would he think when a couple days turned into a couple weeks? I practiced my new mantra. *On the fly, one day at a time.*

My painting class met that evening. I could only imagine paint flying through the air or tired cries begging for sleep. So far, incredibly, I'd only heard Sweetie whimper at night in her sleep. Wasn't it normal for a little kid to cry? I debated about dropping the course until I decided I'd take her one time. If it turned out to be a disaster, the worst that might happen would be my forfeited class fees.

When I walked into the room with Sweetie on my hip, Beau paused midsentence. He quickly collected himself and waved.

I sat Sweetie on the floor with a spiral notebook and a blue crayon. I demonstrated a few blue *loop de loops* and handed her the crayon. She stuck it in her mouth.

"No, honey. That's not food. Do this." I drew a little cat that time. "Kitty cat."

166

She giggled, a sound I'd never heard from her. That time she put crayon to paper.

"Who's your little friend?" Beau crouched and smiled at Sweetie. "Hi, honey."

Sweetie looked at him for a moment and went back to her crayon.

"I have that effect on women." He grinned at me. "Is she yours?"

Why did people keep thinking that? "Watching her for a friend for a few weeks." I redirected Sweetie's crayon from the floor to the paper. "I promise we won't disturb the class. She's pretty quiet for her age. If she's a problem, we'll leave."

"Can she talk?" Beau laughed. "My brother's kids never stop talking."

That gave me pause. Maybe she couldn't speak. Maybe that's why she didn't cry. Wait, hadn't she just giggled?

"Hey, looks like she might be an abstract artist." Beau gazed at the blue lines that jutted in angles and circles.

"You never know."

A sense of relief overcame me when he walked away. Sweetie grabbed my arm just as I dipped my brush into the paint. Crimson paint plopped on my jeans. I dabbed at the stain with a rag, her hand clinging to my arm like it was a lifeline. Then another emotion arose. I felt like a thief. Was I a bungling baby burglar?

On Friday, Dr. Swenson called me into his office. I'd brought Sweetie to work all week and although there hadn't been any problems, I knew it wasn't fair to use the office as a daycare.

"Have a seat, Liza."

Sweetie stood at the side of my chair, clutching my arm.

"What's up?" He looked at me, waiting.

"My mother is still on vacation, and Sweetie's mother hasn't made it back."

Swenson drew his index fingers together and remained silent for several moments.

"I know it's not fair to you," I said quickly. "I'll leave now or I can stay until you find my replacement."

Dr. Swenson glanced at Sweetie and smiled. "She's been as quiet as a mouse. I can't complain about her behavior." He paused and gave a penetrating look, one meant to solicit confession.

He wasn't getting anything out of me. "If Minnie was home, I'm sure she'd watch her but…"

"No worries. Your job isn't in jeopardy. Let's hope your mother returns soon."

I stood and reached for Sweetie's hand. "Thank you, Dr. Swenson."

"In my office, you can call me Kent."

"Thank you, Kent." I returned to the receptionist's counter and offered Sweetie the Duplo blocks we kept for young patients in the waiting room. She shuffled the plastic pieces around but couldn't connect them even after I showed her how they worked. When *would* Minnie return?

On my break, I called Julie. She needed to know someone cared about what she was going through. "How are you, girl?'

"I won't lie, it's hard." A deep sigh came over the line. "Say, can you come by for dinner tonight? I'm making lasagna, and I'd love to talk with you."

"I'm afraid I'm watching a friend's child. Another time?"

"How old?"

"She's a toddler. She's around…I mean, she's a year and a half."

"Bring her. My kids are back, and they love little ones."

"I'll see you around 5:30 then."

"Perfect."

On the drive over to Julie's, I worried I'd made a mistake by accepting the dinner invitation. Would Sweetie be overwhelmed by another home and all the strangers?

Julie opened the door and squatted before us. "Hi, sweetie. What's your name?"

Awkward. "Actually her nickname is Sweetie." I was quick to add, "Her real name is Susannah."

Sure enough, Sweetie shadowed me as if I might abandon her there. When Julie's kids cajoled her to play in their room, she held back. They offered her toys but she'd only touch them briefly and return to clutching my leg.

"I'm afraid she's feeling pretty lost without her family," I said.

"She's definitely shy. Tell me again why they left her with you?"

"A family emergency," I said. "I don't know all the details."

Julie cocked her head and looked at me strangely.

"Anyway, she's no trouble. She never cries."

"That helps," Julie said.

After dinner, Julie and I retreated to the living room where she served two glasses of chardonnay. Sweetie sat on the carpet at my feet, playing at last with a doll Julie's kids had pulled from the toy box.

"So, it's been pretty rough, huh?" I said.

Julie curled her legs beneath her in the recliner. "It's the end of a whole life, and it affects not only me but the kids, too."

"How much time has Jim spent with them since the separation?"

She rolled her eyes. "He asked to see them once." A bitter grin formed. "Bad for the kids, but good for me." The smile vanished. "Does that make me cruel?"

"You're going through a lot of upheaval. You didn't ask for any of this."

"That's the God's truth."

Sweetie climbed into my lap and reached for a long strand of hair. She popped her thumb into her mouth.

"Poor little thing," Julie said. "Bet she misses her mama." She set her glass on the end table. "She sure seems to like you."

I thought about that. The poor kid was probably in survival mode, and I represented the only safety in her little abandoned life. "Hope they come back soon," I said as Sweetie nestled her warm head against my arm. *Did I really?*

"Minnie still vacationing?" Julie refilled our glasses.

The wine worked its spell. Warm and relaxed, I confided that my mother had up and left with only a note. "I don't even know where she went."

Julie straightened in the chair. "That doesn't sound like Minnie."

"You're telling me."

"Wonder what's going on there?" Julie shook her head. "People. Sometimes they're impossible to figure out."

"Mystery mother. Mystery child." I stroked Sweetie's hair.

"What are you talking about?"

Alcohol had never done me any favors which was why I usually avoid the stuff.

"What's going on, Liza?"

I swore her to a blood oath of secrecy minus the messy body fluid and spilled the story.

"Oh, Liza."

I studied her face. "What do you think?"

A serious expression swept over her face. "It's possible the girl means to come back. I can see how you could read that into what she said. But what if she kidnapped the child? What if the real family is looking for her?"

I slumped. I hadn't thought of that.

"Or here's another possibility. Have you considered that the girl might be Sweetie's mother?"

"She looked too young," I said weakly.

Julie made a face that read *really now*.

"Okay, a teenage mother is a possibility." I worried the edges of the sofa pillow. "But why wouldn't she have left the toddler with the grandparents? You hear that on the news all the time, the older generation having to raise their grandchildren."

"Hmm." Julie pondered that for a moment. "Maybe they're not in the picture, you know, deceased. Or maybe the girl's parents ostracized her."

"Don't know about that," I said. "Indian people love children. Doesn't fit the culture."

"What are you going to do?"

"For now, I'm waiting to see if the girl returns." With my index finger, I traced the floral pattern on the sofa.

"How long will you wait?"

"I don't know."

Julie left the chair and slid next to me on the sofa. Sweetie was fast asleep. Julie touched my forearm. "Honey, if you wait too long, you're going to be too attached to this precious little one."

I didn't respond to her statement and took another sip of wine. Something inside said it was already too late.

Overinflated

I woke to the sound of chimes. Sweet and resonant, the music floated on the air. My mind drifted to fountains in lush gardens and waterfalls rushing over cliffs. My alarm clock went off and broke the fantasy. The chiming turned to laughter. Little person laughter. I sat upright and peered into the playpen. Sweetie cradled the doll she'd been allowed to bring home from Julie's house. The most beautiful sound I'd ever heard rippled from her little mouth, and I couldn't help but smile.

I approached the playpen where Sweetie rocked the doll in her arms. "Pretty dolly," I whispered. Sweetie looked up, and for the first time, a smile swept from cheek to cheek. I was completely disarmed.

"Pretty dolly, just like Sweetie."

She giggled and touched the doll's nose.

"Time to go potty." I lifted her into my arms. Amazingly, she hadn't wet her training pants except one night when she drank too much apple juice before bedtime. My fault, I realized later. I carried her down the long stairway from the loft, crossed the main floor, and descended the basement steps. The journey sometimes tested my own morning bladder, but I sat Sweetie on the toilet seat first. Right on cue, she tinkled into the toilet.

"Good girl."

Sweetie and I arrived home to the sound of Bob Dylan singing "Blowin' in the Wind" on an old record player. *Minnie.* My mother waltzed from the front of the store and paused mid-step when she saw us. "And who do we have here?"

I crossed my arms, a proactive barricade to one of Minnie's free-flowing hugs. How dare she dance back into our life without a care? My jaw tightened. She acted like she'd been gone for an hour instead of two weeks. Minnie didn't wait for an explanation and strode up to Sweetie, who was holding my pant leg in a death grip.

"Aren't you cute?" Minnie removed her scarf and draped Sweetie's body in crimson silk. The smell of patchouli oil drifted from my mother's skin.

Sweetie giggled for the second time.

"Whose little girl are you?" Minnie tapped the tip of Sweetie's nose.

"It's a long story," I said. "Would have been nice if you'd told me in person you were leaving. Or where you were going."

"I'm back now, honey. What do you say we order a pizza?"

My teeth clenched like a vice. Obviously, answers would not be forthcoming. "Fine. Pepperoni, thin crust. Sweetie only likes pepperoni pizza." I picked her up and headed to the balcony. My mother was so infuriating. Apparently she didn't worry about losing business after two weeks of being closed Monday through Friday. And how about a thanks for opening on weekends after I'd worked all week? I tossed Sweetie on my bed and bounced the mattress until her laughter erupted over and over again. I couldn't get enough of that happy child.

After dinner Minnie pumped me for the skinny on Sweetie. For a moment, I considered letting her sweat it out. Leave her in limbo without any explanation. I sighed. The need to unburden myself outweighed my thirst for revenge. I told her the whole bizarre story and waited for her reaction. The voice of reason sounded from my mother. "We have to call the authorities."

"But if the girl is coming back for her sister, do we want to tell her, 'Sorry, but the kid's under the custody of social services'? Do you really want to place a toddler in a foster home and put her through another drastic change?"

Minnie glanced at Sweetie asleep in the playpen and smiled. "What exactly did the girl say?"

"She said, 'I'll be back in a couple of weeks.'" I tried to sound convincing, but I remembered the entire conversation. *I'll be back in a couple of weeks. Show you more.* The girl may have said that just to sound like a reputable vendor. Part of me knew it might be nothing more than that, but I maintained my composure.

"You've got something there," Minnie agreed. "But you know—"

"Of course I know." I changed into my pajamas and sat on the edge of my bed. "So why'd you leave so suddenly, Mother?"

Already in bed, Minnie turned on her side and faced the wall. "Just needed a little change of pace," she mumbled into the pillow.

Both of us were holding out.

Much to the relief of my boss, Minnie agreed to watch Sweetie while I worked. I phoned thirty minutes after I arrived at the dental office. "How's she doing? Does she seem nervous? Is she afraid?" That morning I had voiced my concerns that

Sweetie might not be able to deal with my absence. The child clung to me, for Pete's sake. The little thing had had so many upheavals, and I was afraid this might be one too many for the toddler.

"We're having a great time," Minnie said.

A moment of silence.

Was my mother allaying my fears with a half truth? I found it hard to believe Sweetie would warm so quickly to a stranger. I cleared my throat. "I use the playpen when I can't watch her every second. Keeps her safe—"

"I raised you, remember?"

"But it's been a while and she's—"

"Liza, I'm not so old that I can't remember how to take care of a young child."

"You have to really keep an eye out—"

Minnie laughed. "I promise to watch her like a hawk."

"Does she act scared?" Sweetie's laughter in the background answered that question. Was that jealousy elbowing its way into my heart?

"Don't worry. She'll be fine."

"Thanks, Mother. I get off at five."

"See you then, honey." *Click.*

I took a deep breath and returned to printing postcard reminders of upcoming appointments.

At the end of the day, I thought about how easily Sweetie had gone with Minnie. Maybe it was some type of survival mode that deserted kids had. Maybe the connection I felt with Sweetie existed more in my head than in reality. With that idea weighing on me, I trudged into the antique store and found Minnie and Sweetie in front of a full-length mirror (part of the old JCPenney store fixtures) with Sweetie wearing a 1950s pillbox hat. They were both giggling. I could feel my bottom lip protrude, so I sucked it back into position and aimed for a smile.

"Hi, everyone." I flopped my purse on the nearby counter.

Sweetie stretched her arms out to me with a smile that popped her little cheeks into two squeezable balls. "Li-a. Li-a."

"I believe that's you," Minnie said. "Toddlers can't pronounce Zs."

I swept her into my arms, and Sweetie's hands grasped my neck. Her little fingers clung to my hair. *She missed me. She really missed me.* After a few moments, I set her down and placed a 1930 cloche on her head.

"How was she?" I asked.

"We had a good time," Minnie said. "No problems whatsoever. And I can't believe she's potty trained."

"It helps if you anticipate her needs," I said, sounding like an expert on toilet training.

"I have pigs-in-a-blanket and beans warming on the stove. Sweetie helped with the 'blankets'."

Sweetie lifted her arms in supplication, and I set her onto one hip. The three of us headed to the modest kitchen in the back of the store, actually a storage closet in the store's freight room. A lone window that faced the alley kept the room from making me totally claustrophobic, though the weak light from the high, narrow window made me insist the door remain open.

Minnie had absolved a vintage highchair of its porcelain-face doll. I tested the stability of the oak piece and found the chair solid. I preferred antiques that could be put to good use versus museum pieces meant only to be admired. We sat down for our feast of swaddled swine. The room felt cozier than usual, the dandelion-yellow walls cheerier, and even my mother seemed—dare I say it?—more normal.

Raindrops splatted against the storefront windows. June proved to be unpredictable, typical of eastern South Dakota, one day promising picnic weather and the next threatening a thunderstorm. I grew testy at Minnie's questioning of what I planned to do next and Julie's sad expression when she thought I wasn't watching. The Native teenager hadn't returned for her little sister—if she really was her sister—leaving me in a dilemma. What *was* I going to do?

I was manning the store on a Saturday afternoon while Minnie attended an auction. Sweetie played nearby with three dolls I'd picked up at a rummage sale. She lined them up against the playpen and took turns feeding them with a toy bottle.

The bells on the door heralded the arrival of our old friend, Raymond Standing Rock.

"How's it going, Ray?"

He spied the toddler in the playpen. "Who is this little one?"

"Sweetie," I said. "Her name is Sweetie."

"She's a cutie." Ray smiled down on her. "Are you feeding your babies?"

Sweetie studied him longer than she ordinarily assessed a stranger before she went back to feeding her dolls.

Ray glanced down the aisles. "Minnie around?"

"Afraid not. She's at an auction."

Disappointment stamped his forehead.

"Say, Ray." Dare I trust him? Or would he snatch Sweetie away in the blink of a barn owl? "If someone left a child," I began. My throat tightened. I swallowed and took a deep breath.

"An Indian child?" His eyes softened.

So much for pretense. "How long would a person have to wait," I said. "I mean, if they said they were coming back for the child. How long should a person wait?" My face grew hot.

"Indian people love their *wakanheja*." A compassionate expression flooded over Ray's face.

I nodded, my throat constricting. Minnie had told me the word, *wakan,* meant sacred. Children were sacred.

"I know of many grandparents who have raised their own grandchildren."

But not in this case. What made this different, I mused? Something had to be terribly wrong for the girl to leave Sweetie in the care of a stranger.

"How long has it been?" Ray asked.

"A month." I spilled the story then, the words tumbling out.

Raymond drew his brows together and pursed his lips, his eyes staring into space. "I can speak to the tribal authorities and see if anyone has reported a missing child."

My stomach lurched. In that moment, there was no denying I dreaded losing Sweetie. My conscience kicked in—she wasn't mine to keep, yet part of me screamed otherwise. "Thanks, Ray. I appreciate it." Part of me wished I had never disclosed the truth.

Ray looked around as if Minnie might magically appear. One of Sweetie's dolls sailed over the railing of the playpen. I retrieved it and placed the doll back inside. A large hand met my shoulder. I glanced at Ray.

"I'll see what I can find out. I know she's in good hands."

I nodded but dared not speak. The blood in my veins congealed. Throat seized. My heart was breaking.

Minnie called up to the balcony. I had folded the playpen and carried it up there for Sweetie's nap. I leaned over the balcony and held a finger to my lips. "Shh."

My mother motioned me with a wave of her hand. I snapped the child gate shut, actually two wired together, and returned to the front of the store. A man near the counter turned around, and there stood Beau Bartlett smiling at me.

I glanced at Minnie and back at Beau. "Ah, hi Beau."

"Hey. Was strolling down Kemp and thought of you. Have time for a Coke?"

I froze for a moment.

"A beer, a coffee, Kool-Aid?" He raised one eyebrow.

"I have to—"

"No problem." Minnie jangled the store keys that hung on an old jailer's ring. "I planned on closing early today. Go ahead, Liza."

I didn't want to explain why Sweetie was still staying with me, so I decided on a short Coke/beer/coffee/Kool-Aid. To be polite, I introduced Beau to my mother.

"Nice to meet you, Mrs. Murphy."

Minnie had never been married, but she didn't correct him. "Nice to meet you, Beau. I know Liza has enjoyed your classes."

"Your daughter is very talented." He turned to me. "Even if she doesn't know it." He winked. "Shall we?"

I accompanied him outside. I didn't want to go but there I was.

"So what will it be?" He opened the passenger-side door of his Jeep.

It took me a moment to realize what he was asking. "A Coke. That would work."

"Let's see. The Wheel Inn?"

"Sure."

We passed Riverside Park, the expansive lawn beckoning. I'd have to bring Sweetie to the park. She'd love it. Beau pulled into the café's parking lot and found an empty space near the front door. We sat in a booth at the back.

Over the top of the menu, he asked, "How's it going, Liza?"

"Great." I glanced around the room. Several retired men sat around tables and swapped stories.

"Missed you at the last two classes."

"Things came up." I shrugged. "Life happens." Clichés can be so useful at times.

"I'm glad I caught up with you."

Beau produced that winning smile that had made the girls in the first class fall all over themselves. Though he was a good-looking guy, he didn't have that effect on me. I credited my life experience.

"Weather permitting, would you like to do some *plein air* painting next weekend?"

That caught my interest. "Where?"

"Lake Kampeska. I have an extra portable easel."

He was putting candy before a baby. "Let me check with Minnie. See if she needs me to work next weekend." My mother would have to be free to watch Sweetie.

Beau sat back, looking relaxed. We made more trite conversation for a while, and Beau discussed what I'd missed in class. "I'll check with you next Wednesday. May I have your phone number?"

I rattled off the digits, and he paid the check. We drove back to Minnie's amid flashes of lightening in a dark indigo sky. The phone number was the listing for Swenson's Dentistry.

Neon-blue dragonflies skimmed the smooth surface of the lake. The water reflected the cerulean sky and a band of dark trees where the lake curled to the northwest.

Beau had a way of setting me at ease. I should have been intimidated painting beside a professional artist, but he held no airs about him. He produced a disarming smile that might come from your favorite brother. Beau set his easel to face the broad expanse of water to the north. I chose to paint the trees along the shore. He'd picked a perfect morning without a hint of a breeze. I set aside my worries and melted into the scenery around me.

"Ready to paint?" Beau asked.

"I'm up for the challenge." I'd wanted to tackle a lake scene ever since I started taking lessons.

181

I chose to paint the scene with a palette knife. The impressionist technique would free me up to work quickly under the obstacles of sun and bugs, while capturing the scene before the light changed. I glanced back at Beau. A girl would have to be blind not to admire his well-defined upper arms, narrow waist, and thick chestnut hair.

I abandoned all thoughts of Beau as I worked against time to finish my landscape. The light changed so quickly. Two hours later, I stood back and admired the monochromatic color scheme of blue, turquoise, and purple.

Beau continued working on his canvas, so I sat on the beach and watched. His every brushstroke mesmerized me, each stroke made so economically, yet so purposefully. He painted in a realistic way that captured nuances of color I hadn't detected. He finished twenty minutes later.

"I packed a lunch." He jogged to the Jeep and retrieved a picnic basket. I spread the stadium blanket over the sand. Roast beef sandwiches, cheese and crackers, and a bottle of cabernet surfaced from the depths of the basket.

As I relished the unexpected lunch, I couldn't deny this was a classic romantic overture. I didn't have time for starry-eyed entanglements, not when the situation with Sweetie remained unsettled. A soft breeze rose up from the south, and we both remained silent as ripples formed on the water. It was a perfect day, but I'd promised Minnie I'd return before three.

"As much as I could sit here for hours, I have to get back so my mother can attend an auction."

Beau glanced at his watch. "Ten minutes to soak up the sun?"

"Then we pack up."

He leaned back on his elbows and turned his face to the sky. "Let's savor this Van Gogh sunshine."

182

I curled my arms around my knees and soaked up the delicious weather. With my eyes closed and the sun on my face, I was grateful Beau didn't pursue conversation. What a strange sensation. Though fully aware of his presence, I experienced the serenity of enjoying the moment on my own.

On the drive back, Beau looked over at me. "I find this slow pace addictive. I'll have a hard time getting back into my schedule next semester."

I knew he'd be returning to Brookings in the fall, so why did I feel disappointed? "I'm sure you'll fall right back into it."

"I plan on coming back every other weekend." He tossed a meaningful look.

I turned from his handsome face and gazed ahead at the road as if I hadn't heard.

"It's only forty-five miles away."

"Mm-hmm."

"I plan on seeing you, you know."

Though secretly pleased, something inside me still didn't trust handsome men.

It was happening more frequently. People who didn't know me often assumed I was Sweetie's mother.

"She looks like her mother," an elderly customer in the store said one day. "She has your eyes."

In the milk aisle at the grocery store, a middle-age woman commented, "She has your hair."

"Your daughter is so adorable," the young clerk at the drug store said.

At first, I corrected these well-meaning strangers but soon decided it wasn't worth the trouble. Did I enjoy pretending she was mine? My growing sense of guilt expanded like an overinflated tire.

I acquired a habit of reading a book to Sweetie every night. She had a fondness for any story with animals. Any book where an animal didn't appear by page three, she pushed from my hands. Dr. Seuss qualified since Sweetie considered all imaginary creatures as legitimate as any farm animal or wild creature.

Many nights, she fell asleep in my bed before the second book was finished. I was tempted to curl up beside her and join her in sleep, but my heart fluttered a warning, and I placed her gently in the crib. Minnie had upgraded the playpen to a real crib she'd found at a secondhand store. Sweetie's little round cheeks, button nose, and black lashes made an image I longed to paint, but some things refused to be captured.

Soap Opera Scripts

Low light from sconces blotched the back booth at the Sunnyside Tavern. Julie's mother watched her kids, and Minnie kept Sweetie, so we could have a girl's afternoon out. The waitress placed two glasses of white zinfandel before us. Halfway through the wine, I spilled—not my wine—but my recent exchange with Raymond Standing Rock.

Julie peered at me over her long-stemmed glass. "That sounds like a good start."

"Mm-hmm." I studied the swirling zin as if an answer would surface in the pink elixir. "Why would the girl leave her little sister? If she really is her sister."

"Abusive parents?" Julie offered. "Neglect perhaps? Maybe the parents weren't providing enough food."

"They could be transients, and the teenager wanted a better life for her sister."

"And they were living out of the car," Julie stared into space, "and the teenager loves her sister enough to give her a better life."

Silence hung between us for a few minutes. We sounded like script writers for a soap opera.

A bad soap opera.

"How many teenagers could make those kind of decisions?" I asked.

Julie shrugged. "Not many. Maybe she *is* coming back."

"It's been six weeks," I said flatly.

"Have you heard back from Ray?" Julie set down her glass. "Maybe he's learned something."

"He should be back in town anytime now." Part of me wished he'd never return and that I'd never mentioned Sweetie in the first place. Good time to change the subject. "How are the divorce proceedings going?"

"Would you believe that Jim's come to realize what he's lost? I'm suddenly attractive again."

I bit my lip. Was she considering taking him back? "So-o-o?"

"Are you kidding me?" She rolled her eyes. "I saw him at the mall with some redhead last week. He's just having buyer's remorse."

"Buyer's remorse?"

"His shiny new conquest suddenly seems a bit tarnished."

"Hmm." My mind was torn between pending news from Raymond and the friend before me. "Tarnished?"

She tilted her head. "The grass is always greener…"

"I get it. So you're definitely not considering reconciliation?"

"Looking back, I think the signs were always there. After the babies came, I couldn't even consider the fact that my husband and the father of my children could be anything but a stellar person. I was so in denial." Tears perked in Julie's eyes.

I reached for her hand. "Any woman would have trouble accepting that." I recalled the months I struggled to accept what was going wrong with my marriage. "It's a process. Sometimes it's difficult to accept the truth."

I thought of Sweetie. Every day that went by left me grappling between what I wanted and what in the end would be.

The clock behind the reception counter read 5:00 p.m. I cleared my desk and carried my coffee mug to the staff lounge. Kent continually warned us about the staining properties of coffee, but Amber and I ignored him and used whitening toothpaste. I passed Kent in the hallway.

"Good timing," he said. "Say, I'm making barbeque ribs tonight. Care to join me?"

"Well, I...actually I'm still watching Sweetie."

"She's still with you?" His eyes grew wide for a moment but then he recovered. "Did the mother leave the country or something?"

"I have to rinse out my mug." I hoped he got the hint.

"Bring her," he said. "I like kids. My brother has a passel of them. I promise, I'll do all the cooking, and you can relax."

Kent produced a smile that made me feel like everything was going to be all right. It wasn't like I had anything else to do. It was Friday night. Minnie had a card party that evening, and I sure didn't feel like cooking. But would my acceptance send the wrong message?

He raised both hands in the air. "No strings attached. Just want to share a meal with someone for a change."

"Okay. Sure. What time?"

"Come out within the hour. I'll have the grill going and Margaritas on the deck."

Minnie always said I'd do anything to finagle my way out of cooking. It wasn't that I didn't know how. I just didn't like to take the time if there was a frozen TV dinner available—or better yet, someone else's offer to cook.

Sweetie ran to me as soon as I entered the store. I lifted her off her feet and spun her around. "How's the cutest little girl in the world?"

She giggled and nuzzled her nose into my neck.

"What's your plan for dinner?" Minnie asked. Since Sweetie's arrival, she had made sure there was always food on the agenda and the cupboards were stocked.

"I'm eating with a friend."

"Did you forget I'm playing cards tonight?"

Minnie didn't let anything stand in the way of her card parties. She was wearing a sarong in a colorful palm tree print and traditional Japanese getas, a mix between clogs and flip-flops.

"I'm taking Sweetie with me."

My mother looked relieved. "Has Ray gotten back with you?"

"No, Mother."

"It's been quite a while now. Don't you think—"

I started to walk away. "He'll get back to us."

"Nothing endures but change," Minnie cited Heraclitus. The Greek philosopher had been quoted many times throughout my childhood.

"Maybe you should call him." Minnie's voice followed me, rising above the clacking of her getas. "Honey, I just don't want you to be hurt when—"

"Give it a rest, Mother." That Margarita was sounding better all the time.

* * *

By the time I arrived at Kent's lake house, my stomach had twisted into knots. The truth was I couldn't bear the thought of losing Sweetie. I unfastened her from the car seat and held her hand as we approached the front door. The temperature had risen to the mid-eighties, typical for July. From the backyard, towering pines rose above the house. I rang the doorbell and waited. After two more tries, I figured he was out back on the deck. We entered the tiled foyer.

"Hello! Kent, it's me, Liza." Still no answer. We passed the formal living room with its classic white upholstery and entered the great room with a view of the backyard. On the patio, Kent stood over the gas grill. The slide of the glass door over the track announced our arrival.

"Welcome ladies." Kent lowered the hood and approached Sweetie, who backed up into my legs. "Remember me?" He offered Sweetie a cookie from a plate on the serving table. He'd found her weakness. She loved chocolate chip cookies. "Have a seat and make yourself comfortable, Liza."

I took his advice, flipped off my sandals, and chose the padded chaise on the cobblestone patio. Several shade trees offered relief from the sun. A chilled glass with a strawberry margarita was placed in my hand.

"I need to grab a few things from the kitchen." He patted Sweetie's head and sprinted to the house. "Be right back," he said over his shoulder.

The late afternoon sun sparkled over the calm water, truly a Kodak moment. Mallards flocked in the distance. A canopy of giant cottonwoods bordered the far shore. A seagull flew overhead. I sighed. A gal could get used to this. Sweetie played with colored straws I had snatched from Kent's portable bar. I remembered playing Pick-Up Stix as a kid.

With a skip in his step and a broad smile, Kent returned with a tray of meat.

"This is the life," I said. "I bet you love coming home to this panorama every day."

"I read the paper out here in the evening. There's nothing like listening to the gulls and the waves lap up on shore."

"Do you fish?"

"Occasionally I fish from the dock. What I really need is a boat. My neighbor caught a mess of perch and walleye in the middle of the lake." He pointed to where a fishing boat trolled across the water.

The rolling lap of the waves mesmerized me. I would have preferred just staring at the lake but that would be impolite. I forced myself to engage in conversation. "Do you have family in South Dakota?"

"One of my brothers lives in Sioux Falls, and my parents are in Minneapolis. My folks are coming out in a few weeks to see my place. My sister, Tess, is planning to visit next month. I'm not sure when I can talk my older brother to visit. He lives back East. My nieces and nephews would love it here."

"Living on the lake, I'm sure you'll have more company than you might like."

Kent placed ribs on the grill. "Not a problem for me." He winked. "I love get-togethers. Can I freshen your drink?"

"I'm good." A measure of guilt threatened to surface. I could tell as Amber had warned, Kent was interested in me. I pushed the thought aside. I was enjoying this way too much. Sweetie crawled into my lap. I took another sip of my frosty drink and sighed. *Don't worry about tomorrow; tomorrow will worry about itself.* Was that quote from the Bible?

The next morning Sweetie played with wooden blocks in the playpen as I hoisted a box of miscellaneous items onto the counter, one of Minnie's purchases from a recent estate auction. The opened lid revealed a plethora of small pieces, like with like items, my mother always said. I spied an old metal bottle opener and nearby, another opener with a red and white wooden handle, the kind popular for kitchen tools in the 50s. I pilfered through dice, playing cards, gaudy jewelry, and tin measuring spoons until I excavated a bright red Bakelite bottle opener and then another with Hamm's beer advertising on the handle.

Minnie staggered up, hefting another box from the back room. She set it down and helped Sweetie stack blocks. Sweetie smiled at my mother. Both had become fond of each other. My stomach flipped as I once again considered the dynamics of the situation. What if they took Sweetie? I stuffed the panic down.

"Harold Bagley's sitting on a gold mine," Minnie said.

"How's that?" Here came another of my mother's tall tales.

"His son gave him a metal detector for his birthday, and he found a gold dollar in his lawn. His wife, Sharon, says he's digging holes all over the yard."

I laughed. "That doesn't make a gold mine. Maybe he can sell all the night crawlers he finds to fishermen."

"In my grandparents' time, people buried their money." Minnie shot me a look that declared she knew about these things. "They'd bury bullion in the dirt floor of a barn or hide it in the garage or even out back in the lawn."

"Bet they died without telling anyone where they buried the loot." I chuckled. "And after a while they probably forgot where they buried it."

"You won't be laughing when Harold's a rich man." Minnie pressed the key to open the cash register. She lifted a tray and removed a yellowed paper.

I glanced over her shoulder and said facetiously, "Did Harold bequeath his treasure map to you?"

Minnie gingerly unfolded the aged document. "This, my young skeptic, was your great-grandfather's chart of where he hid his money during the Depression."

She had my attention. "How much did they find?"

"You can see there was quite a bit at one time." She pointed to several spots on the map. "But it was hard times. Most of the coins were dug up to buy necessities."

Aha, another of Minnie's exaggerated stories.

She refolded the map and placed it in the register. Minnie looked me in the eye. "There was enough left that my father was able to buy his store. It kept him in business for years."

That was something. "Maybe Harold will make out good, too," I said more to appease my mother than anything.

"Li-a," Sweetie called with her arms in the air. I picked her up and nuzzled her neck until she giggled.

The sleigh bells broke the special moment between us. Raymond Standing Rock entered the store, and my heart plunged. I chastened myself. He might bring good news.

"Ray," Minnie said. "How are you?" There was more warmth in her voice than usual, possibly because of Sweetie.

"Minnie. Good to see you."

"Hey, Ray." I swallowed hard. "Any news?"

He walked up to Sweetie, and my breath caught. For a minute, I thought he'd sweep her from my arms. Instead, he held out a hand. Sweetie smiled and curled her fingers over his thumb.

Minnie and I stood silent, both of us on edge.

"No one has reported a missing Dakota or Yankton Sioux child," he said.

Was my deep sigh obvious?

"I put out a search for Minnesota and west of the Missouri."

My chest constricted.

"I've contacted the Sioux, Ojibwa, and Winnebago tribes in Minnesota," Ray said. "In South Dakota, I've written the nine tribal governments, and I'm waiting for them to get back to me."

With Sweetie squirming in my too-tight embrace, I plunked down on the stool. With all those choices of families, there was bound to be someone who'd claim a little Indian girl.

Minnie rounded the end of the counter and stood before Ray. "Can't we do some kind of DNA testing to find out what tribe she's from?"

Ray shook his head. "People always assume that's possible, but DNA can only determine family connection. It doesn't tell your tribal background."

A heavy silence fell over all of us.

"She looks healthy." Ray smiled at Sweetie. "You're a happy little thing, aren't you?" He glanced at me. "Thanks for taking such good care of her, Liza."

I glanced away. I wasn't just a babysitter. Deep inside, I'd become her mother.

Minnie walked Ray to the door. They stood there for a few moments, talking quietly. I couldn't make out what they were saying.

Minnie returned to the counter. "Eleanor Roosevelt said…"

Here we go.

"Women are like tea bags." She cast a pointed look my way. "They don't know how strong they are until they get into hot water."

My mother meant well. She wanted to reassure me that I could deal with whatever the outcome—even the loss of Sweetie.

I watched a car pass outside the storefront window and fantasized running away. Just me and Sweetie. It could work. Not well, I'm no fool, but it could work. What was keeping me here anyway?

I chose to take Eleanor's quote another way. I was willing to jump into hot water for Sweetie. I was even willing to go on the run for her.

Tribal Concerns

G oing on the lam would not happen immediately. There were preparations to be made. And there was the off chance—God make it so—that no one would come forward and claim Sweetie.

Under a hot sun, I shuffled through rows of used cars and paused before a blue and white classic 1977 Volkswagen van. The vehicle came with a popup top, a sink, and stove burners. Definitely cramped living quarters, but I reasoned Sweetie could live anywhere, and we could move on when necessity mandated. I was even willing to homeschool when the time came. On the bright side, our front yard could be a lake, the forest, or even the ocean. Sweetie would be a well-rounded girl, citizen of the entire country, and I would get to see more of the world.

Ironically, my house fund went to a hippie van.

I parked the VW in the back alley as Minnie took out the garbage.

"Interesting choice of vehicles." Minnie stood with elbows flared.

"Always wanted one," I said.

My mother turned her piercing eyes on me. Minnie was many things, a mind reader, I hoped she was not.

Julie and I sat under the shade of a big cottonwood to escape the late August heat. Jimmy played on the swing set while Annie and Sweetie made castles in the sandbox. Julie had demonstrated how to pack the sand into plastic buckets and turn them over to create forms. So far, their success rate was one out of five.

"Jim has agreed to turn over the house to me," Julie said.

"That's good news."

"Not if you consider the mortgage has twenty years of payments left."

Annie squealed in delight as her latest form stayed intact. "That's a problem."

"I found a part-time job with the school district, and my mother has agreed to babysit, thank heaven. The cost of paying a sitter would counteract the small check I'll make."

Questions formed in my mind about my situation. It was hard to believe that I might have to revert to living in a VW bus sometime in the near future. I counted the costs: food, clothing, gas, RV rental space…would a part-time job cover *my* expenses if Sweetie and I lived like gypsies? "You'll get child support, right?"

"Of course, but that won't cover a mortgage payment, utilities, clothes, and food." Julie refused to work fulltime with the kids so young.

"What are you going to do?"

"I'm going to ask my dad if he'd be willing to pay part of my mortgage. If he doesn't, I'm looking at subsidized housing. An apartment, somewhere." Julie teared up.

"Let's hope he agrees," I said. There was a good chance her father would help. He had recently retired and sold his construction business.

Julie looked forlornly at her children. "This isn't how I expected my life to go."

"We do what we have to do." I hadn't told Julie about my alternate plans if the courts tried to take Sweetie from me.

"So have you heard anything from Ray?" she asked, wiping away her tears.

"He wants us to talk to the tribal government and see what our options are." My jaw tightened even as the words formed.

"That makes sense. When are you doing that?"

"He has an appointment set up in two weeks."

Julie reached for my arm. "You need to know what's legally feasible."

"Mm hmm." I needed to work on my backup plan was more like it.

"Here I'm thinking my life is so bad but you might lose—"

Julie knew where my heart was when it came to Sweetie. "Don't say it."

Julie straightened. "Okay, change of subject. How's it going with that handsome art professor?"

When Beau had taken me out for lunch a few weeks ago, she'd seen us together. "He's back in Brookings. Classes have started up again." All those cute college girls must fawn over an instructor like Beau, not to mention the single professors, single waitresses, single barmaids, etc.

"Didn't you say he owns a place here?"

"He stays here in the summer." I didn't mention his claim of returning on the weekends. I didn't trust any of it.

Sweetie toddled over to where we sat in lawn chairs and tugged my hand. "See."

Lately, my thoughts had taken a desperate twist. I'd even considered marrying Kent if that meant his money could win legal battles over Sweetie. Maybe I could find a Native American man who might be interested in a flat-broke white woman with an Indian child. Although I had agreed to the meeting with the tribe to learn my options, I was already considering if I should take off before it went any further.

September arrived too soon. Minnie, Sweetie, and I drove to meet Ray at the Peever exit off I-29. Kent had no problem giving me the day off. To Minnie's chagrin I refused to eat breakfast that morning, afraid I'd lose it in the meeting. Just across the overpass, Ray's brown Chevy waited on the shoulder. He waved out the driver's side window for us to follow.

After four miles, we turned onto an unpaved road. Sooner than I liked, we arrived at Agency Village. We followed Ray into the tribal office and sat in the waiting room as he checked in at a nearby desk. Brown faces that matched Sweetie's surrounded us. That was when it struck me—was I being fair to Sweetie?

She sat on my lap, appearing overwhelmed by the strange surroundings and snuggled closer. The old saying that love is colorblind flashed through my mind and eased my conscience. Minnie placed her hand on my shoulder and for once didn't say anything. Raymond returned and conversed with some men sitting across from us.

Twenty minutes later, a woman approached and pointed to a door. I felt like I was going to trial except the jury was out, literally out—the room held rows of empty chairs. At the far end, a lone man sat behind a desk. Inwardly, I laughed. Maybe they were all out eating warm fry bread dripping with honey. Granted a bad stereotype, but my stomach was empty.

Ray shook hands with the man and introduced us to John Eagle Feather.

"Have a seat," John said. His long hair was pulled into a ponytail, and he wore a plaid shirt with a western yoke. "Liza, why don't you give us a little background to the situation."

His kind eyes encouraged me to tell the story of Sweetie's unusual entrance into my life. After what seemed an eternity, I sighed. "That's about it."

John glanced at Sweetie, who was now sitting on Minnie's lap. "Raymond told me you've taken very good care of our little girl. I can see she feels safe."

Why did he say "our" little girl? It hadn't been confirmed she belonged to any tribe.

John Eagle Feather brought his hands together over the desk, his index fingers forming a teepee. "In 1978, the ICWA was formed. That's the Indian Child Welfare Act. There is a placement preference for adoption of Indian children. First preference is that a child would go with a member of the extended family. Second preference would be a member of the child's tribe, and lastly, another Indian family of another tribe." He paused and cleared his throat.

I swallowed hard. I didn't qualify for any of those categories.

"Of course, we are presented with an unusual situation here." John leaned back in his chair. "No one, as of yet, has come forward to report a missing child. Second, to complicate matters, we don't know which tribe she's from." He tapped his index finger on the desk and his gaze went inward.

My stomach knotted, and I feared I would puke in front of the man despite my empty stomach, a revolt of stomach juices or something equally disgusting. Sweetie climbed back on my lap, and I hoped the added weight would hold my stomach down.

"Raymond has vouched for your character and your wonderful care of the child." John turned to Ray. "Would you be willing to sign a paper that states you will accept full responsibility for Liza's temporary custody of the girl? Then it's a matter of waiting to see if any out-of-state tribes report a missing child."

"Certainly, John. As I've said, I vouch for this family. The child has had excellent care and attention."

"It involves monthly paperwork on your part."

"No problem." Ray smiled at Minnie.

John Eagle Feather glanced over at Sweetie. "I can see the child has become attached to you, Miss Murphy. But you must realize, if anyone comes forward…"

I nodded and looked down at Sweetie to avoid his eyes.

"Legally, if the child is found to be abandoned for one year, you could then initiate adoption procedures."

I swung my head up. That was the best news I'd heard so far.

On the drive back to Watertown, Minnie was remarkably quiet and tuned the radio to a seventies rock and roll station. Meanwhile, I ruminated over everything John Eagle Feather had said. Now my days—and nights—would be haunted by worries of missing child reports and relatives claiming a sweet little girl with brown eyes.

I had just sat down with a bowl of popcorn when Minnie handed me the phone.

"Hi, Liza," Beau said. "How's the painting going?"

"I haven't done much lately." I wound the cord around my finger. "How are your classes this semester?" I couldn't think of anything else to say. Frankly, I was surprised he had called at all.

"I'm going to be in Watertown this weekend. How about a pizza and a movie Saturday night?"

He told me he'd be back, but I thought it was all talk. Never figured he'd return this soon. "Okay."

"Don't sound so excited," he said.

"Sorry, it's been a long week."

"It's only Wednesday. Sounds like you need to get out. I'll pick you up at six-thirty."

"I'll meet you at Franco's Pizza. See you then." I didn't want a college professor picking me up at the antique store even though I'd confessed that's where I lived. I had my pride.

The following night, Sweetie and I drove to the lake. Kent promised burgers on the grill and root-beer floats. I had expressed an interest in painting his beachfront view of Lake Kampeska, and he had countered by offering to buy my painting.

"It could take several tries." I set up my portable easel on his patio. "Watercolor is a very unforgiving medium."

"That will give me more grilling opportunities." He offered Sweetie an Oreo cookie. New toys appeared upon each visit. Kent had even invested in a toy box by the sliding glass doors. What was getting my attention, though, were his great biceps. At the office, he always wore a traditional long-sleeve dress shirt with the cuffs rolled up. Obviously, he worked out on a regular basis.

I didn't want to encourage anything with my boss, but I desperately needed a diversion from my worries and the promise of my first art sale prodded me forward. I did worry that Kent was growing on Sweetie. It wasn't fair to involve children in a relationship that might end in the near future. Next *plein air* visit, I vowed to keep Sweetie home with Minnie.

I captured the sky with its three distant clouds and set my brush down. Watercolors required drying time in between stages of painting, otherwise my lake would bleed into the still damp sky. Kent walked up with a frosty Margarita in hand. "Could I have a Coke, instead?"

"Of course," he said. "Smart girl. You have to drive home."

Sweetie had changed a lot of things in my life. Responsibility to her wellbeing came first.

Kent served burgers and deli potato salad on the patio table. After dinner, classical music played from outside speakers. Kent's lake house always provided a relaxing escape from the world.

An hour later clouds had formed on the horizon, and the setting sun mocked me with its masterful strokes of color. I pulled a smaller watercolor pad from my bag and tried to capture the shades of plum, rose, and violet. My painting was pretty but nothing in comparison to the real thing before me.

Sweetie became fussy, a sign I now recognized. She was tired. I thanked Kent for another great barbeque, and he walked us to the van. He ran his hand over the door and got a dreamy look in his eye. "Man, this thing brings back fond memories." He reminisced about the VW bug he'd driven back in his college days.

He waved to Sweetie now safely secured in her car seat and held the driver's side door open for me. "We should go camping in this some time. You know, test it out and explore another lake."

Unable to speak, I smiled and waved to Kent before backing out of his drive. This relationship was headed where I never wanted it to go. I sighed. My chimera at Kent's lakeside villa had officially come to an end.

Sweet Tea

I woke to find Sweetie pulling the bedcovers from my face. "Lia. Lia."

Through blurry eyes, I realized she had managed to climb out of the crib. Thank goodness she didn't fall. "Is it time to wake up, Sweetie?"

"Hungy."

One of the drawbacks of living in a store open for business was I couldn't put on a robe and head for the kitchen. I threw on a crumpled pair of jeans and a faded t-shirt. That was as far as I'd go for Minnie's customers. With Sweetie in my arms, I unlatched the child gate and trudged down the thirteen steps to the main floor and eighteen stairs to the basement. First things first.

Once we arrived in the kitchen, I pulled three boxes of cereal onto the table. Sweetie liked variety with her breakfast, sometimes mixing two different brands in her bowl. I was pouring milk into her Trix and corn flakes when Minnie waltzed in with Ray on her heels.

"Morning, sleepy heads." Minnie kissed Sweetie on the cheek and me on the crown.

"Good morning, girls," Ray echoed.

Was he here for a welfare inspection?

"Liza, would you mind taking over the store for a while?" Minnie glanced at our cereal bowls. "After you finish your cereal, of course."

"What's up?" I looked at Ray who was placing a kid's pair of beaded moccasins on Sweetie's feet. "Aren't those pretty? Can you say thank you to Ray?"

"'ank you." She kicked her feet up and down, staring at the colorful shoes.

"Ray has invited me out for breakfast." Minnie glanced at Ray and smiled. "Won't be gone long."

"We'll bring our breakfast to the front counter." I cleared a wheeled cart and replaced the toaster and bread with bowls, cereal boxes, and milk. With Sweetie on one hip, I wondered if living in the VW wouldn't be so bad after all.

Minnie and Ray walked in front of us. Was that a sassy wink Minnie tossed in his direction? Looked like the *Minnie*sota Freeze had thawed.

That evening Minnie repaid the favor by watching Sweetie, so I could meet Beau for dinner. I entered Franco's Pizza and scanned the room. Beau waved from the back. By the time I made it to the booth, he was standing. He gave me a quick hug.

"Good to see you again." In blue jeans and t-shirt, he could have been any ordinary guy.

"How's campus life?"

"The same as always. You have the usual wiseacre freshman who thinks he's a Rembrandt and a large percentage of abstract artists, students who think they don't need to know the basics of drawing." Beau ran his fingers through his hair, a slight air of exasperation on his face.

204

I'd never considered there'd be aspects of his job that would be mundane or frustrating. Guess every job had its highs and lows, even that of a professor.

"Let's decide on a pizza and get that out of the way." He studied the menu. "We'll each choose our top two favorites and see what we come up with."

After a little deliberation, I voted for the Bunny Rabbit Pizza, a thin-crust vegetarian, and Alice in Wonderland, a pan-crust mushroom, onion, and pepperoni.

"Good selections," he said. "You pick."

"Okay, Alice in Wonderland it is." Beau was obviously being a gentleman by going with my choice. The waitress appeared at that opportune moment and took our order.

He leaned over the table and smiled. "So what's new with you?"

"You know that little girl I brought to class? Someone deserted her, and I want to adopt her."

"Whoa!" He leaned back against the booth.

I surprised myself by unloading all the facts. I was tired of worrying that Sweetie's relatives would surface and want her back; I was tired of my pretenses with my boss; and I was tired of carrying the weight of loving someone I could easily lose at any moment. "And I'll do anything—"

"Wait, this calls for a beer." Beau raised his voice as the waitress passed. "Ma'am, could you change our sodas to two drafts of Bud?"

I started crying.

"Oh, man." Beau moved to my side of the booth. "I'm sorry, I didn't mean to upset you."

The waitress set two frosty mugs in front of us, but they went untouched.

"Sweetie's such a precious child," I said, "and we've become attached to each other."

205

Beau offered me a paper napkin in lieu of a tissue. "Someone actually abandoned her?"

"Left her right in the store." I sniffled. "My mother's antique store. Can you believe it?"

He shook his head in disbelief.

"I didn't want to send her to a foster home. You know, what if they came back for her? But four months have passed and nothing."

"So now what?" He took a swig of Bud.

"Minnie, that's my mother, has a Native American friend who helped us with the tribal authorities. No one has reported a missing child locally, so they're looking at other tribes in bordering states. If someone does come forward,"—I looked him straight in the eyes—"I've decided to run away with her."

Beau's eyes widened, and he was silent for a moment. "You really love her, don't you?"

I gulped and nodded, unable to speak. That's when I decided I liked this man. He didn't lecture me about what was right or the trouble I could get myself into, no legal ramifications shoved in my face. I realized his hand had covered mine for the last fifteen minutes. The waitress arrived with our pizza.

"Think you can eat?"

He considered my feelings before his own stomach. What man does that?

"Starving." I smiled. Admitting everything to Beau had freed me of some of the burden I'd carried for weeks. I took a big bite and saw that Beau had a smear of tomato sauce above his upper lip. He'd never looked so handsome.

Saturday morning, I made French toast while Minnie prepared coffee. Sweetie played with a rubber duck in her high chair. Preoccupying her with a toy kept her from playing Houdini and slipping beneath the tray.

"You won't believe what I saw yesterday." Clad in a wild violet caftan, Minnie wore her hair on top of her head bound with a purple scarf. "I was driving back from the Wilkerson auction ten miles north of town. Did I tell you I got a great buy on a camel-back trunk? Anyway, I'm on a gravel road about a quarter mile from turning onto Highway 81 when I passed the Johnson farm."

Another of Minnie's meandering stories. I sighed and flipped a piece of toast in the frying pan.

"It was a beautiful day, and I was admiring the sky. You know that color you artists call ultramarine blue? Well, I passed the windmill and would you believe someone had climbed to the top? I slowed down and sure enough, there was Janice Johnson, shielding her eyes to gaze over the horizon like a pirate. I stopped the car and got out. 'Janice,' I shouted. 'Are you okay?'" Minnie stopped for a dramatic pause. "You won't believe what she said."

"What did she say, Mother?"

"She said, 'I do this every Friday morning, Minnie.'"

My chest heaved with laughter as I stacked the French toast on a plate. I glanced over. My mother's right eyebrow rose. I refrained from laughing any further.

Minnie whispered, "I think there's something wrong with that woman." She circled her index finger next to her ear. Sweetie giggled and mimicked the gesture.

I hated to think what else the child was picking up from my mother. "Sounds dangerous to me," I said. "Those windmills are pretty high."

"Exactly." Minnie placed butter and syrup on the table.

"They're ready. Let's eat."

Sweetie continued spinning her little hand next to her ear. I met Minnie's eyes, and we broke out laughing.

Later that morning, I gathered sweaters for a visit to Riverside Park. Sweetie loved to feed the geese along the Sioux River. The swing sets were a big drawing point, too. I punched the till for change for the pop machine.

I looked up to see Ray approaching the counter. My stomach flipped. "Hey, Ray."

"Hi, Liza." He stooped to pat Sweetie's head. "Hey, there's that cute little girl."

"Say hi to Ray, Sweetie."

"Ray ray."

Behind the counter, I stood frozen, the cash drawer open. I forced myself to ask, "Any news?"

"Nope, nothing."

Minnie walked up at that moment. "Raymond. How's it going?"

"I brought you something." Ray reached into a canvas bag and pulled out a beaded necklace.

"Ooh, that's pretty. How much?" Minnie fingered the red and purple necklace.

"It's a gift," he said. "The colors made me think of you."

"Why thank you, Ray." She draped it over her head. "You needn't have." Minnie admired the beadwork in a mirror propped on the jewelry case. "You shouldn't have," she repeated. Her smile said otherwise.

Ray dug in the bag and drew out a pair of earrings. "These are for you, Liza."

The four-inch dangling earrings weren't the kind I'd ordinarily wear but they were pretty, a pattern of blue and green beads. "Thanks, Ray. They're beautiful."

"I have some business in town, Minnie, and I wondered if you'd care to have dinner later tonight?"

Minnie angled her head and smiled. "Won't turn down a free meal." Was she flirting with Ray? She played with the hair at her temple. Definitely flirting.

"Pick you up at six. See you, Liza." Ray waved at Sweetie.

The door shut. "Jewelry and dinner, huh?"

"He gave you jewelry, too." She spun around and straightened some cedar boxes.

I had another thought. "Do you think he's checking up on me? You know, with taking care of Sweetie."

"He trusts you implicitly. He told me so."

I closed my eyes and sighed. His recommendation would come in handy for an adoption proceeding. "We're off to explore the park."

"Have fun, girls." Minnie turned back to the boxes. As we exited the store, Minnie was humming a happy tune.

In the VW, I strapped Sweetie in her car seat and drove down Kemp Avenue. Two blocks down we passed the bank. Beau stepped from the double doors accompanied by a beautiful blonde, statuesque as a model. I took a double take. They were definitely together. I sped up and pretended I hadn't seen him. My cheeks flushed. What a fool I was.

Parked along the Sioux River, I realized Beau viewed me as a friend. Only a friend. I could deal with that. Everyone could use more friends. What got into me to think a guy like that would be interested in a small-town girl? I undid the straps of the car seat. Sweetie held out her arms and puckered her lips for a kiss.

"Aw, my little sweet tea." Who needed anything more?

Where Your Treasure Is

Minnie skipped up the stairs to the balcony.

"How was dinner?" I asked.

She kicked off her shoes and pulled a nightgown from the dresser. "The ribs were great."

"Did you have a good time with Ray?"

"It was just a dinner, Liza." Her mouth compressed into a single thin line. Obviously, the highlights of her date wouldn't be forthcoming.

Minnie folded back the quilt and plumped the pillow. "It is by going down into the abyss that we recover the treasures of life."

"Huh?" I clamped my mouth shut, but it was too late.

"Where you stumble, there lies your treasure." Her head disappeared beneath the rising dress.

"What's that, Confucius?"

"Joseph Campbell." Minnie slipped the dress on a hanger. "But it fits Joyce Schmidt."

"Your bridge partner?"

Minnie slipped on her nightgown. "She found a treasure in her basement while she was cleaning out her cold storage room, the kind with a dirt floor where people store their apples and potatoes for winter."

"And?" I couldn't help but get caught up in Minnie's stories, despite myself.

"Her house was built in 1901. She's lived there for ten years, but she just got around to a thorough cleaning of the cellar. Joyce was preparing to store apples she ordered from that farm place two miles out of town."

"The Thacker's orchard?"

"Right. Anyway, she poked the broom under the lowest shelf when she heard a ping. Joyce got down on her hands and knees, but it was so dark she had to fetch a flashlight. She was practically lying on the dirt floor, shining that light. Seven old Mason canning jars were lined up along the wall. Joyce had to reach through cobwebs to pull out the quart jars." Minnie stopped. "What do you think was in those jars?"

"Oil. Black Gold. Texas tea. Now Jeb's a millionaire." I could be a smart aleck when I wanted.

"Close," Minnie said. "Three jars of Liberty gold dollars and four jars of Morgan silver dollars."

"I was hoping for oil."

"Just for your information," Minnie narrowed her eyes, "they don't make those coins anymore. She's going to have them assessed by a coin expert."

"So they've been hidden there quite a while?"

"You betcha. I examined the jars myself. They have the old lids with the metal clasp. The mold numbers on the bottom of the jars point to the 1930s."

"Why would someone put money in a dirt cellar?"

"It was the Depression. I've talked with you about those days."

Minnie stared into space. "All those hidden treasures that will never be found."

"Maybe we should buy a metal detector," I quipped.

"Now you're making fun of me." Minnie crawled into bed and pulled the covers to her chin.

"I'm sorry. Good night, Mother."

"Where you stumble, there lies your treasure," Minnie mumbled again as she turned out the light.

Sunday morning, I took two quarters from the front register, so Sweetie could drop coins in the offering plate at church. Something about having children made a person reconsider her spiritual wellbeing. Plus, I always enjoyed Sunday school as a kid. I glanced out the front display windows and saw a dark blue vehicle through the drizzle running down the glass. Something was familiar about that faded hood. A young girl stepped out.

The Indian girl who had left Sweetie!

My stomach sank. I ducked behind the counter and held my breath. The pounding in my chest rose and clutched my throat in a stranglehold. The girl knocked on the glass. As a rule, the store was closed on Sundays. I prayed Minnie couldn't hear the rapping from the back room. Unfortunately, my mother had excellent hearing. Oh, God. The tapping continued despite the closed sign on the door. Finally all went silent, and I peered over the counter's edge.

The girl reentered the car, and the vehicle backed away from the curb.

"Was there someone at the door?" Minnie called from the back.

"There's no one there." I headed to the back room. "Ready to go?"

My nerves blazed all throughout Sunday service at St. Martin's. My heart revved to maximum speed. I couldn't pray.

My conscious told me I had no right; I refused to give up what didn't belong to me. Sinner that I was, I spent the entire service planning what to take on our coming exodus.

Minnie glanced over with a frown as I scribbled notes on the church bulletin. I turned the paper away from her. More questions demanded my attention. How could I afford childcare if I escaped to another state? I could see right away I hadn't thought this through. My thoughts spun from despair to the hope that the older girl would be discouraged by our absence and wouldn't return. By the end of the service and the final blessing, I decided I would pack our bare necessities just in case we had to bolt. At the risk of losing my job, I'd call in sick. I couldn't have Minnie willy-nilly giving Sweetie back while I was at work. If the girl returned, Sweetie and I were out of there.

The usher dismissed our row. "Are you all right?" Minnie whispered in the church foyer. "You fidgeted through the whole service."

I held Sweetie in a death grip, and she whimpered. "I'm fine. Let's get to the car before it starts raining again." Minnie had trouble keeping up as I speed-walked to the parking lot.

"Hold on," she said. "Where's the fire?"

I took all of us out to dinner at the Wheel Inn, as far from Kemp as I could manage. Then to Minnie's surprise, I treated us to a matinee movie afterwards. Anything to avoid another visit from the past.

"You're sure generous today," Minnie remarked with a suspicious glint in her eye.

"I thought it was time," I said. "You're always doing things for us."

That evening Minnie headed to the grocery for that night's barbeque sandwiches, I took a case of bottled water and two jugs of juice to the van. I was glad Minnie took Sweetie with her to the store. Sweetie tends to become fussy when she sees me stressed.

I would be ready in case the girl returned. Second trip, I carried winter coats. It could be a decade before I came this way again. For several weeks, I'd kept the gas tank full. On my third trip, I threw in three jars of peanut butter—Minnie liked to stock up when it was on sale—and also stole a loaf of bread. My mother would forgive me. I wasn't so sure about God.

While Minnie cooked dinner that evening, I smash-packed enough clothes for Sweetie and myself to last five days. I crept out the front door and slid around the corner to the alley to avoid Minnie's detection. Couldn't have her catch me carrying a suitcase to the van. After a dinner of barbeque sandwiches and chips, one of my favorite meals, I complained about indigestion. By bedtime, I grumbled about feeling sick to my stomach. As if in collusion with my fake symptoms, my stomach roiled with anxiety. The coming week would determine whether I stayed in Watertown. My whole future hung on the appearance or disappearance of a teenage girl.

The next morning I called in sick as planned. Amber wished me a speedy recovery. Minnie offered to take Sweetie up front so I could rest.

"I'm not sleepy right now," I said with my best languid expression. "I'd rather she keep me company."

"If it's a virus, you don't want her to catch it," Minnie said.

"My stomach's okay this morning. I just have a terrific headache."

Minnie gave me a sideways look and headed toward the front of the store. She paused. "If you get tired, let me know."

"Thanks, Mother. I will." Rest would definitely not be on my agenda. Every time the sleigh bells rang, I peered over the balcony to see who had entered the store. It was going to be a very long day.

215

At noon Minnie delivered a tray of chicken noodle soup, the canned variety, and a peanut butter sandwich for Sweetie. "I need to run to Billy Townsend's and check on some things she wants to sell. I'll close the store until I get back."

"Good idea. I'm pretty sleepy." The odds of anyone coming in around noon on a Monday were slim, but I couldn't risk the girl returning for Sweetie.

"I'll be back as quick as I can." Minnie knitted her brows. "Sure you're okay?"

"Positive, just feeling weak."

Minnie headed for the stairway and paused. "Shoot. I forgot the utility bill in the kitchen. I hate it when I have to backtrack." She glanced over her shoulder. "I'll check on you when I get back." A few minutes later, the bells registered Minnie's exit.

The store remained blissfully quiet. As I contemplated a little nap for Sweetie and me, the bells jangled. Dang. That meant Minnie forgot to lock the door. I peered over the balcony and froze—the Indian princess was back. My stomach sank. I glanced at Sweetie lying on the sofa, her eyelids hanging low. In a moment, she'd be asleep. I looked again. The teenager walked down the aisle, looking for someone in charge or maybe in hopes of spotting Sweetie in the next display. I ducked down as the girl's head lifted.

Faint footsteps continued toward the back of the store. Stealthy, I mused, like moccasin-footed Indians in old Westerns. The footfalls came louder, closer. Escape from the balcony could only occur in full view from the main floor. I peeked over the partial wall of the balcony, and the teenager stood staring at the PRIVATE sign on the chain that closed the upstairs to the public. Could she hear the drumbeat of my heart? I pressed my forehead against the lower part of the wall and hoped Sweetie wouldn't wake and start giggling as she was prone to do. At retreating footsteps, I peered over the balcony. The teenager strode toward the front of the store. At the front register, she paused as if someone might magically appear. After a moment, the bells announced her departure.

For Whom the Bell Tolls. Like the famous novel, a lingering sense of incrimination rolled over the quiet store.

I half stood and watched the girl enter the same decrepit car. With unspeakable relief, I gathered Sweetie in my arms, clutched my purse, and ran downstairs. I rushed to the kitchen in the back room and retrieved a pen from my purse. On a paper napkin, I wrote a quick note to Minnie. A moment later, I pulled out of the alley and drove through the drive-through window at the bank to withdraw cash.

The message left on the table for my mother was terse and a bit more than ridiculous.

Minnie,
Feeling better. Need a vacation.
Call you later.

Love,
Liza and Sweetie

Guess sudden leavings ran in the family.

On the Run

I slowed the VW bus upon approaching Henry, a blink of a town on Highway 212. A few miles later, I turned south onto Highway 25. Along with an endless blue sky, the rolling acres of tall field corn and cut hay fields carried a sense of freedom. Ochre, umber, ultramarine—I had a sudden desire to capture the idyllic scene in paint. But there'd be no stopping until there were miles between us and the antique store. With the driver's side window open, sweet, crisp air whipped against my face. I could breathe again.

I glanced back at Sweetie who took in the sights like she did most of life: with acceptance and wonder. "We're going on vacation, Sweetie. We'll have lots of fun."

"Fun," she repeated.

"Fun," I said. "Lots of fun."

I recalled the Buick parked out front on Sunday morning. The car had New Jersey plates. That meant they were probably coming back from wherever they'd gone after the girl dropped off Sweetie. I hoped after a day or two of searching for the toddler, they'd give up and head back East. And if they questioned Minnie, what could she say? She had no idea where we'd gone. Besides, I reasoned, what right did they have after deserting a poor child? Then it dawned on me, *I* could be accused of kidnaping. I shoved the thought aside.

I remembered my original reason for not reporting Sweetie to the authorities. Ironically, I had hoped the girl would return for her. I clenched my jaw. The girl had stayed away for too long. It wasn't fair to Sweetie. It wasn't fair to me.

My escape plans remained fuzzy, but gypsies didn't require an itinerary. In the back of my mind, an image of the Black Hills arose. My church group had a retreat there when I was fifteen, and I'd always longed to go back. Besides, how fitting that Lakota Indians believed the Hills to be sacred grounds? I glanced in the rearview mirror. With my dark hair and lingering summer tan, I could pass as Sweetie's biological mother. I smiled and accelerated over the empty country road to the tune of Bryan Adam's (*Everything I Do*) *I Do it For You.*

My mother came to mind. Is this how she'd felt all those years ago when she left everything behind? Perhaps the air had blown through her hair as she drove to California, a young woman, carefree and ready for whatever came her way. When she finally returned home, she had a little dark-haired child with her. I smiled at the irony. I was my mother's child, after all, duplicating the process in reverse.

I was in no hurry. Tucked safely in my purse, the money left over after buying the van offered a small measure of reassurance. Besides, I didn't want to keep a two-year-old strapped in a car seat all day. In the middle of the afternoon, we pulled into Mitchell. We landed at one of those old motels from the sixties where a guest can drive up to the door of his room.

The dated avocado shag carpet and flamingo paintings made for an economical lodging fee.

I drew back the comforter and blanket, figuring the sheets were cleaner than the bedspread, and placed Sweetie there with a canvas bag of toys. With pillows stacked behind me, I leaned back, put up my feet, and browsed the tourist brochure I'd taken from the motel office.

"The Corn Palace is here, Sweetie," I said. "We'll check it out tomorrow."

"Corn?" Sweetie perked up at the word. She loved corn smothered in butter.

I peered over the top of the brochure. "Are you getting hungry?"

"Hungy." She patted her stomach.

"We'll find a place to eat in a few minutes."

Sweetie crawled into my arms. "Home?"

I kissed her cheek, guilt creeping in for taking Sweetie away from what had become her security over the last few months. "We're on vacation now. Taking a road trip. We'll go home later." I bounced her up and down on the mattress until she giggled. "Let's find something to eat."

I placed her in the car seat and blew a raspberry on her tummy. "I love Sweetie." With the sweetest sound ringing in my ears, I snapped the seatbelt. I closed the door upon her giggles and found myself wishing, like Sweetie, that we were home.

The price of admittance to the Corn Palace came as a pleasant surprise—free. The brochure stated the first Corn Palace was held in 1892 to celebrate the harvest, and the tradition had continued ever since. With Sweetie in hand, I stared up at the Moorish minarets and kiosks made entirely from ears of corn and grain. I never realized there were so many colors of corn.

221

"Look, Sweetie." I pointed at the exterior walls. "They use corn to make the murals. Did you know corn came in so many colors?" I didn't. Red, brown, black, blue, white, orange, calico, and yellow—whew!

According to the article, the corn was nailed ear by ear. The theme changed every year, the current theme: South Dakota— The Good Life. I laughed. As eager as I had been to leave home at eighteen, I had to admit I'd grown to appreciate my roots. After a quick tour of the palace, we hit the road again, making good time on I-70 West.

Seventy minutes later we approached the town of Chamberlain. A sign announced the new Akta Lakota Museum & Cultural Center. I glanced over my shoulder. Sweetie was staring out the window, taking in the open prairie. I refused to keep Sweetie from her Indian heritage. I swerved and turned off at the exit and drove to the museum.

Once parked, I spotted a large teepee on the grounds. "Let's check that out." I took her hand and ducked inside the tent. "Your people used to live in these. See the fire pit? That kept them warm. They would sleep around the campfire."

Sweetie explored the teepee by running in circles around the pit. By the fifth round, I grabbed her shoulders. "Okay, okay, you like it. Let's go into the museum." We entered the octagonal building where a sculptural display of an Indian brave in buckskin and beads rose life-size. The Indian led a paint horse harnessed with a travois. Glass cases displayed arrowheads and other artifacts. Paintings created by Lakota Indians hung on the wall. One painting portrayed a native woman with three children. I pointed to the youngest child. "Sweetie is an Indian."

"Inyun," she repeated. She pointed to me. "Inyun." I let that go. She was too young for explanations. We meandered to the gift shop which had Native American crafts, everything from moccasins to jewelry. I purchased an inexpensive bead necklace for Sweetie and fastened it around her neck. The blue bead design looked good on her.

The Native clerk leaned over the counter and studied Sweetie. I panicked. What if these were Sweetie's people?

"Your daughter is so cute."

I sighed. "Thank you." In my heart, Sweetie truly was my daughter.

"What tribe are you?" the young woman asked.

Raymond's tribe came to mind. "Dakota Sioux."

"I thought so," she said and placed the bills in the register.

We ambled back to the van. I hoped Sweetie would think we looked alike as she grew older. Could be worse. I might have been a blue-eyed blonde or a dramatic redhead. Back on the interstate, we approached the bridge that spanned the Missouri River. Dark cobalt clouds formed on the horizon as I drove across the five-span bridge, its arches making the VW seem small and inconsequential. Sweetie was asleep in the backseat. Clouds built over the expansive Dakota sky, and self-doubt overwhelmed me.

Would love alone make all our horizons clear?

We made Rapid City by six o'clock that evening. With dinner reservations courtesy of Mickey D's, we washed up in their restroom. A park we'd passed on the way into town would provide a stopping point for the night, our lodging courtesy of Rapid City public streets and the sleeping accommodations of the old van.

At nine, I tucked Sweetie into her sleeping bag and crawled into mine. I tossed a lofty quilt over both our bags in case the temperatures dropped further that night.

"We're camping, Sweetie," I said.

"Campin'," she said in a sleepy voice. I usually put her to bed by eight.

Weeks ago I made makeshift curtains in the back, pine-tree print fabric hung with a coiled wire attached to thin metal brackets. I drew the curtain aside and stared at the sky. Unfortunately, the streetlights competed with the galaxy of stars overhead. Sleep didn't come easily. I kept battling the fact the young girl had come back to reclaim Sweetie. I debated back and forth. Why did she abandon Sweetie in the first place—how dare she? The next moment, who was I to make a judgement over a child's life?

With no winner in that battle, I moved on to plan our vacation. The presidents awaited on the mountain. That was a definite destination point. Reptile Garden or Bear Country? I'd let Sweetie decide from the color brochures I'd taken from the last gas station. I would have more fun watching Sweetie's reactions to the sights anyway. I vowed to follow an old Indian saying I read somewhere: *Every day is a good day.*

After breakfast at McDonalds and fifteen minutes for Sweetie to explore the play area, I showed her the tourist brochures. "That's Jewel Cave and there's also a Rushmore Cave. Reptile Garden has all kinds of snakes and slippery creatures. Bear Country has real bears. Big bears and baby bears."

"Baby bears!" Sweetie exclaimed.

"Good choice." I'd hoped she'd like Bear Country since I wasn't much for reptiles.

After a quick survey of the tourist trinkets in the gas station, I considered a souvenir for each of us, a mug for me and a coin purse with Mount Rushmore printed on it for Sweetie, neither too expensive. An unexpected wave of panic pummeled over me. Other than for the next few days, I had no destination. Had no idea when I'd find a job that would accommodate having a small child. I needed to hang on to my money and quickly diverted Sweetie's attention from the souvenirs with the promise of a candy bar. We headed to the van. I strapped Sweetie into her car seat and started the engine. "Bear Country or bust!"

"Bust," Sweetie echoed. "Baby bears!"

"Yup, we're going to see baby bears."

Once out of city limits, pines laced the hills on either side of the highway. A momentary sense of guilt engulfed me. Would Minnie be worried about us? Her own disappearance came to mind, and I set my jaw. Feeling justified that I'd given her as much information as she gave me, I pressed foot to pedal and gained another hill. Like litter, my guilt flew out the window like fast-food packaging.

The sun warmed the van's interior, but I followed Bear Country rules and refused to crack a window. I was becoming one of those overly protective mothers, but driving in the midst of full-grown bears proved intimidating. Fully committed to the idea, a bear could break into a vehicle with those powerful claws.

Turns out black bears come in all shades and colors, different shades of brown and even blond, though black predominated. The older baby bears tended to congregate together, like children who prefer their own company. They were adorable.

"Babies, babies!" Sweetie jumped up and down on the passenger side of the van.

"Aren't they cute?"

"Sweetie play." Her hand moved to the door handle.

I braked. "Sweetie can't play with these babies. They have long claws and sharp teeth. They might hurt Sweetie." I growled and demonstrated with curled fingers raking the air.

She mimicked my growl and pretended to claw me.

I idled the van for several minutes, so Sweetie could get her fill of juvenile bears before we moved on to the adults, soaking up the midday sun. After our tour through Bear Country, we visited the souvenir shop. Sweetie ran up to the stuffed bear shelf as soon as we entered the store. How could anyone deny a child a teddy bear? I knew we weren't leaving without one.

I stooped to her level. "Which one do you want?"

I never would have expected such a serious deliberation from a toddler, but she took her time. She finally chose a black bear holding its own little brown teddy bear.

"Aw, momma bear and baby bear."

She clutched the stuffed bears as if I would steal them from her. Sweetie wouldn't release the bears even for the clerk at the register.

"It's all right," the young woman said. "I'll go check on the price."

From Bear Country, I drove down Highway 16 to our next destination, Hill City. "We're going to ride a train, Sweetie. Choo choo!"

"Choo choo," she echoed.

The tourist train took three hours round trip to Keystone and back. Upon arrival I searched for a parking spot along the city park, the best bet for our sleeping arrangements that evening. Sleeping in the van kept the costs down, a wise decision since I had no idea where we were headed in the near future. We walked to the 1880 Train and purchased our ticket.

Sweetie stood on my lap and stared out the train window. Even I enjoyed the winding track through the pine forest. With her bears clutched in her arms, Sweetie fell asleep thirty minutes into our trip. I covered her with a blanket I'd brought in anticipation of such an event. I leaned back and enjoyed the scenery.

In Keystone, the train attendant announced a forty-five minute break for lunch. Sweetie awoke rejuvenated, and we strolled down the sidewalk in search of a quick burger and fries.

After eating, we had exactly ten minutes to window shop. I soon learned every stop in the Black Hills offered souvenirs. I bought Sweetie a cheap beaded bracelet but forewent a leather belt for myself. The belts with "made in Hong Kong" Indian bead designs were cliché tourist items, but as evident in Minnie's Antique Shoppe, they'd been around for decades.

On the return trip, Sweetie cradled the bears as she had all day. She'd kiss the momma bear and then kiss the baby and rock the two bears like they were both babies. It looked like the stuffed animals would go everywhere with us for the rest of our trip. She fell asleep shortly after I placed her in the car seat. I wondered if she was giving those bears the love she had missed as an infant. I'd do my best to make up for everything she might have gone through in her little life and swore I'd give her all the love she needed. And more.

Bear Den

My destination decisions formed on a whim now. Under a dazzling cerulean sky, I steered the VW up Highway 244 headed for the classic, absolutely could not miss, Mount Rushmore National Memorial. The morning traffic was light, one advantage to vacationing after the summer tourist season.

I parked the van at the edge of the parking lot for a quick getaway. Though it was no longer summer, a wave of late-season tourists might descend on the memorial, and I hated backing up in a crowded lot. With eyes closed, I inhaled the scent of pine. I unfastened Sweetie from her car seat. "Do you smell the trees?"

She closed her eyes and sniffed—she must have been watching me. "Twees."

We crossed the parking lot and headed to the amphitheater where the granite faces of Abe, George, Tom, and Teddy looked down on us. Sweetie stretched out her arm and pointed. "Nose. Big nose."

"Big faces. Big noses."

An older couple equipped with binoculars and camera glanced over at us.

"She's so cute," the trim sixty-something lady said. "She looks just like you."

"Thank you." If I was considered a child abductor, at least I traveled incognito.

"Big nose," Sweetie said.

The woman's expression fell. She did have a rather long nose. "She means the presidents," I added quickly.

"Oh, yes," Mrs. Retirement-and-Loving-It said. "They do have big noses. Big ears for that matter."

I glanced at Mr. Retirement. He had unusually long-lobed ears. Sweetie pointed at the man, and I shuffled a few feet away to divert her attention to the granite faces. Sweetie pulled at my earlobes.

"Liddle ears," she said.

I burst out laughing, and she joined in. The more I laughed, the louder her laughter. We spent twenty minutes assessing the presidents and another fifteen in the gift shop, before we left for our second destination spot of the day.

Thirty minutes later we pulled into the open parking lot of the Crazy Horse Memorial—again, the joys of off-season vacationing. I pointed to the distant mountaintop. "See the horse's head? That's a very big horse, isn't it?"

Sweetie nodded. "Big nose."

I laughed. "Yes, another big nose." We entered the exhibit buildings where several sculptures were on display. The family of the deceased sculptor, Korczak Ziolkowski, continued to work on the decades-long project. A display showed a futuristic drawing of the completed memorial. The finished size of the monument made Mount Rushmore shrink in proportion.

"This says Crazy Horse Memorial honors all Native American tribes." I pointed out the window at the monument. "This is for Sweetie, too."

She tugged at my shirt, Sweetie talk for pick me up. All our sightseeing had worn her out. Many of the employees at the memorial were Lakota Indians. Their eyes flashed from Sweetie to me. Were they judging me for raising a Native child? I pretended to ignore their glances as I carried Sweetie into the gift shop. I milled around the glass cases for a few minutes but with Sweetie now asleep in my arms, looking for trinkets had lost its appeal. My arms ached from holding her limp body. A sign over a doorway announced a café, so I purchased a cup of coffee and lay Sweetie on one side of the booth.

"I envy the ability of children to sleep anywhere." A middle-age Indian woman wiped a nearby table with a cloth.

"Wish I could do that." I slipped off my shoes.

The woman peered at Sweetie. "So sweet."

"She's pretty tuckered out," I said. The woman didn't appear to judge me.

"She looks just like you," the woman said. "No mistaking who her mama is."

Didn't she notice my lighter skin? I went with it and willed my heart to stop pounding. "Thank you."

When I was young, one of Minnie's friends had said, "With her full head of dark hair, Liza could pass as a little Indian." Then the woman laughed. It made me mad, but Minnie told me to take her words as a compliment: Indian children were beautiful. If my hair made me look like Sweetie's mother, how could I complain?

I finished a free refill and checked the time. Five o'clock. Time had passed so quickly, and I hadn't thought ahead to where we'd spend the night. As I lifted Sweetie into my arms, her body heat radiated against me. Kids were so warm blooded. I carried her across the parking lot. Her eyelids flickered, but she didn't wake. I unlocked the VW and thought to feel her forehead. Sure enough, she was burning up.

My hands shook. *Think. What had Minnie done when I was sick? A lukewarm bath, cool damp cloths on my forehead, anything to bring down the fever*. With the key in the ignition, a plan developed. I'd drive back to Hill City and spend the dough on a motel where I could put Sweetie in the bathtub. I turned the key and the engine sputtered. I moaned.

"Come on." I tried again with the same result. I pounded the steering wheel. "Not now! This isn't the time to act up." The engine spit and popped. On the next try the engine went dead. "Shit!"

Only five cars remained in the lot without a single male in sight. I grabbed Sweetie from her car seat. Hot as a boiled egg, she muttered in her sleep. I nearly ran to the main building and prayed it was still open. A dark-skinned man twisted the sign on the door to CLOSED.

"Please, I have a sick child."

The Native man waved me in and yelled for someone named Clara. The table-wiping lady I'd spoken to earlier appeared in the doorway to the kitchen.

"Sick kid," he yelled.

"Bring her over here." Clara flapped her cloth like she was starting the Indie 500.

"She has a fever," I rambled, "and my van won't start. I don't know what to do." Now I was crying like a baby. Who did I think I was to raise a child? I certainly didn't know what I was doing. Maybe all this traveling…Minnie would have known what to do…this was all my fault.

"Everything will be fine," Clara said. "Young mothers get so panicky. That's why you need us elders. I've nursed five of my own back to health and another ten of my grandkids." She turned to the man. "Frank, help carry this child to my car."

When Frank took Sweetie from my arms, I almost sobbed.

Clara wrapped an arm around my shoulder and guided me to a car parked at the side of the building. "Shh, shh. Everything will be okay. I promise. You can spend the night with me."

As she drove to Custer, I began to relax. Clara looked unfazed. She'd raised five kids, hadn't she? I knew my little girl was going to be all right with this kind Lakota woman. Still, I wouldn't quit worrying until Sweetie's temperature went down.

Clara turned the radio dial until Native music chanted from the airwaves. "This is one of our local Indian channels. This music always brings me peace."

And it did for me, too. The pine forest spun past us on the winding road, and my muscles slowly loosened. I was in Sweetie's country, the sacred land of the early Indians. The land would surely work its magic on my little Indian princess. Clara glanced over and smiled reassuringly. "Everything will be all right. What's your name, by the way?"

"Liza."

"What tribe are you?"

Oh, boy. I used Raymond Standing Rock once again. "Dakota," I blurted. "Dakota Sioux."

"Welcome sister to *Pahá Sápa.*"

I must have given her a blank look.

"That's Lakota for Black Hills."

I smiled. I'd have to remember that for Sweetie.

Clara looked over. "What brings you out to these parts?"

"Ah...a road trip." The warmth from Sweetie's feverish body felt like a heating pad against my chest. "Just needed a little vacation."

We entered Custer city limits. Clara's house sat on the edge of town. The one-story clapboard house looked cozy and well maintained. I traipsed behind Clara through a living room decorated in outdated avocado carpet and into a bedroom with floral wallpaper. Everything was clean, though definitely out of style. But who was I to judge, the girl who lived in a store?

Clara filled the bathtub with water while I undressed Sweetie, limp like a little rag doll.

"This will cool her down," Clara said. "We may have to do this a few more times tonight. It'll bring down that fever."

Afterwards, I dried and dressed Sweetie. We met Clara in the living room where a Native man now sat in an easy chair.

"This is my husband, Clarence," Clara said. "Clarence, this is Liza and Sweetie."

"How's it going?" Clarence smiled and turned back to watching the local news.

No questions, no critical glances. He treated me like I was family.

"Make yourself comfortable. I'll warm up the chicken soup. Made a big pot this morning." Clara smiled. "It's like it was planned." She winked.

Minnie always served canned chicken-noodle soup when one of us came down with a cold, but Clara's soup turned out to be the real thing—homemade noodles and all. With Sweetie looking out of half-mast eyes, I sat on the couch with her cradled in my arms.

I managed to get several spoonfuls of broth into Sweetie and half a glass of orange juice. We repeated the cool bath twice before Clara checked the thermometer. She frowned. "Let me check again. Clara shook the thermometer and waited a few minutes, before she took her temperature again. "Her fever went up. It's 104.8."

Concern etched her face and I panicked. "What do we do?"

"We need to get her to a hospital."

234

"All the way into Rapid?" My nerves stretched like thin, brittle taffy. That would take too long.

"We have a hospital in Custer."

We piled into Clara's car, and within minutes, we were rushing into the emergency room. At the desk, I was given paperwork to fill out. Name—I printed the fictional name of Sweetie Murphy, address—the store, of course, but I had nothing to fill in for insurance carrier. Why hadn't I thought of coverage for Sweetie? What if something was seriously wrong with her? One of Minnie's friends claimed if you blinked in a hospital it cost a thousand bucks. After purchasing the van, the little remaining money I'd saved for my future house would now go to the medical bill. House schmouse—a house meant nothing if I didn't have Sweetie.

I shoved the paperwork across the counter. The woman looked over the form.

"No insurance?"

I shook my head. "I'll pay cash. Well, I mean I'll pay by check." Was it my imagination or did the clerk give me the evil eye?

The woman held out the form. "We need your tribal information. Then take a seat and we'll call your name."

"But she's burning up. She needs help now." This time the woman definitely gave me the stink eye and repeated the same instructions. In tears, I returned to where Clara sat with Sweetie, the paper still in my hand. Clara wiped her forehead with a moist cloth she'd brought.

"We have to wait." My voice stretched thin and whinny. "Isn't it dangerous for young children to have high fevers?" Fever could cause seizures. I'd heard that from somewhere. From Julie, maybe?

"Here, you take her." Clara handed Sweetie's limp body into my arms and strode over to the desk.

I couldn't make out the words, but Clara didn't sound happy. She walked back and the clerk made a phone call. A few minutes later, we were called into an exam room and seated behind a beige curtain.

"My brother's on the hospital board. Thank God for inside connections."

We waited several minutes. Considering we were in an emergency room, things moved incredibly slowly. At last, a tall slim doctor in blue scrubs introduced himself. His blond hair was prematurely thinning.

"I'm Dr. Harrington. And who do we have here?"

"Her name is Sweetie." My hands were shaking.

"Hi, Sweetie. I'm going to take a look at you, so we can get you feeling better. Is that okay with you?"

Sweetie's eyes rolled up at me.

"It's okay, honey. He's going to help you feel better."

He looked in Sweetie's mouth. "Her throat is inflamed." He checked her ears and listened to her heart. "I'm going to do a rapid strep test."

"Strep throat?" My voice cracked.

"That's what I want to determine. Don't worry." He winked. "We have a cure for that."

We waited behind the bland curtain for fifteen minutes until the results came back. Dr. Harrington brushed aside the curtain. "As I suspected, your little girl has strep throat. I'll put her on antibiotics. And I recommend an over-the-counter throat spray to relieve the soreness."

"She's going to be okay?" I said with tears in my eyes.

Dr. Harrington smiled. "She'll be just fine."

Clara glanced at the hospital form clutched in my hand. "Let's drop that off and head home."

"I don't…I'm not registered with the tribe," I blurted.

"You need to get that done, girl." Clara took the paperwork from me. "My brother will take care of it."

"I'll give you my address and mail you—"

Clara shook her head. "Bill will make it disappear. Don't worry that pretty head of yours."

As we drove to Clara's house, I was overcome with a wired weariness from all the stress of the day. Clara showed us to a spare bedroom that by the looks of it, had been one of her son's. I crawled into the full-size bed with Sweetie. The smell of Tide detergent lifted from the clean sheets. I imagined this was my home, a simple but quaint old house where Clara, my traditional mother, and Clarence, my stalwart but kind father, kept the home fires burning. Sweetie and I slept like bears in hibernation.

Running on Empty

At Chamberlain I drove over the Missouri River once again, this time eager to get home. Clarence and Clara Eagle Claw had shown their warm hospitality for two days. Clara insisted we give Sweetie an extra day of recuperation. Clarence repaired the VW. It turned out to be a loose battery cable. Clara made me promise to stop in if we were ever back that way.

Our fugitive flight had ended. Though Sweetie had recovered in high spirits and the van was working fine, I didn't want to push my luck. When things had gone wrong so far from home, I had felt incredibly vulnerable.

With relief, I pulled into Watertown city limits. I glanced at the fuel indicator that hovered a hair above empty. Guilt bubbled up. What if we'd been on a lonely country road and ran out of gas? Now that I had Sweetie, I swore to be more responsible. I swung into the Sinclair station and filled up.

As the gallons mounted on the readout screen, a voice came from behind.

"Long time no see."

I spun around. Jim Bailey leaned against the gas pump. "Hi, Jim." This chance encounter was more than uncomfortable considering Julie and Jim's pending divorce.

"How's it going?" He stood far too close for comfort.

"Working for a dollar. One day at a time."

Sweetie chose that moment to announce she was awake. She never cried full force like most children; instead the sound came more like a mournful whimper. Jim walked over to the van and peered inside.

"I see you've been busy." His eyebrow rose deviously. "Find yourself a Native buck, did you?"

I narrowed my eyes and glared. "I'm watching her for a friend."

"She sure looks like you."

I hung up the pump nozzle and my hand flinched. I wanted to slap that sneer off his face. Jim stepped closer. Too close.

"You know, I'll soon be officially available," he said. "Maybe we can go to a movie sometime."

I crossed my arms. "That's never going to happen. Julie is my friend."

He headed to his truck parked one pump over. "If you change your mind…"

I climbed inside the van and slammed the door, peeling out of the lot like a teenage boy with raging hormones. Julie had to be told. I'd kept silent about Jim's earlier advances, but as a true friend, I had to tell her.

We arrived home at six that evening and found Minnie heating up homemade beef stew. Upon seeing us, she shrieked and came running. "You're home!"

I set Sweetie down, and she toddled into Minnie's arms. After my mother embraced me, she placed Sweetie in the high chair.

"Sit down, Liza, and I'll scoop you up a big bowl of stew." She opened the cupboard and retrieved two bowls.

I told her Sweetie was recovering from strep throat.

"I added peppers to the stew. That'll cure any ailment," Minnie said, pulling out the silverware drawer. "So where in the world have you two been?" She tossed a pointed look in my direction.

"Out and around, back and forth," I said glibly.

Minnie stopped mid-step and narrowed her eyes.

I sat at the table. "Like Mother, like daughter."

Minnie paused for a moment but didn't say anything. She knew her own clandestine trip had never been explained.

"Someone keeps calling," Minnie said.

My first thought was the Indian girl. My heart dropped. Could she still be in town?

"Beau seems like a nice fellow," she continued. "Said he'd call next time he was in town."

Relief flooded over me like water over Niagara Falls.

"Oh, and the dental office called three times to ask if you were feeling better," Minnie said as she passed the corn muffins.

"What did you say?" I'd hate to lose that job though it would serve me right.

"I said I'll keep making homemade soup, but I knew you were steering in the right direction." She winked.

"Thanks, Mother."

"Everything okay?" she asked.

"Everything's good."

I was glad to be home. Glad to sleep in my own bed. Glad my mother would be there to help me with Sweetie if I needed it. I had never been so happy to be home.

* * *

241

Saturday morning I had just settled Sweetie behind the counter with a coloring book and crayons when June Johansson popped in.

"Hi, June," I said. "Looking for Minnie? She's chasing antiques at an estate sale this morning."

"Good for her." June straightened her shirtwaist dress. Bright red peonies danced over her wide hips. "My sister's 40th anniversary is next week, and she collects yellow ware." She pressed her bottom lip up. "I don't see the attraction of old things myself, but Sarah loves those bowls. It's almost an addiction. Do you have any?"

I picked up Sweetie and slid around the counter. "Let me show you that booth."

"My, who is that?" June's left eyebrow rose scandalously.

I realized then that Minnie had not blabbed our newest resident to her bridge buddies. Bless her heart. I had newfound respect for my mother. "Taking care of her for a friend."

"Oh, my," June said. "For a moment, I thought you followed in your mother's..." She pursed her lips. "Where did you say I could find the yellow ware?"

I led the way. *Mother's footsteps.* I finished June's thought in my head. No wonder Minnie hadn't mentioned Sweetie to her bridge group.

Along with being judgmental, June proved to be a spendthrift. She bypassed a beautiful large bowl with decorative trim for one small enough to hold a can of cranberries. On the way back to the cash register, I couldn't resist. "So, I hear you lived in Las Vegas," I said over my shoulder.

"That was a long time ago. I worked as a dealer at a casino there."

At the counter, I wrapped the bowl in tissue paper and placed it in a paper sack. June plopped her purse on the counter.

"I was quite a looker back then." June looked wistfully out the front window. "I could have married Lenny Giovanni, the owner of the casino."

My head jerked up. It was true then. I collected myself. "You didn't love him?"

"Oh, I loved the man; that was for sure." June leaned over the counter and whispered, "But he was part of the *Giovanni* family. I didn't want to wake up some day with my husband's head shipped to me in a box."

I nearly dropped the yellow ware.

"Ten years later, that casino burned to the ground. The Vegas papers said the fire was suspicious although nothing was ever proved." June narrowed her eyes and nodded.

As June left the store, I forgot to say thank you. This was one story that my mother hadn't fabricated or to be more generous, embellished. At least, in the mind of June Johansson, every word had been the gospel truth.

Monday morning found me swarmed with questions and concerns about my health as boxes of sample toothbrushes obscured the reception counter.

"That must have been some flu," Amber said.

"I credit my mother's homemade soup." I draped my sweater across the chair.

"You should take vitamin C. Lots of vitamin C," Dr. Swenson said. "We're glad you're back. We're booked to the gills this week." He pointed to the taxidermy big mouth bass on the wall. Amber rolled her eyes. Sometimes I just had to smile at his corny jokes.

Kent wasn't kidding about being busy that week. We were overbooked with at least one emergency visit every day and three appointments erroneously double-booked by the previous receptionist. I made the best of it by serving herbal tea, asking older patients if they had any antiques for sale (I was feeling especially conciliatory about Minnie ever since my return) and generally getting people to talk about themselves. That usually kept them preoccupied.

Our oldest patient that day was Rosemary Humphrey, Grace Humphrey's grandmother.

"I heard you're moving into town." I leaned closer in case she had trouble hearing.

"They want me where they can keep an eye on me," the fragile ninety-five year old said. "But I'm still capable of doing for myself."

"I'm sure you are. We have some of your old wooden clothespins in our antique store. I loved seeing the names written on the pins."

"That would be Ruth, Andrea, Elizabeth, and of course, myself. Nothing like the clean smell of clothes dried on the line."

I had never pinned fresh laundry to a clothesline, but I nodded in agreement.

"Andrea was a real livewire," Rosemary said, looking up with faded blue eyes. "Shortly after she moved out of our apartment, she robbed a drugstore. Can you believe it?"

So that part was true, but what about the rest of the story. "Who did she marry?"

"After she served a little time in the local jail, she married Thomas Wellington, a druggist." Rosemary giggled. "Can you believe that after what she did?"

"Incredible."

"She stole some drugs from the store and left town. And people think drug problems are a recent phenomenon." Rosemary shook her head. "How that man loved her. Waited for her to come back every single day."

"That's quite a story, Rosemary." But Minnie had said the man divorced the woman. "So the druggist didn't divorce her?"

244

"After she didn't return for two years, he most certainly did. Isn't it funny, I've never forgotten that story?"

Amber entered the reception area and announced the dentist was ready for Rosemary.

So Minnie's far-fetched stories held more than a thread of truth. Was it possible, my mother wasn't as crazy as I'd always thought?

At five o'clock, I cut out before everyone. I'm sure they assumed I wanted to rest after my lengthy illness. I did long to put up my feet and relax, but when I arrived home, I found Raymond Standing Rock sipping tea in our kitchen.

My heart plunged. Lately, I couldn't escape the constant feeling of being found out. "Ray," I said, wearily.

"Liza. You're looking good."

"Ray has some good news," Minnie said, bouncing Sweetie on her knee. "Cup of tea?"

"No, thanks. I'll get a Coke." I leaned over and kissed Sweetie.

"No missing child reports in the surrounding five state region," Ray said. "Checked with all the reservations."

"Isn't that good news, Liza?" Minnie said.

By this time, Minnie was firmly attached to Sweetie. We had no sooner exchanged smiles when Ray brought the good news down a notch.

"Our tribal chief suggested a final check," he said. "President Reagan opened a National Center for Missing & Exploited Children."

I stared across the table at Ray. *You've got to be kidding me.*

"Just to make sure," he said and turned from my eyes.

Blame it on just getting back from my trip, the things that had gone awry towards the end of my vacation, the first day back at work, or whatever you will, but I fled the room in tears.

A few minutes later, Minnie appeared in the balcony where I'd flung myself face down on the bed. "They probably won't find anything there either. You have to keep a positive outlook."

I propped myself up on one arm and looked at Minnie through tear-clouded eyes. "But what if they do? I couldn't bear giving her up."

"I know, dear." Minnie stroked my temple. "I know how much you love her. But you have to think positive."

"Tell Ray I'm sorry." I sniffled. "It's just so hard." Absently, I raked my fingers across the bedspread, the lines of chenille like planted rows of corn.

"He'll understand." At the top of the stairs, she paused and offered one of her many quotes. "Today is the tomorrow you worried about yesterday."

I waited for the credit due the originator of the quotation. My mother descended the wide staircase, each step creaking upon every footfall, but said nothing more. This saying apparently came from an anonymous source.

All this worry about being found out; the real mother appearing or another family member, heaven forbid; a visit from social services; the odds against a white, single woman getting custody; and a myriad of other worries had flagellated my tortured mind. I was exhausted. How many nights did I wake at 3 a.m.? I was due for an ulcer or a nervous breakdown. Even my divorce hadn't been this brutal. Loving a child, well, there's nothing quite like it.

Options

Despite how busy I'd been with a new job and an instant child, not to mention my spur of the moment trip, my creative urges hadn't left me altogether. All around me, ideas and objects for collage surrounded me in Minnie's store. Along with strokes of paint and bits of fabric from hankies or aprons, my stretched canvases now included vintage ephemera: old train tickets, yellowed cards and letters, movie tickets, bits of patterned wallpaper, and sepia photos of unnamed people long forgotten. The collages provided an outlet for my creativity with an added bonus: I never worried when I was creating.

Minnie was as surprised as I when the first piece sold. I'd hung it behind the front counter for my own pleasure, but Minnie called me the next day at the dental office and asked if I'd be willing to sell it.

"I suppose," I said, in shock. "How much do you think I should sell it for?"

"That's your decision. You're the artist."

A patient walked in the office and approached the counter. Pressured to get off the phone, I said, "Fifty dollars?" Since I'd just finished the piece the day before, I didn't really want to part with it. I figured the price would scare off the would-be buyer.

That evening, Minnie announced over meatloaf and mashed potatoes that my picture had sold. "Reverend Baker's wife didn't hesitate at your price."

"She actually bought it?" Minnie handed me a President Grant over the table.

The next day the local newspaper announced the library was accepting artwork for an exhibit of local artists. I called the head librarian and asked if they would accept collages.

"Of course, dear. I'll mail you the entry form."

I produced two collages for the exhibit and created two more for sale at the antique store. Play-Doh and coloring books kept Sweetie preoccupied while I worked in a corner of the balcony. Minnie scrounged up an old floor lamp with lights that swiveled in different directions. Evenings found me working amid the saucy fragrance of Play-Doh, acrylic medium, and oil paint. I'd never been so happy living in Minnie's Antique and Curiosity Shoppe. Go figure.

Julie invited me to dinner that week. I was eager to tell her about my trip, but I vowed to tell her about Jim, too.

We dined on homemade lasagna, garlic bread, and red wine. Julie's kids loved having Sweetie over, and by this time, they all played well together. Julie had new highlights in her hair and a perky attitude. I was glad to see her smiling again. Maybe she had finally realized her life would be better off without Jim. We had retreated to the sofa with a glass of wine when she announced they'd gotten together.

I stared, speechless. Had I heard correctly? "When did this happen?"

"Last week. You know, he regrets breaking up our marriage, and he misses the kids horribly. He wants me to consider a reconciliation."

"You're not—"

"I can't take the dissolution of our marriage lightly. There's the kids to consider. And I have a lot invested, too."

Before I lost my nerve, I blurted, "Jim asked me out a couple of days ago."

"What?"

"He also came on to me when I first moved back to town, but I didn't have the courage to tell you then."

Julie narrowed her eyes. "Are you attracted to my husband?"

"No way!" My hands clenched. My lingering high school crush had long ago been squelched by the lecherous lout.

"You've been single too long. I bet you're desperate for a man." She crossed her arms and glared.

"Julie, I wanted you to know the truth—"

She looked away.

"Please let me explain." My pulse raced, pounding at the base of my throat. "I thought you should know."

She glared at me. "I think you better leave."

With tears in my eyes, I picked up Sweetie.

"Does she have to go?" Jimmy asked.

"Afraid so." I hurried to the door. Sweetie started crying. That made both of us as I pulled away from the curb. I believed honesty was important between friends, but evidently I was wrong. I had just lost my best friend.

Beau called that evening, but I shook my head when Minnie tried to hand me the phone. I was in a funk, still hurting from what Julie had said to me. After dinner, I retreated to my corner studio in the balcony and worked on a collage that turned out to be a pretty dark piece. Great design, but gloomy colors and sharp paint strokes made for a depressing effect. By the time I finished, some of my angst had dissipated. I glanced at the clock. Minnie had put Sweetie to bed, and that was my destination after I carried my paint and canvas downstairs. Minnie had complained before about the smell of paint and medium so close to where we slept.

When I slipped into bed, my thoughts swirled like brushstrokes. I tried to close down my mind but tossed and turned for hours. I stirred every time Sweetie turned over in her crib and counted the cycle of snores coming from Minnie's bed. Tomorrow I'd be sucking down coffee like it was soda pop just to make it through the day.

Riverside Park called to me that Saturday afternoon. Stretched out over a plaid stadium blanket, I watched the clouds on their slow slide across the sky. Sunshine fell luxuriously over my skin one moment and disappeared the next as an occasional cloud passed overhead. Nearby, Sweetie stuffed autumn leaves in the tote bag that had carried the blanket. She dragged her colorful leaf collection towards me.

"Such pretty colors," I said. "When I was a kid, I jumped in a huge mound of leaves." I stretched my arms wide. That occurred at a friend's house, another negative of living in a store—no yard. "My friend and I took turns burying each other in leaves." Sweetie's eyes widened as she doubled her efforts at filling the bag. I succumbed to the warm rays on my face and closed my eyes.

Dry leaves rustled over my stomach. I opened one eye. Sweetie scooped handful after handful of leaves over my body. At least, she was keeping busy as I relaxed in the sun. Sweetie dragged the bag beneath a nearby cottonwood for another refill of leaves that would soon be dumped on me. Satisfied that she'd be kept preoccupied for a few minutes, I studied clouds as they formed the face of an old man.

Obsessed with her newfound activity, Sweetie returned again and again with more leaves until only my shoes and head were visible. I allowed her to cover my feet, but the growing leaf cocoon would end there.

"I've heard of duck blinds, but this is going to an all new level."

My eyes flashed open to the sight of Beau gazing down with a look of amusement. I sat up, leaves crackling around me.

"Saw your van and thought I'd say hello." His thick hair was a little longer than the last time I saw him, and his unsymmetrical smile still had that same allure.

I shook my head to free any lingering leaves and brushed my t-shirt.

Beau tipped his head at Sweetie and smiled. "How are you, little one?"

Sweetie looked at him and went back to scooping more leaves.

"She loves the park," I said. "Great day, huh?"

"Beautiful." Behind Beau geese swooped down and landed on the river. "Been doing any artwork?"

"I started doing collages."

"Really? I'd love to see them."

"I have a show coming up…guess I should say, my work will be in a public show at the library next month."

"That's great. I'll be sure to check it out." He picked up a leaf and turned it in his hand. "Could I interest you two ladies in a treat at Dairy Queen?"

I wanted to keep Sweetie away from any of my dates, which were as rare as an albino deer, but he caught me at a weak moment. I was feeling sad about the drift between Julie and me.

Besides, I reminded myself Beau saw me only as a friend. "I'm up for that. Sweetie, how would you like an ice cream cone?"

Beau crouched down as she approached. "Remember me? What's your name?"

She peered at him in a studious way.

"Her name is Sweetie."

"That's her name? I thought you…" He turned back to her. "Hi, Sweetie."

But she had already moved to the safety of my side. She took a fistful of my t-shirt and wasn't about to let go anytime soon. I stood and brushed the remaining leaves from my shirt. Beau shook out the stadium blanket and folded it.

"Thanks." I dumped the remnants from the bag and tucked the blanket inside.

We took the van because of the car seat.

"I like your retro ride," Beau said from the passenger side.

"It's great for camping."

At the DQ, we ordered three vanilla cones: one double, one regular, and one kid size. We sat in a corner booth.

"You seem down," Beau said.

"I told a friend something she didn't want to hear." I refused to go into details.

"But you evidently thought it important to tell her."

"I'd want someone to tell me." I gazed out the window.

"What if you hadn't told her?" he asked.

"I'd feel I was keeping something from her. It wouldn't be right."

"Give it some time. Gut reactions have a tendency to cool down over time."

"Maybe. So what's new with you?"

Beau went into a litany of who was retiring in his department, that fall's starry-eyed freshmen, and a new steak place that had opened in Brookings. He popped the bottom of the cone into his mouth. "Am I boring you?"

"Not at all." I smiled. Anything was better than worrying about a future without Sweetie or about my lost friendship with Julie. When we parted ways, I realized the sophisticated blonde at the bank suited the good-looking college professor. Me, I was just a small town nobody.

Back home in the grand old JCPenney building, Minnie asked me to watch the front counter while she ran to the grocery store. Sweetie was napping upstairs. A few minutes later, Raymond Standing Rock entered the store.

"Hi, Raymond. Afraid you just missed Minnie. She's grocery shopping, but she should return any minute."

"I came to talk to you."

My stomach twisted. Had someone recognized Sweetie's face on the back of a milk carton? I felt lightheaded.

He held up a hand. "No, no, nothing's been reported."

My face always betrayed my emotions. I started to breathe again.

"I talked to the tribal chief again. Nothing has surfaced." Ray shifted his feet and turned his gaze to the counter. "He said we could look into our options after some time has passed."

"How much time?" My hands shook as I straightened some invoices on the counter.

"He said legally we need to wait a year before taking further steps."

Part of me wanted to shake the big man and make him spell out our options in detail. Just when I was comfortable being back home, my thoughts returned to the possibility of living life on the lam.

"A year?" My words vibrated strangely.

"A year from the time she was abandoned."

I collected myself. "Sure you don't want to wait for Minnie?" I asked.

"I came down with a friend," Ray said. "He's in a hurry to get home. Tell Minnie I'll see her in a couple of weeks."

"I'll tell her."

Outside, Ray stepped into a pickup idling at the curb. Looked like a '65 Chevy. I turned around to throw an errant gum wrapper in the basket when I caught my image in the ornate mirror on the wall. Mouth downtrodden, eyes drooping, it wasn't hard to envision the newspaper headlines: "Fugitive on the Run. Wanted for Kidnapping a Native child." The first line of the article would read: *If you have any information about Liza Murphy, please contact the authorities immediately.*

Giving Thanks

Julie called me at work. "Can you stop by on your way home?"

My heart raced. I couldn't speak. She had accused me of cheating with her husband.

"Please, Liza. We need to talk."

A patient entered the reception area and approached the counter. I said into the phone, "I suppose I could drop by for a minute."

"Thanks. See you then."

After Mrs. Walters checked in for her afternoon appointment, I wondered about Julie's call. I could nurse my offense or offer her grace. She was a woman whose life had been ripped apart, and with two children between them, I couldn't blame Julie for doing everything possible to reconcile her marriage. If she chose to get back together with that womanizer, I'd have to swallow my firm belief that the man would never change. Keep my mouth shut. Even sadder I'd have to watch him hurt her all over again. One of Minnie's quotes ran through my head. *None so blind as those that will not see.* Matthew Henry if I recalled correctly.

At 5:15 I pulled up outside Julie's house and took a deep breath. She met me in the doorway and hugged me before I could step inside. We moved into the living room and sat on the couch. Julie sighed. "I need to apologize."

"It's okay," I said. "I understand."

"Understand what a fool I am?" Her mouth drooped.

"Hope springs eternal," I quoted. "Alexander Pope." I *was* my mother, attributions and all.

"A young teacher from my church took me aside and told me Jim had hit on her, too."

"I'm sorry, but that man's incorrigible." I sighed.

"It's been hard to admit my husband and the father of my children is a womanizer."

I could relate all too well. "No one wants to believe that about the man she loves."

"Forgive me?" Tears brimmed in Julie's eyes.

"Why wouldn't I? You accept me as a future fugitive from justice." I'd finally confessed my plans to run away with Sweetie if it came to that.

"That's right, I do have that over you." Julie's eyes twinkled. She ran into the kitchen and returned with a wine bottle and two glasses.

We toasted to our renewed friendship.

November brought pink cheeks, cold noses, and a trip to Goodwill for clothes for Sweetie. I zipped up her coat. She was adorable in the pink parka that Minnie bought on sale at JCPenney. The fake-fur trim framed her little face. She was growing and needed just about everything in a bigger size.

One evening after I'd finished another collage, I showed Sweetie how to make a hand turkey. I dipped her palm into tempera paint and pressed it to construction paper. "Now we let it dry for a few minutes."

I helped her paint feathers and a turkey head. Sweetie insisted on making a dozen turkeys, which we hung in the storefront window along with a collection of yellow ware bowls filled with apples, gourds, and pinecones.

After I put Sweetie down for a nap, Beau called with an invitation for dinner at Sunnyside. Unsure how to dress for dinner, I finally settled on a pretty blouse, dark jeans, and heels. My hair escaped its usual confinement in a scrunchie and fell loose over my shoulders. When I met him at the door, his cologne drifted over. He smelled really good and was way too good looking for a friend.

Beau had never brought up the subject of his blonde girlfriend. I certainly didn't want to get involved in the middle of a lover's spat or worse, the wrong end of a jealous lover. I broached the subject over the candlelit table.

"So will you spend the holidays with your girlfriend?"

"What are you talking about?"

"I saw you together at the bank. The pretty blonde. I don't understand why you never mentioned her." Definitely not fair to the woman whoever she was.

"Blonde?" Beau appeared genuinely puzzled.

Please don't lie to me, I thought. Friends need to be honest with each other.

"Oh, Jessica. Jessica Larson." He leaned back and smiled. "She's the wife of the new vice president of the bank. She was showing me where she wanted to display the painting they purchased from me."

"Oh, that's nice."

"You thought…" Beau laughed. "I can see how you might think that."

I swiped a line through the condensation on my water glass. "Well, it didn't matter. We're just friends after all."

"I never said that," Beau said. "Here come our steaks. Hope you're hungry." He reached across the table and touched my hand.

And that was how we left it.

I worked at Minnie's on Saturday, wanting to replenish my house—or fugitive—fund, whichever fate decreed. That afternoon customers swamped the store, both locals and out of town relatives home for the Thanksgiving holiday. By late afternoon, foot traffic finally slowed. At the counter Minnie painstakingly wrapped a set of china, piece by piece, purchased by a couple from Ortonville while I made a second trip outside to a customer's truck with the top mirror of a walnut dresser.

"Thanks for your help," Esther White said. Her eight-year-old son played with a toy truck on the sidewalk.

"Hope you enjoy it."

"It will look beautiful in my guest bedroom."

I reentered the store as Minnie put the last piece of china in the box. The husband struggled with the heavy carton, so I held the door for him.

Minnie blew a piece of hair from her forehead. "Quite the day, wasn't it?"

"Holidays are good for business," I said. "Very few lookie-loos. Almost everyone made a purchase." I glanced at the playpen behind the counter. Sweetie must have fallen asleep. I stepped closer and found the playpen empty. "Where's Sweetie?"

Minnie glanced around. "She was just there in the playpen. Oh, dear. Looks like she crawled out."

We each took one side of the store and made a wild search for Sweetie. Our voices echoed as we yelled out her name. At the rear of the store, I checked that the back door was locked. I met Minnie at the end of her aisle. Her face said it all.

"I'll check the basement," I said. "You check the main floor again." Frantic, I searched behind every dresser, rocking chair, and trunk, found the bathroom empty, and ran back upstairs.

"Maybe she followed you outside," Minnie said.

I raced outside with Minnie in fast pursuit. Visions of a car hitting Sweetie hurtled through my mind, but a glance up and down the empty street proved my fear needless. A lone car approached at the far end of the block. The sidewalks were vacant except for a man walking a terrier on the opposite side of the street. I glanced at Minnie, feeling as helpless as during Sweetie's flu episode in the Black Hills, except this time Minnie was present and nearly as panicked as I.

Minnie flew into action. "I'll run around the block. You look in the alley across the street."

With a heavy ache growing in the pit of my stomach, I checked behind every dumpster and garbage can. I raced around the block in case she'd wandered that far. The 35° chill didn't faze me. It could have been twenty below, and I wouldn't have noticed. I returned to Minnie's Antique and Curiosity Shoppe just as my mother came huffing around the corner, empty handed.

"What do we do now?" A million things went through my mind—child abductors, Sweetie lying hurt somewhere, and the possibility the Native teenager had returned in the midst of our holiday rush. And to make matters worse, if we called the cops, I'd be labeled as an unfit person for adoption. Who leaves a child unattended? "Mother, tell me what to do!"

"Stop shouting," Minnie said. "Calm yourself. Let's look in every store on this block. I'll check across the street. You check this side."

A warm wave of cinnamon, caramel, and yeast hit me as I opened the door to the bakery, empty except for an elderly woman eating a scone at a table by the window. I raced on to the next building and after that, the dime store. Up and down the aisles, I skirted dawdling customers and yelled at the wrong children. After checking the rest of the block, my blood pressure threatened to explode and an inner voice whispered you'll never survive this loss. You'll never forgive yourself.

I burst out the door and met Minnie halfway down the block. By the time I caught up with her, I was sobbing. Minnie wrapped an arm around me. "Let's go back and call the police. There's nothing more we can do."

We passed the bakery when Minnie stopped and clutched my arm. She pointed. Through the window, we could see Sally in her hairnet leaning over the glass display case filled with baked goods. Sweetie had her nosed pressed to the glass as she gestured for a sweet roll. I rushed in the store.

"Sweetie, we've been looking all over for you." I grabbed her by the hand.

She looked at me strangely and pointed to my eyes.

"Yes, I'm crying. I thought I lost you. You made Lia sad."

Sweetie started crying.

"Oh, for heaven's sake," Minnie admonished me. "Pick up the child and quit scaring her."

I obeyed the first part of her order, but I couldn't quit crying. A shower of tears continued all the way to the antique store and didn't stop until we reached the balcony.

"Go dry your face and compose yourself. You're frightening the child." Minnie took her from my arms, and I reluctantly did as I was told. I regretted upsetting Sweetie, but I had been scared to death. In the back room, I splashed cold water on my face and chugged a half-frozen Coke. By the time I reached the balcony, I had a brain freeze and Sweetie was asleep.

I slumped on the edge of my bed.

"One time," Minnie whispered, "I lost you at Falls Park in Sioux Falls. I thought you were nearby playing with my cousin's kids, but you were a little maverick even back then. After searching for ten minutes, I was convinced you had drowned under the waterfall, and it was my fault. I didn't let you out of my sight for months afterwards." She joined me on the bed and wrapped her arms around me. "It happens to the best of us. Children can be very slippery creatures."

Two days later we celebrated Thanksgiving with roasted turkey and all the trimmings. Indulging in pumpkin pie with whipped cream, I had more than a little to be thankful for. One thing was certain, I needed Sweetie in my life.

I was working the counter when Holly entered the store the following Saturday. Her hair retained the brown rinse, so I assumed she was still dating the farmer from Clark. She disappeared down the aisle. Before long Holly lugged a 1906 Remington typewriter to the counter. On that lofty Standard Model No. 6, the paper roller stood high above the keyboard.

"Still seeing Henry?" I asked.

"Oh, yes," Holly said. "We're a regular couple now."

"That's nice, Hol." I pulled the tag from the typewriter.

"So that's the child I've been hearing about." Holly peered behind me where Sweetie colored completely out of the lines in a coloring book.

My spine stiffened. "What have you heard?"

She ignored my question. "Oh, she's Indian."

"What was your first clue?" I said, sarcastically, and followed it with my typical line, "I'm watching her for a friend." I looked Holly straight on. "So what have people been saying?"

Holly met my gaze. "Some people think you're following in your mother's footsteps."

261

"Holly, come on now. Have you seen me pregnant?" My blood pressure soared.

"You've been back less than a year and a half." Holly took another glance at Sweetie. "She's definitely older than that, isn't she?"

Deadly quiet, I fumed like a volcano on the brink of eruption. Holly reached into her coin purse for her wad of folded bills.

"Jeez, Holly, I'm sorry but this one's not for sale."

Her head jerked up. "But there was a price tag on it. Two hundred and fifty dollars."

"It's spoken for," a deep voice said. Raymond Standing Rock stood to the side of me. Ray, all six feet of his Native American self, looked down on Holly.

"Well, it was in the booth." She propped her hands at her waist. "I carried it up here."

"Sorry, Holly, *Native Americans* have first pick at Minnie's Antique and Curiosity Shoppe." I folded my arms over my chest.

Holly tore out the door in a huff.

"I overheard everything," Ray said.

"No way I'd sell her that typewriter after the gossip she spewed."

"Native Americans have first pick," Ray said. "That was a good one, Liza."

"About time, don't you think?" I smiled up at Ray.

"Long overdue." He winked.

Minnie came flying up the aisle in a long fringed skirt and boots. "We're going out for lunch," she said. "Anything we can bring you back?"

"No, thanks. Sweetie has put in an order for peanut butter and jelly."

"See you later," Ray said. Minnie kissed the top of Sweetie's head, and the pair headed to Ray's truck parked at the curb.

I had lost all anxiety over Ray's visits and no longer feared they were meant to check up on me. Ray and Minnie had been spending a lot of time together lately. And the dating marathon? My mother had not gone out with anyone else for weeks. Something was definitely brewing between the two. Fine with me. I liked Ray. Besides, his affection for my mother gave me that much more influence with the Tribal Authority. John Eagle Feather appeared to respect Ray's opinion, and I would use every reference, endorsement, and good word I could find.

The Michelin Man

Bundled up like the Michelin man, Sweetie dug in the snowbank at Riverside Park. December could be day after day of wind and snow, so I figured we'd make good use of the calm, sunny morning. I rolled a snowball until it reached the respectable size for a head and crowned the body of the snowman.

As a kid I had lived for snow days. Elementary school would dismiss early due to an unexpected blizzard, and as soon as I arrived home, I jumped into my snowsuit and tugged on my mittens and boots. Minnie always wrapped a long scarf around my face to ward off frostbite. We lived in the secondhand store, so I was warned against crossing the curb and instead, played along the sidewalks of closed businesses.

Howling winds formed snowdrifts against storefront windows and packed entryways four-foot high. I created snow forts by digging into the drifts, and when I tired of that, I'd jump in a fresh pile for a soft landing. Kids will make do with what they have, their imaginations transforming almost anything into fun. But the town park with its big open spaces and towering trees provided a much better snow arena for Sweetie.

"Sweetie, let's add buttons to our snowman." I demonstrated how to push a rock into the snowman's belly and laughed. "That tickles his tummy."

Sweetie followed my example and giggled. "Tickle, tickle."

Two sticks formed the arms. "Now we need to make his face."

Sweetie imbedded a rock at the bottom of the head, so we worked on the mouth. I'd brought a carrot for a pointy nose. After we finished, I posed Sweetie in front of Mr. Frosty and snapped a picture with Minnie's camera. I had become a member of that elite group of freeze-the-moment mothers.

Clouds had gathered in the last twenty minutes, and each time one passed over the sun, it felt like the temperature dropped ten degrees. "Time to head home. How would Sweetie like a cup of hot cocoa when we get back?"

"Mellos, too."

Sweetie preferred the little colored ones. "Of course, we'll top it with marshmallows."

That night was my official workplace Christmas party. Weeks earlier, Kent insisted he wanted to throw a party for his loyal workers. A picture formed in my head of Kent renting a reception room at a local hotel. It seemed silly with only three employees, Kent, Amber, and me, especially since none of us had spouses or dates. To my relief, he had announced the event would be at his house.

Back at Minnie's, I made PB & J sandwiches to go with our hot cocoa. My mother came waltzing in the back door.

"Hey, everyone. Look what I have." Minnie manhandled a six-foot evergreen into the kitchen, its branches compressed with twine.

"Look, Sweetie, a real Christmas tree."

Minnie stood back and admired it. "It's a beauty, isn't it?"

"Thanks Mother, that means a lot to me."

Minnie had suggested a silver aluminum tree she found among the many items waiting to be priced in the stockroom. I insisted on a live tree. This might be Sweetie's first real Christmas, and I wanted everything to be perfect. My stomach turned squeamish. This could be my only Christmas with Sweetie.

After sharing a cup of cocoa with Minnie, we decorated the tree in the balcony. Minnie produced a box of vintage ornaments. We hung those on the highest branches out of reach of tiny fingers. I had purchased some plastic Walt Disney ornaments and helped Sweetie hang those on the lower limbs.

Pungent pine floated in serendipitous currents across the balcony. "Doesn't the tree smell wonderful, Sweetie?" I took her hand and drew her closer to the evergreen.

Minnie sat on the bed and twisted red sheer curtains into a garland, which she draped over the balcony railing, giving a festive look to the store. I carried a vintage sled upstairs and set it beside the tree. Even the steering mechanism consisted of wood. The sled was probably a holiday-issue model given the faded holly design on the body. Sweetie sacrificed, for the moment anyway, her Bear Country souvenir and set mama and baby bear under the tree. Colorful lights draped along the walls made the room magical. I was definitely in the Christmas spirit.

I manned the counter while Minnie put Sweetie down for a nap. We did a brisk business that afternoon. The holidays drew out-of-town relatives and locals doing seasonal shopping.

A mustached man in a cowboy hat ambled through the door and approached the counter. "Hey there, pretty lady. Could you tell me if there's a western memorabilia section?"

"You're in luck." I rounded the counter. The cowboy's eyes frisked me head to toe, which made me uncomfortable as I led him down the aisle. He was probably checking out my ass. The cowpoke had to be close to my mother's age. "Here's our western section. Anything specific you're looking for?"

"I collect spurs and old saddles."

If I was in my forties, I might have considered the guy attractive. He had that tough, wiry build of a stereotypical cowboy. The buckle on his tooled western belt emphasized a flat stomach and narrow hips.

He winked, his eyes smoky blue. "You'd look good in a saddle."

The guy was definitely flirting. "I've never ridden a horse in my life."

"You'd pick it up easy."

Time to make an exit. "Let me know if you have any questions."

"I'll do that."

Where's Minnie when I need her? I rushed back to where an older lady placed a floral teacup and saucer on the counter. "Nice pick. Is it for you?" I pulled out tissue paper and wrapped the set for her.

"It's for my best friend, Florence. She loves her china."

"This will be a nice gift."

I checked out two more customers and pulled out a magazine, anticipating a lag in sales but to no avail. The cowboy stepped up to the counter and plunked a pair of spurs on the counter.

"You have good taste," I said. He had chosen a pair with intricate etching in the silver. Brass accents shone at several points. He also picked the most expensive pair. The tag read three hundred and fifty dollars.

"I definitely do." He looked straight at me and winked.

I busied myself with wrapping the ornate spurs. "Do you farm around here?"

268

"Oh, honey, I'm no farmer. I'm visiting my daughter and her husband in Estelline. I have a ranch west of the Missouri." He handed me an American Express card and a five dollar bill.

I glanced up puzzled.

"I know American Express charges vendors an extra fee. That should cover it."

"Thanks, that's very considerate."

He caught me with those eyes, and I tore myself away.

"Those riding lessons still stand if you ever make it out my way."

I bet his daughter wasn't much older than me.

"Here's my card, darlin'." The business card read Lincoln Cattle Co. in silver font over a black background. James McMillian appeared on the second line.

He winked again. "My phone number's on there along with my email address. Shoot me a line sometime." He turned and exited the store.

Backup plan No. 139: Sweetie and me on a painted horse roaming the prairie. We'd wear matching cowboy hats, of course.

"How's it going?" Minnie and a wide awake Sweetie joined me at the counter.

"Yippee ki yay."

Minnie looked at me strangely.

"It's been busy."

Sweetie held up her arms, and I took her from Minnie.

"I'm glad you're keeping a sense of humor," my mother said. "Sometimes the holidays can be trying."

I caught a ride with Amber, ensuring we'd leave the party together. As we headed to Kent's lakeside house, Amber looked cheery in a red plaid coat and crimson blouse. She wore jeans, although her black pants were dressier than my indigo Levi's.

269

At Minnie's cajoling, I wore her candy-cane print blouse that tied in a bow at the neck. It wasn't my style, but I acquiesced to the spirit of the season.

We pulled into Kent's drive lined in luminaries, candles flickering in brown paper sacks. Evergreen wreaths adorned the double doors.

"Kind of strange, isn't it?" Amber said. "Just the three of us."

I shrugged. "Guess he's lonely."

Kent answered the door in a gray dress shirt and bright red tie with holly leaves running down the middle. "Merry Christmas!"

He ushered us past the formal dining room where the table was set with a red tablecloth, three place settings, and white pillar candles, and led us to the great room. The gas fireplace was blazing. Red decorative pillows had been added to his gray sectional. In the corner, ornaments swamped an artificial tree to the point of obliterating the branches. Lit candles glimmered on the counter and cooking island, all anchored with evergreen branches. The scent of fresh pine and cinnamon candles filled the air. Kent had gone out of his way to decorate the house.

Amber whispered over my shoulder, "He should have his own decorating show."

"I thought we'd have drinks before dinner." He popped the top from a champagne bottle and poured pink bubbly in our glasses. Amber poked me in the ribs and pointed her chin. Between the great room and dining room, a strand of mistletoe hung. No pausing in that doorway.

"Here's to us and a bright holiday season." Kent raised his glass and we all toasted.

"Your tree is pretty," I said.

"The whole house looks nice," Amber added.

"Thank you. I really like to get into the spirit."

Poor Kent. He needed a nice little wife. I imagined a country club type with perfect hair—and teeth—who followed the latest fashions.

There was a period of uncomfortable silence until Kent played some Christmas tunes that rang out from multiple speakers. Another painful pause in the conversation had me surveying the room and wondering what to say next.

"Good champagne," I said.

"Yeah, great champagne," Amber said.

"The liquor store clerk claimed this was the best brand." Kent looked uncertain. "I don't usually drink champagne."

"It's great," I said. It was very dry champagne. The few times I'd tasted champagne it was at least sweet.

"Yeah, great," Amber echoed. As Kent gazed out the window, she grimaced upon a second sip.

Reassured, Kent turned back and smiled.

"So what's for dinner?" Amber asked.

"I have a treat for you, ladies," Kent said. "I had the food catered in. Roast duckling, new herbed potatoes, and the best artisan bread you've ever tasted. And a special dessert, but that will remain a surprise."

Amber glanced at me doubtfully.

"Sounds wonderful, Kent."

He offered refills of champagne, and I waited to see if Amber would have another glass.

"No more for me," Amber said. "I'm driving."

"I'll have one more," I said, not wishing to hurt his feelings.

After admiring individual tree ornaments, complimenting Kent's tie, and gushing about the colored lights on the back patio that reflected off the ice, I was relieved when he announced dinner would be served. Would this night never end? I scooted ahead of Amber, clearing the mistletoe in record time. Amber hurried on my heels.

He seated Amber and me on either side of the dining room table, which left Kent to sit at the head of the table. A strange image of a sultan and his harem or an early-stage polygamous marriage came to mind.

Kent returned to the dining room wearing an apron fashioned to look like a tuxedo and served us individual bowls of salad. He joined us and offered a short blessing.

I glanced around the room. "I like your paintings, Kent."

"All by our local artist, Terry Redlin," Kent said, pleased. "I thought you'd like them, Liza. They're a great mix of local history and regional scenery. I know you like barns." He pointed to a print we'd had at one time in the store. The painting portrayed a farmhouse and barn with three mallards in flight backlit by a colorful sunrise.

"That's one of my favorites." I hoped he hadn't purchased it with me in mind. Had he?

Amber picked at the duck and scooted pieces to the edge of her plate. She tucked one morsel under a half-eaten dinner roll. The quiet was disconcerting, so I asked Kent about dental school. His response filled the next twenty minutes. Amber nodded off once and caught herself with a jerk of the head.

"It's time for dessert," he announced at last. He delivered coffee in a silver urn and returned for the surprise dessert.

I poured a cup. This was Minneapolis coffee house quality. I bet Kent had a commercial coffee maker somewhere in his gourmet kitchen. He returned with a smile and a silver tray.

"Voilà! Baked Alaska." He beamed.

Amber perked up at the sight. "I've always wanted to try that."

In keeping with the season, festive cherry sauce topped the browned meringue. I forked my first bite. "You've outdone yourself, Kent. Delicious."

"I like it, too." Amber dug into the concoction for another bite, the most she'd eaten all evening.

After dessert, Kent suggested we take our coffee to the great room and sit by the fire. How much more small talk could we possible tolerate? When Kent wasn't looking, Amber rolled her eyes.

For lack of conversation, I drank more coffee than I should have; I'd be up all night on a caffeine high. Thirty minutes later, Amber stood.

"I'm going to warm up the car," she said and made a hasty exit.

"I could take you home, Liza." Kent smiled warmly.

"I should be going, too," I said. "Might have to help Minnie check in new stock in the morning." I glanced at my watch.

Amber evidently chose to shiver outside in the frigid car versus strive for more mundane talk with her boss.

"You know, I could make a good life for you and Sweetie." Kent looked at me eagerly.

Oh, boy. Amber must have told him about Sweetie. I needed to watch what I said to that girl. "I'm still getting over my divorce, Kent. I can't even think about a new relationship." My standard go-to excuse.

"But it's been almost two—"

Amber, bless her soul, reentered the room at that opportune moment. "Ready, Liza?"

"Thanks for everything, Kent," I said. "This was wonderful."

"Yeah, great," Amber said. We headed to the front door. As Amber crossed the threshold, Kent softly grabbed my arm.

"Think about what I said," he whispered.

Backup plan No. 140.

"Good night, Kent." I scurried down the sidewalk and jumped in the car. Helen Reddy's *I am Woman* played on the radio. Miss Reddy would be disappointed with my list of plans, most definitely not of the "hear me roar" quality. I saw myself cleaning motel rooms, wearing one of those tidy housekeeping aprons, Sweetie in a stroller that I rolled from room to room along with my cleaning cart. Would that be better, Miss Reddy, than marrying a mild-mannered dentist or a ramrod rancher west of the Missouri? Would you roar under any of those circumstances, Helen?

Snow Magic

Wind whipped snow in every direction as it descended in clouds of giant flakes. School was cancelled, banks closed, and the mayor advised everyone to stay inside except for emergencies. Kent made the call to close the dental office for the day. Traversing icy roads threatened his patients more than tooth decay and gum disease.

By the end of January, I was winter weary. The subzero cold, gusty winds, and gray skies wore on me like a bad head cold. Would winter ever end?

The wind whistled around the corner of the building. A foot of snow blanketed the occasional parked car on Kemp. Most of the vehicles belonged to residents of upstairs apartments. Sweetie pointed. "Snow fort?"

"Not today, honey. Too much wind." With wind-chill factor, the temperature was twenty below zero. I wouldn't risk frostbite on those precious little cheeks.

If you didn't have to travel, South Dakota blizzards brought something magical. Snow obscured the ordinary world and transformed it into a wonderland of white beauty. Strange new forms appeared as snow concealed fire hydrants and parking meters. Soft edges made everything sculptural and mystical.

Minnie was in the stockroom, sorting her latest treasures. I set Sweetie's toys on the rug behind the counter. She had progressed from wooden blocks to being able to manipulate Duplo bricks. Since we didn't know her true age, I had made a trip to the library and done some research. After reading about early childhood development, I figured Sweetie must be at least two-years-old. Her vocabulary had increased, and she was now forming short sentences. Her repertoire of facial expressions now included anger, sorrow, and happiness. She could ride the small plastic trike Minnie had found by scooting her feet across the floor. Who knew? She might even be nearing two and a half.

I preferred to watch snow flurries from the front windows rather than spend the day in the balcony. The lack of natural light upstairs made me feel like a caged animal. I lit a gingerbread candle and soon the spicy scent lent a cheery atmosphere. Shuffling through magazines behind the counter, I came across a hard-cover copy of Watertown Arrows Yearbook 1964. A quick jiggle of mental math affirmed the book was my mother's senior yearbook. The "Dear Margaret" quips signed inside the front cover further confirmed it.

Dear Margaret,
Will miss your kooky sense of humor. Wishing you all the best,
Mavis

Dear Maggie—
You're still one of the cutest girls in the senior class. Look me up this summer.
Frank

Mag:
I'll never forget science lab. You kept me laughing even though Mr. Hanson never fully appreciated your lack of respect for his specimens.
Mary T.

Margaret—
What a blast we had at the lake. And we never got caught! You might consider becoming a counterfeiter with your skill at forging my mother's signature.
All the best.
Love, Bonnie

Obviously, my mother had a more spirited experience in high school than I had, but that didn't surprise me. Minnie's official senior picture revealed a Jackie Kennedy flip with lots of poof on top. Someone had written beside it: *Most likely to become a fashion designer.* My mother's eccentric wardrobe had proved that person wrong.

I paged through the yearbook and glanced at group pictures. One photograph had Minnie standing between two guys, both grinning like madmen. The caption read: *Fearless Yearbook Committee Members.* I studied the faces of both young men, searching for any signs of resemblance. After careful deliberation, I found no likeness whatsoever in their eyes, noses, or lips. I considered scrutinizing the photograph of every senior boy in her class, but what if my biological father was a junior or worse yet, someone who had already graduated? Considering the painstaking prospect of looking at all those faces, I gave up.

I flipped a few more pages. On the next page, a folded piece of paper stuck to the binding. I opened the yellowed note.

277

Maggie,

I think about you all the time. Your beautiful face is always on my mind. Make my dreams come true and go to the prom with me.

Yours always and ever—

Minnie trudged up the aisle, her arms weighed down with a box that rose to her nose. I hurried to help her place her latest finds on the counter.

"Thanks. That was getting heavy." She blew air up her forehead and brushed dust from her palms.

I held up the note and smirked. "Who wrote the love letter?"

She clenched her jaw. "Never mind." Minnie yanked the paper from my hand.

"He sure had a crush on you."

My mother grabbed the yearbook, tucked it beneath her arm, and marched to the back of the store. Case closed. She wouldn't talk.

It was indisputable. My mystery father would remain forever in the shadows.

A snowstorm raged outside the storefront windows the next morning. Few if any customers would leave the comfort of home today. I was about to look for Minnie and suggest we close the store when I saw her coming down the aisle.

"Hey, you two. Tea Time." Minnie pushed a cart down the aisle, a china teapot and matching cups and saucers jingling as the cart rolled our way. Sweetie looked up. The Bear Country stuffed animals sat center stage on the cart. Minnie had thought of everything. "We're having a tea party, Sweetie." My mother passed us and headed to the display window. She moved a stack of midcentury suitcases to the side and spread a 50s camp blanket. The teapot and accompaniments were placed in the center.

"Come on, girls." She waved us over and held up a sweater for me and a parka for Sweetie. The cold transferred through the expansive storefront window, and a current of chilled air rolled over us. I brought the gingerbread candle and set it out of Sweetie's reach.

So there we sat in the display window with snow whipping outside in a furious dance of white. I poured two tablespoons of peppermint tea into Sweetie's cup and made sure it was lukewarm before I allowed her to sip it. She made a face and stuck out her tongue.

Minnie laughed and sprinkled sugar over it. "Try it again. It's sweet now."

Sweetie clapped her hand over her mouth.

"One more time," I said. "If you don't like it, you don't have to drink anymore."

She tentatively stuck her tongue in the cup. "No like." She shook her head emphatically.

We laughed. "No more for Sweetie," I said and nudged the cup away.

"No, no. Bear drink." Sweetie gestured for the cup.

I brought the thimbleful of tea back, and she drew the cup to Mama bear's snout. "Bear no like." She wrinkled her nose. On the other hand, neither she nor the bears had any trouble with the sugar cookies.

I had a new appreciation for all the little adventures Minnie had provided during my childhood. As snow continued to fall outside the window, we succumbed to the snow fairy's spell of magic and mystery.

Beau called the first of February. "How's everything going?"

"Barely surviving," I said.

"How's that?"

"Tired of winter. Aren't you?"

"If I lived in Watertown fulltime, I'd definitely take up ice fishing."

"Hmm. Cooped up in a little shack, atop a layer of ice, the only thing between you and deep, frigid water." I raised and lowered my palms like weighted scales. "I'd prefer a roaring fire and a hot toddy."

Beau laughed. "That sounds good, too."

He hadn't been back to Watertown since early December, but he had called every few weeks, small talk mostly, but it gave me something to look forward to during the long dark nights of winter. I recalled his remark when I referred to us being friends. *I never said that.* His words inferred we were more than friends. Or maybe he meant, we *could* be more than friends. Whatever the meaning, he wasn't pressuring me. Friends were pretty much all I could deal with at the moment.

I hung up the phone just as a pretty Indian woman stepped up to the counter. "May I help you?"

The woman clutched a plastic sack. She appeared to be around my mother's age. "I have something for Minnie Murphy."

"I'm afraid she's out at the moment."

"Can I leave this with you?"

"Sure, I'm her daughter. I'll give it to her as soon as she returns."

She placed the sack on the counter. "Tell her it's from Raymond Standing Rock."

I nodded at the attractive stranger. My mother had said Ray had too many women. If that was the case, why had Minnie changed her mind about him? I shook my head. Most of the time, I avoided trying to figure out my mother. Minnie was Minnie.

I considered peeking inside the bag but valor won out and I refrained. Though what would it hurt to feel the outside of the sack? Something slightly curved and beaded formed under my fingers. Best guess: a barrette.

Minnie walked up. "What's that?"

"A woman left this for you. She said it was from Ray."

Minnie looked inside the bag but said nothing. "I'm going to the movie this afternoon."

"What are you going to see?"

Minnie rolled the top of the bag closed. "*What About Bob?*"

"What about him?"

"That's the title of the movie, silly. It's starring Bill Murray and Richard Dreyfuss."

"Who are you going with?" I asked.

"Reverend Wright."

That was an interesting development. "Have a good time."

"Thanks, dear." Minnie grabbed her purse from behind the counter and kissed Sweetie.

Did the pretty woman who delivered the package have anything to do with this new development? "Sweetie, let's go bake some cookies."

"Cookies. Yum yum." Her face lit up and she rubbed her tummy. I'd taught her that.

A March wind howled outside the window as Julie served meatballs and spaghetti in the humid kitchen. Spaghetti sauce smeared Sweetie's face like makeup on a clown. Jimmy pointed at her and laughed. Sweetie smiled, making her look even more like a circus performer.

"How're the divorce procedures going?" I asked.

Julie blotted the corner of her mouth with a napkin. "Jim agreed to give me primary custody with two days a week visitation for him. That part goes into effect immediately, but so far he's only taken the kids for a few hours on his day off."

"Why does that not surprise me?"

Julie glanced at the kids who were busy talking among themselves. She whispered, "Can't have the kids interfere with his social life, now can we?"

"Maybe in time," I said.

"We can hope for the kids' sake," Julie said. "On a brighter note, there's only two months to go before you can start adoption proceedings."

"I'm glad the required year is coming to a close." I scooted my plate away. "But I'm last on the order of preferred adoptive parents."

"But Ray will vouch for you, so will I if that helps."

"Don't forget, I'm white, single, and without a traditional residence."

"Maybe you can get a cheap apartment," Julie said.

"That's what I'm thinking. I better start looking."

"Good plan, girlfriend."

"Kent hit me up for a date again."

Julie shook her head and smiled. "That guy doesn't give up, does he?"

"I hope he's starting to realize it's not going anywhere. But this last time was a little tempting."

"How's that?"

"He offered concert tickets for Don Henley."

"Wow, that *would* be tempting. Where's the concert?"

"He said we could catch Henley anywhere he's on tour."

"Maybe you can put in a good word for me." Julie laughed. "I could use a nice trip out of state."

"I think he finally got the hint. He knows how much I'd like to see Don Henley in concert, so to turn down tickets…"

"Mm-hmm. He has to know now," Julie agreed. "Hey, kids. How about strawberry shortcake?"

The kids ran up, giggling. Jimmy hollered for extra whipped cream. Julie looked more composed than I'd seen her in weeks. She was going to be all right. The question was—was I?

More Tall Tales

O n arrival home, I found Minnie and Sweetie making Easter eggs. I tossed my jacket over a chair and surveyed the table. "Interesting colors."

"I used natural dyes." Minnie pointed to each bowl. "This color's from yellow onion, that one's from red onion. Beet, turmeric, and grapes."

I took a seat and watched her work. Minnie held Sweetie's hand and guided the white wax crayon over a hard-boiled egg. She drew a cross on one egg, a long-eared bunny on another, and stripes on the next egg. With a serving spoon, Minnie scooped an egg and dipped it into the turmeric dye. After a moment, she spooned the egg out and set it on a wire rack to dry. The egg was now a rich amber orange.

By this time, Sweetie crawled into my lap and cuddled. I whispered in her ear, "Sweetie's making pretty eggs."

"Wait until we show you Sweetie's Easter dress." Minnie dipped the last egg and washed her hands. "Let's go show Liza."

At the front counter, Minnie retrieved a plastic sack and withdrew a bright purple dress. I held up the garment. Knowing it came from a secondhand store, I wanted to check for stains or tears. The dress appeared in excellent condition. White lace trimmed the collar and sleeves. The skirt splayed like an open umbrella from an under layer of tulle. A self-fabric belt tied at the back. "It's adorable. Did she try it on?"

"Fits like a dream," Minnie said.

"'Dorble." Sweetie fingered the tulle.

"And I bought these." Minnie held up purple hair ribbons.

"Perfect. I'll weave the ribbons in her braid," I said.

"I better clean up the kitchen." Minnie returned to the back room.

It was fifteen minutes to closing without a customer in sight. The bell rang, and I looked up as two young Indian women entered the store. Even though they were beyond their teenage years, their appearance gave me a start. I never knew when someone might appear and claim Sweetie. The older of the two approached the counter.

"I have something for Minnie Murphy," she said.

"She's in the back." I said. "I'll go get her."

"No problem. Just see that she gets this." The beautiful Native woman had high cheekbones and flawless skin the color of cocoa. The younger woman looked closer to my age and was just as pretty.

"Tell her it's from Ray." The women turned and exited the store.

Too many women. I could see why Minnie started to date Reverend Wright again although he didn't seem her type. They say opposites attract but Minnie and a conservative preacher?

With a slight nod to superstition, I waited until after April Fool's Day to begin a search for an apartment. On April 2nd, I combed the want ads. We could get by with one bedroom, but

286

anticipating a rule from social services that required a child to have her own room, I narrowed it to two bedrooms to be safe.

Several listings for duplexes appeared, but they were more expensive. I found an apartment in an older house that had been divided into four residences. Only three blocks from Minnie's Antique and Curiosity Shoppe, the location would be convenient for dropping off Sweetie on my way to work. I liked the idea of being close to Minnie. The irony of this thought was not lost on me. I had left Watertown smoking rubber, eager to escape my hometown and my mother. Now I needed Minnie. Needed her to watch Sweetie while I worked, needed her motherly advice in raising a child, but maybe more than anything, I wanted my mother to be part of my life.

I put down a deposit. The apartment would come available in two weeks. I looked forward to having my own place, yet part of me would miss—hard to admit—living in the antique store. The three of us had been happy over the last eleven months. Each day brought something novel: new customers, changing merchandise, and with Minnie, there was never a dull day.

I dreaded telling my mother we were moving out, but it had to be done. I spilled the news after dinner that evening. Amid the lingering aroma of garlic burgers, I carried our dishes to the sink. "I have something to tell you."

Minnie set the casserole down and plopped on the chair. "You're moving." Her mouth drooped, and a glaze fell over her eyes.

She'd seen it coming.

I sat beside her at the table. "It's not like we're moving out of town. But if I want to adopt Sweetie, they're going to expect me to be self-sufficient. You know—that I have a stable job and can provide an adequate home."

She stared at the table. "I suppose you're right."

287

"You'll still watch Sweetie every day," I said. "And do you want to hear the good news?"

Minnie looked up hopefully.

"The apartment is only three blocks from here." I gave directions to where we'd be living.

A smile wiped the sadness from her face. "That will be nice."

I took my mother's hand. "To tell the truth, I'm going to miss living here."

She squeezed my hand. "You gals can always come over for a slumber party."

"We'll do that." I kissed her on the cheek. "We'll definitely do that, won't we, Sweetie?"

Sweetie wedged between us. She kissed both our cheeks and giggled.

Minnie wrapped us in her arms and Sweetie laughed harder.

On my first morning in the apartment, I surveyed the living room. A midcentury western rocker with embroidered steer horns flanked a slightly worn upholstered sofa. Minnie's housewarming gift of a steamer trunk served dual purpose as storage container and coffee table. A used toy box sat in a corner. Along the wall, stacked boxes forewarned of days—weeks—of unpacking. Secondhand furniture mixed with the few vintage pieces, but the room still looked empty.

"What do you think, Sweetie?" I asked. The room definitely didn't feel like home.

"Juice," she said and yawned. Sweetie slumped back against the sofa.

I'd forgotten to stock the refrigerator. I wasn't even sure if it was turned on. "Let's go see Minnie."

"Min-nie." She parroted.

I slid Sweetie's parka over her pajamas and shoved snow boots over her footed PJs. After a brisk walk in the chilly air, we arrived in the alley behind Minnie's Antiques. I used my key to open the backdoor.

"Well, look who's here," Minnie said, not looking one bit surprised.

Sweetie scurried over to Minnie for a hug.

"That coffee sure smells good," I said, eyeing the coffee maker.

"I mixed a batch of blueberry pancake batter," she said. "Bet I know someone who likes pancakes."

Sweetie bobbed her head. And so went our first morning in my new apartment.

April teased with sunny afternoons and warmer temperatures, getting our hopes up and our lightweight sweaters out. We made plans for the season's first picnic only to be greeted by windy, overcast skies.

I soon discovered the drawbacks of moving and spent most of the month unpacking, stocking the kitchen, and basically trying to find a place for everything. On the weekends we rolled into a routine where we watched old movies with Minnie. These evenings usually turned into the foreseen slumber party. Exceptions were made on nights Minnie had a date with Reverend Wright. Sunday mornings we attended church together.

One Saturday afternoon Ray paid a visit to the store. "Hi, Liza. Minnie." He dropped to one knee. "And here's our little shining star."

By this time, Sweetie had warmed to Ray. She smiled brightly. "Ray-ray."

"I talked to John Eagle Feather," he said. "We have a date set for the initial adoption proceedings. May 23rd."

"So, Ray, what do you think my chances are?" Not waiting for his answer, I rattled off the reasons why the court should see me as an ideal mother: my solid job at Swenson Dentistry, my newfound apartment, and the fact that I had my own wheels.

Minnie jumped in. "Those are all good things. Right, Ray?"

"Good, solid things," he agreed. "But they'll also want references."

Minnie turned to me. "Reverend Wright will vouch for you."

That was unexpected. I didn't even know the guy except for a few hellos and goodbyes as the two headed out somewhere.

"My friend, Julie, said I could use her as a character reference. She has two kids of her own," I said. "My boss might vouch for me, too."

"That's great." Ray glanced at Minnie. "I plan on putting in a good word, too." He winked at her, but she quickly turned away.

"That's nice, Ray," Minnie mumbled.

"So what do you think my chances are?" I repeated. This time I paused to let him answer.

"I think it'll turn out the best for everyone," Ray said. "I'll be in touch." He exited the store.

That was an odd response. "Mother, what do you think?"

She hugged me. "I'm saying prayers every night for you."

Why did that not reassure me?

Now that May had arrived, the pending tribal meeting hung over me like a bad virus. Beau was in town for the weekend and suggested a drive around the lake. I jumped at the opportunity to divert my worries. Along Highway 212, fields of ankle-high corn swept past, rows like parted hair weaving over the land. The wind blasted our faces through open windows as we turned onto the road that skirted the lake. It was good to see trees leafing out and grass greening. I enjoyed getting out of town and told Beau how nervous I was about the upcoming meeting.

"You told me this Ray fellow's on your side," he said. "That has to carry a lot of weight. And like you said, you've got a stable job and an apartment."

"Yeah," I said. "I just hope it's enough."

"And they have to see how attached the child is to you." He glanced over the seat. "That has to mean something."

We passed Memorial Park in silence. After a few moments, Beau said, "I have a gut feeling it's going to be all right."

I glanced over at him. My mother didn't have a gut feeling. I certainly wished I did. What did a man know about these things?

We drove without talking. I studied the passing lake houses, some mere cottages, and others grander constructions.

"Been doing any artwork?" he asked at last.

"I'm still unpacking." I couldn't possibly think of creating anything until all this was settled with Sweetie. A wave of anxiety swept over me. My chest constricted. I had trouble breathing. "Please take me home," I managed to say.

He looked over, startled. "Was it something I said?"

"I just can't—I mean—until this is all settled." I leaned out the window, hoping the fresh air would help me breathe. On top of everything, I was on the verge of tears and certainly didn't want to cry in front of him.

He pulled the car over to the side of the road. "I understand. This is life and death to you."

I nodded and looked down at the floor mat.

Beau turned the car around. "I know this is difficult for you. I wish I could do something."

Silence hung between us on the drive back. Beau didn't deserve this. I reached for his hand.

He smiled. We left it at that.

"Remember Harold Bagley's find?" my mother asked. Behind the counter, Sweetie was building a castle of sorts with her Duplo bricks or maybe it was a New York high-rise.

I wondered if Minnie told her friends tall tales about me. With a quiet sigh, I helped her unwrap the red transferware from an estate sale. "Is there any grass left?"

"Sharon said he made a mess of the yard. They'll have to reseed or add sod next spring."

I imagined his pockmarked lawn. "Bet he didn't find another coin, did he?"

"Always the skeptic." Minnie shook her head. "Actually, he had the coin appraised. Turns out it's a 1933 Indian Head Gold Eagle."

I unwrapped a cup and set it on its matching saucer. "Will it pay for the new sod he needs?"

"If it had been in mint condition, it would be valued at $500,000."

I reached for another dish. "I assume it wasn't mint condition considering he found it buried in his lawn."

"You're correct. It's only worth $6,492."

I swung my head up. "You're kidding, right?"

Minnie smiled slyly. "Sharon says they're going to take a cruise to the Bahamas or maybe fly to Europe in the fall."

I was speechless. Now I understood why Minnie always carried the red book for coins when she hit auctions. I unwrapped more pieces and stacked the dinner plates. That got me thinking about another of Minnie's tall tales.

"The day you saw Janice Johnson at the top of the windmill," I said. "Did you ever find out what that was about?"

"There were lots of rumors floating around for a while," Minnie said. "I didn't pay them much mind. Rumors are—"

"The devil's handiwork," I finished for her.

"Exactly. And sometimes simply the work of idle people," Minnie said. "Janice filed for divorce last week, something to do with a neighboring farmer's wife and a roll in the—"

"Hay?"

"I was going to say, a roll in the field."

"And thus the high vantage point of the windmill."

Minnie nodded.

"So her words, 'I do this every day' weren't just for sarcastic effect."

"I believe Janice stopped climbing once she had her evidence."

"Poor woman," I said.

Minnie tsked. "They'd been married for twenty-five years. What a shame."

That Sunday on Mother's Day, I grilled T-bones on the charcoal grill in the alley and set a bouquet of daisies, Minnie's favorite flower, on the table. Sweetie helped me sprinkle brown sugar and chopped walnuts on top of baked sweet potatoes. I cheated and bought coleslaw from the deli section of the grocery.

After dinner, I handed Minnie an envelope. "From Sweetie and me."

Minnie opened the card and laughed. "I love it."

Instead of signatures, Sweetie and I had put on lipstick and kissed the inside of the card.

Sweetie tugged Minnie's dress. "Sweetie, too."

"I see that," Minnie said. "Thank you."

"And for dessert, we have a unique dining experience." I pulled the concoction from the oven. I had spent a pretty penny, as Minnie would say, on buying the dessert from Kent's caterer. "For my mother, only the best. Baked Alaska."

"Oh, my. You've definitely surprised me this year."

A sense of guilt crept over me. In the past, I was doing good if I remembered to buy a card. Minnie rushed over and gave me a bear hug. That was the thing about mothers, they so easily forgave.

A dark shadow hovered over the celebration. Exactly eleven days remained before fate would have its way in the adoption proceedings. The possibility that I might never be Sweetie's mother haunted me.

Unknown to my mother, my primary backup plan remained in full force. For weeks the VW van had been packed with clothes, sleeping bags, pillows, toys, bottled water, juice, granola bars, paper plates, peanut butter and crackers. I never let the gas tank drop below three-quarters full. I had dreams about the van being stolen since all my savings were rolled up inside empty water bottles—the colored kind kids use on their bicycles—and stuffed beneath the seats.

In the meantime, I asked Julie and Kent to provide certified reference letters. I had the bank print out the past twelve months of my statements, made a copy of the title to the van, and a copy of my apartment lease agreement. I even hunted down my senior-year math teacher, Miss Woods. She had always liked me and told me I had great potential. Retired for the last five years, she was more than happy to write a letter for me. Minnie considered that a longshot since what did math ability have to do with raising a child? Undeterred, I stockpiled every endorsement I could get.

The week prior to the tribal meeting was pure torture. I had no appetite but forced myself to eat a little so I wouldn't look emaciated at the meeting. I woke at odd times of the night and had trouble falling back to sleep. Nightmares became a regular occurrence, something that hadn't happened since I was a kid.

When I found myself on the cold kitchen floor at 3 a.m., I knew it was bad. I hadn't sleepwalked since the age of eleven.

Two days later I woke in the bathtub, no water but with a heck of a neck kink. Thank goodness the deadbolt tended to stick, or I may have ended up on a neighbor's doorstep. I never told anyone, especially Minnie, just in case the court called upon her for a character witness, and she had to swear on the Bible to my competence. By the time the long awaited day arrived, I couldn't wait to get it over with and return to normal—even if normal meant a cleaning cart and living in a VW van.

The excruciating ride to tribal headquarters lasted forever. I didn't know which was worse, the unnerving silences or Minnie's chirpy attempts to lighten the mood. The heaviness in my stomach reminded me of the gravity of the situation. Even Minnie's face held a strained quality I'd never seen.

We met Ray in the lobby, and the three of us waited like a family anticipating the outcome of emergency surgery. Outside the windows, the sun alternately shone and then disappeared behind fast moving clouds, mirroring my emotions—one minute hope and the next despair.

"Taking part in the rodeo this year, Ray?" Minnie asked.

"Yup. Calf roping and horse races."

"That's nice." Minnie picked up a magazine.

Skillful horseman and rides like the wind. Another of Minnie's embellished stories turned into reality.

At last we were called into John Eagle Feather's office. He stood and shook hands with each of us. "Please have a seat."

Sweetie sat on my lap and played with her Bear Country bruins. Minnie held the folder containing all my paperwork and references like it was fragile glassware.

"I'll remind you this is only a preliminary meeting for adoption proceedings," John said. "This is a complicated case. Ordinarily, the first step would be the relinquishment of child custody signed in front of a judge. Obviously, we have no information on family in this case. Then there's the fact that some tribes do not allow adoption outside the tribe." He scanned our faces. "Again, we don't know the child's membership."

John Eagle Feather turned his attention to me. "From information I've gained from Ray, Miss Murphy, you have taken exemplary care of the child." He cleared his throat. "I also know the child has become very attached to you."

I swallowed hard. Where was this leading?

"Let me give you some background information that might make our required procedures more clear. In 1978, the ICWA, Indian Child Welfare Act, made adoption of Native American children by non-native people extremely difficult. This act erected barriers to anyone who wanted to adopt an Indian child without having tribal affiliation."

My heart raced. So I couldn't adopt Sweetie? My mind threatened to close down. I had trouble understanding his words. I heard him speak but I couldn't comprehend what he was saying. "I-I'm sorry," I stuttered. "Would you repeat that last statement?"

"We may be forced to offer adoption of this child to other tribes."

Tears ran down my cheeks. "You mean all tribes?" Ray had said there were over 500 tribes recognized by the federal government. My backup plan lit up like a projection screen at the movie theater, but what if they took Sweetie away today?

"Ray." Minnie grabbed his arm, her eyes wide in fear.

Ray searched my mother's face. "Are you sure?" She nodded and lowered her head.

"John, there's another twist to this case."

John Eagle Feather frowned. "As if it's not complicated enough?"

"Liza is half Dakota Sioux."

I swung my head toward Ray. He maintained eye contact with John Eagle Feather as I stared. My mother lifted her head and met my gaze, her eyes rimmed in red.

"That certainly adds a new element to the equation." John leaned back and braced his hands on the armrests. "Why wasn't this brought up in the first place?"

"I'm afraid she's not a registered member of the tribe."

"I see," John said. "So do we have birth records?"

Minnie wrung her hands. "I didn't put the father on the birth certificate."

"So we have no legal proof that Liza is Native American. You people are making this very difficult, aren't you?"

Ray glanced at Minnie again, and she nodded. He turned to me and spoke softly, "I'm Liza's father." Though my mind was jumbled, I definitely heard that part.

"Would you be willing to submit to a DNA test, Raymond?"

"I would, John."

John Eagle Feather shook his head. "That will have to be our first step then. Second step will be to enroll Liza into the tribe so she has legal affiliation." He shuffled papers on his desk, shook his head again, and sighed. "I guess that's it for today, folks. We can schedule another meeting after you've fulfilled those requirements. Good day."

Like a zombie, I followed Minnie from the office, clutching Sweetie in my arms. Raymond Standing Rock, my father? The stone in my stomach became a heaviness that rolled into my foggy head. Under a hazy sky, Ray turned to Minnie. "I'll touch base with you later. I'm sure you and Liza have a lot to talk about." Minnie nodded and guided me by the elbow. She escorted me to her van, which was a good thing because at that moment I wouldn't have recognized her vehicle from a John Deere tractor.

I fastened the straps of Sweetie's car seat. Minnie slipped into the driver's seat. The front doors slammed shut, first Minnie's, then mine. I glanced over. "It's true?"

She nodded but said nothing more. At that moment, I couldn't have handled any further information. We drove back to Watertown in silence. This was one heck of a way to ensure my adoption of Sweetie.

As we entered Watertown city limits, I asked one question—my only question that day. "All those years ago—the man at the movies—that was Ray?" She stared out the windshield. For a moment, I thought she hadn't heard me. Then a faint nod admitted she had kept my father from me all those years.

A Sweet Perfume

The following week I went to work as usual with one exception. I dropped Sweetie off at Julie's house. She agreed to watch Sweetie until I was ready to tackle the inevitable talk with my mother. Minnie didn't call or visit my apartment, and I didn't stop by the antique store. And I didn't show up on Saturday to work.

"Min-nie?" Sweetie asked at least three times a day.

"Later, honey," I said. "We'll see her later."

I felt indescribable anger toward my mother. How hard would it have been to tell the truth? Teenage pregnancies happen. Why hadn't she been up-front with me? But realizing I might have known my father all these years was the deepest cut.

How many times as a child had I ached to have a father like the rest of my friends? A man to hold me on his knee, to tell me I was his precious little girl. Instead my mother had kept all that from me.

Amber leaned over the counter, her brows knitted together. "Are you all right?"

"Just tired, I guess." I took a deep breath. In fact, I obsessed 24/7 about what it might have been like as a child to know my father, something I could never get back.

I shuffled through my emotions for several days. Minnie hadn't intentionally wanted to hurt me. She thought she was doing the right thing for everyone. I considered the extent I'd been willing to go through for Sweetie. Not all the best decisions made there. Most of all, I missed Minnie.

The following weekend I called my mother. "Can we meet Sunday afternoon?"

"Of course, honey and bring Sweetie."

"I'm dropping her off at Julie's. You and I need to talk alone."

Minnie's voice dropped to just above a whisper. "Whatever you think is best."

The disappointment in her voice was palpable. I weakened. "Do you want to keep watching Sweetie while I work?"

"Of course. I love taking care of her."

I couldn't keep infringing on Julie, and the cost of daycare would take a nasty bite out of my paycheck. "I'll bring her over Monday on my way to work. See you tomorrow around one."

"I'll be here."

I planned on asking my mother to tell the whole story of Ray. How much would my mother share? She'd always been so mysterious. Was she ready to be honest?

I entered the back door to the store. The smell of freshly baked cookies hung in the air. Minnie had the teakettle on and a tray of oatmeal chocolate chip cookies, my favorite, sitting on the table. The situation certainly didn't call for a tea party, but I consented to a cup of tea. There was something about having a physical object in hand when conversation turned to silence and truth became difficult to swallow.

"Ginger herbal tea," Minnie said as she filled our cups.

"I had the DNA test," I said. "They swab the inside of your cheek and send it off for testing."

"That's good." Minnie sat across the table from me and stared at her hands. Her loud sigh broke the silence. "I guess the best place to start is at the beginning." She flicked her eyes at me and lowered them to her hands. "I met Ray during my senior year. I hung out with a small group of friends and met Ray through Billy James, who used to live in Sisseton. After a football game one weekend, Ray asked me out, and we dated exclusively after that." She sighed deeply and massaged the space between her brows. "This is difficult for me. It brings up so many old feelings."

I remained silent and sipped at my tea. I wasn't about to make this easy for her.

"Ray and I fell hard for each other. Shortly before graduation I discovered I was pregnant. My father didn't know anything about Ray and me. This might be hard for you to understand, but times were different in the 60s. My father staunchly opposed interracial marriages. He would never have accepted Ray. And it wasn't just my father. A lot of people would have looked down on our marriage, including Ray's own family."

"What did Ray think about all this?" I asked. This wasn't just about Minnie.

Minnie's face tensed. "Ray wanted to marry me despite his parents' objections. They preferred an Indian wife, of course."

"But you were pregnant."

Minnie lowered her head. "Ray didn't know."

"You didn't tell him?"

"I was thinking of you, too. Mixed-race children weren't accepted. Prejudice ran rampant against Indians back then."

My words rushed out in judgement. "So you just ran away."

"At first, I thought I'd give myself some time to figure it all out. I was pretty confused. Weeks turned into months. I had a job as a waitress near the pier, and I was making good tips. After you were born and I saw you would pass as a white child, I figured I could come home, and the only question would be 'who is the father,' not 'Minnie had an Indian baby.'"

Silence fell between us like a wet quilt. Her story painted an entirely different picture of my mother. My image of a carefree young woman caught up in the hippie culture was completely dispelled. I recalled her senior picture. Behind that smile hid a young woman, pregnant and confused. "So when you came back, did you contact Ray?"

Minnie reached across the table and covered my hand. "Don't blame Ray. I made no effort to contact him for a year. He was heartbroken. A month before I moved back, Ray had married a beautiful young woman from his tribe. By the time he realized you must be his child, he was married and his wife was pregnant. There was nothing to be done about it."

Had Minnie regretted her decision? Surely she had still been in love with him. But the sadness that hung behind her eyes kept me from asking.

Life went back to what it had been before. I worked Monday through Friday and Minnie watched Sweetie, who was overjoyed to be back with my mother during the day. I continued to work Saturdays at the antique store for some extra money.

Ray called Minnie and reported that the DNA test verified he was my biological father. The next time he stopped in with some beadwork, he acted like he always did. But on my part, a new tension surfaced. I had liked Ray as Ray, but I didn't know this man who was my father. One afternoon, he strode into the store with some paperwork for Minnie.

"You need to fill this part out and sign it before a notary." He turned to me. "This is the first step to enrolling you in the tribe, Liza."

I smiled weakly.

"This little one is going to have a bona fide Dakota Sioux mother." He patted Sweetie's head and glanced at me. "We're almost there."

"Thank you, Ray." Who would ever have guessed my own father would help me adopt Sweetie? Life could be so absurd and unpredictable.

Minnie swept me into her arms. "She's a great little *ina*."

His eyes fell softly over Minnie at the mention of the Dakota word for mother. "I'll let you know when the paperwork is finalized."

"Thanks, Ray." Minnie escorted him to the door. They stepped outside for a few minutes.

I felt sorry for Minnie. Ray had a large family, and Minnie only had me. I stopped—that wasn't true. She had Sweetie and me.

Minnie returned to the store. "One step closer," she said.

On a whim, I asked, "Where was I born?"

Minnie smiled. "A girlfriend and I were touring the San Francisco Botanical Garden when my contractions started. Ellen ran for help while I sat beneath a palm tree clutching my stomach. You were in a hurry to come into this world, and I was one of those lucky women who had a short labor. Before Ellen could make it back, you were born." Minnie had a faraway look. "I still remember the smell of magnolias surrounding us. The scent was intoxicating, citrusy sweet and magical. I knew from that moment you were special."

True to her word, my mother had treated me as someone unique and treasured throughout my childhood. It was a gift she had.

"Did you know the bark and flower buds of the magnolia are used in traditional Chinese medicine?" Minnie winked.

I laughed. "I never knew that."

Later that night in bed, I recalled the old story Minnie had often told me about my birth. She'd whisper in my ear. *You were born a flower child, birthed beneath the shade of a tall palm tree. Himalayan magnolias bloomed around your sweet little face.*

I splashed water over my face and grabbed the towel. My image reflected back from the mirror: the high cheekbones and dark eyes were definitely Native American. My black hair came from Ray, too. In high school, an acquaintance said she loved my olive skin, and I often received compliments on my shiny dark hair. A coworker in Minneapolis raved about my high cheekbones and claimed I should be a model. But I had never suspected I was Indian, not with a blonde fair-skinned mother and an anonymous father.

By August, my anxiety about Sweetie had lessened with the news that my heritage would ensure the adoption. That Saturday I dressed Sweetie and headed to the antique store to work. We stood at the front door and waved at Minnie, who rushed over and unlocked the door.

Minnie picked up Sweetie and hugged her. "I have a pie baking in the oven."

I set my purse behind the counter. "What kind?"

"Rhubarb—"

"Pucker pie," I finished for her. I looked at Sweetie and pursed my lips, like I was sucking on a lemon. "Does Sweetie want rhubarb pucker pie?"

Sweetie stuck her lips out and made kissing sounds.

"Even with sugar," I said, "I don't think she'll like it."

The bells rang out, and Ray's tall frame filled the doorway.

Minnie rushed over to greet him. She hadn't been seeing Reverend Wright for months. Who could figure out this woman?

They approached the counter together, and Ray held out his arms for Sweetie. She smiled and ran to him. It dawned on me that Sweetie would be his granddaughter, by adoption anyway.

"I brought you something, Liza." He handed me a large manila envelope.

I unhooked the clasp and withdrew the papers. Smiling, I looked up. "It's official. I'm a registered member of the Sisseton Wahpeton Oyate tribe."

Ray stepped up and wrapped me in an uncharacteristic hug. "Welcome to the tribe. I have something else for you." He pulled a small buckskin pouch from his pocket and placed a bracelet on my wrist.

The colorful bracelet had blue, yellow, red, orange, and white beads. "It's beautiful."

"It's to commemorate your entry into the tribe. The glass beads are sewn on a piece of flexible metal. It's made with Peyote stitching. Each bead is attached to the next so be careful not to hit the bracelet against something or all the beads will loosen."

"Thank you. I'll save it for special occasions."

"Now the adoption can proceed. I don't foresee any problems with gaining permanent custody of Sweetie."

"How long does it take?" I bit my lip. Tomorrow wouldn't be too soon.

"The tribal elders said it could take anywhere from six months to two years," Ray said.

I slumped.

"There's no family to contact or to contest the adoption. I'd say sooner than later in this case."

Minnie's hand rested on Ray's arm. "That's good news. Thank you for letting us know."

"I'd like to take you out for lunch, Minnie."

"Go ahead, Mother," I said. "Sweetie and I will man the store."

My mother's face glowed. I imagined her as a young woman in love. So much had transpired since that time. I couldn't help but feel heartache for what she had gone through all those years ago.

Faint beeping sounded in the distance. The aroma of baking. The pie! I swept Sweetie into my arms and ran to the back room. The timer had gone off. I set Sweetie at the table and found a hot pad. Fortunately, the pie crust came out unscathed.

"We have to let the pucker pie cool now." I made fish lips. Sweetie mimicked me.

"Pucka pie." She giggled.

Months ago I had promised myself to encourage Sweetie's Indian heritage. How wonderful that I, Sweetie's adopted mother, was actually a Native American. I thought of the Princess and the pea story, where the young woman awakes to find herself a princess. There was much I wanted to learn about my heritage, and I had many questions for Ray. Maybe I'd even change my name to Ray's surname. Of course, why hadn't I thought of that before? Sweetie needed a strong Native American name. I'd make a request at the adoption proceedings—her last name would be Standing Rock.

Over the last few weeks, Julie and I didn't seen much of each other. I'd been busy with legal paperwork, and she had been traveling. In June she visited family on the West Coast and in July she vacationed in Montana with her sister. When we finally caught up with each other, I related everything that had transpired in her absence.

That explains it." Julie poured milk for the kids. "Mixed races make the most beautiful people."

Was she talking about me? "Thanks, but I think that's going a bit far."

"Even in high school, I thought you were exotic looking. You should have been a model."

"Minnie claims I walk like a man. She says I stride across a room when I should slow down and glide."

"I'm sure models are taught how to walk like that," Julie said. "I don't think they were born that way."

"Modeling's out of the question. I'm going to be a mother, you know."

"I'm so happy for you and Sweetie. You make a great mother."

Holly Jones's crude assessment still rang in my head. It was good to hear that Julie thought otherwise. I trusted her opinion. She was mother to two beautiful, well-behaved children.

Sweetie rushed up to me with her latest crayon creation. "That's pretty. I like the colors you used." Pleased with herself, she walked back to join Annie and Jimmy coloring at the kitchen table.

"Are you still seeing Beau?" Julie asked.

"We were never *seeing* each other," I said. "He's just a friend."

Julie narrowed her eyes. "Mm hmm."

"Just because he's good looking, you think there's something up?"

"Uh huh."

I threw a cloth coaster at her. "I have far too much on my plate to worry about boyfriends."

"Once the adoption is official, life will go back to normal," Julie said.

What was normal? It seemed the only constant in life was change.

"Ray said the adoption might be completed as soon as the first of the year."

"That's right around the corner." Julie winked.

I shrugged. "Better than two years, I guess." But to me, it felt like a decade.

A few weeks later, Ray stopped in the store.

"I'd like to learn more about my heritage," I said. "I want to be able to teach Sweetie things about our people."

"That's good to hear," Ray said. "The women have a sweat-lodge ceremony coming up soon. You and Minnie should attend. My daughters would be happy to have you as guests."

I glanced at Minnie and back again. "Do they know about us?"

"I told them about both of you months ago."

"Won't they resent us? I mean…their mother and all."

"Indian people accept the uncertainty of life and recognize the path is often winding. They'll accept you with open arms." Ray placed a hand on my shoulder. "After all, you are their half-sister."

"How many children do you have?" I asked.

"Four daughters and two sons," he said. "You've seen two of my daughters. They dropped things off with you at the store."

He has too many women around him as it is. Minnie must have meant his daughters.

"I'll find out the date and let you know," Ray said.

"We'd love to." Minnie placed an arm around me. "How exciting. That's something I've always wanted to do."

Ray paused at the door and glanced back. "I'm a blessed man. My family keeps growing with beautiful women."

Minnie flushed.

I hoped in time to get to know my father better.

* * *

Three weeks later, Minnie and I drove to Ray's ranch located seven miles south of Sisseton. The van's headlights cut through the darkness of predawn. Julie had taken Sweetie overnight since we were leaving so early. I prayed everything would go smoothly. Despite what Ray had said about his daughters, I worried that resentment would linger. How would I feel if I discovered my father had a first love before my mother and another child to boot?

The ping of gravel hitting the undercarriage carried us the last mile to Ray's house. The headlights lit up the name on the rural mailbox: Standing Rock. I pulled up to the two-story farmhouse and before I switched off the ignition, two women appeared on the porch. Minnie and I approached the house.

"Halloo!" Minnie waved.

Laughter rang in the dark. Guess they had to know my eccentric mother from the start. The two young women were joined by two more. The next moment the dark-skinned women surrounded us, and we were embraced.

"Come in," one said.

Ray sat at the kitchen table. "Greetings, ladies." I recognized the younger women who had come into the store delivering packages from Ray. He introduced us to his daughters: May, Pearl, Star, and Sunflower. The oldest, May, appeared close to my age, which made sense if he'd married a year after Minnie's escape to California.

A woman entered the room, and Ray introduced her. "And this is my sister, Annie." The older woman who had left a package at the store that day! His sister, not a mistress.

"We need to hurry before the sun rises," Star said. "You can change in the back." She directed us to a bedroom, and we changed into loose fitting cotton nightgowns that Star provided. The sisters waited for us on the front porch as a faint sliver of light appeared on the horizon. We followed them behind the house where a light glowed from a low structure built of logs and canvas. The cool earth registered on my bare feet as we walked on a narrow path. Following the Standing Rock sisters' cues, Minnie and I faced east. The pale butter light of the rising sun melted across the sky.

"In our tradition," Star said, "the opening of the sweat lodge faces east to await another sun to rise." One by one, the women ducked and entered the lodge. We sat around the low campfire. In the center, stones baked in hot coals.

"The trail that leads to the lodge," Pearl said, her attention focused on Minnie, "is called the sacred path of life. It signifies a plea for mercy and protection throughout the days of your life."

"The darkness of the lodge," Sunflower added, "represents man's ignorance, and your exit later this morning, symbolizes a reawakening to life."

Minnie leaned over and whispered. "I like that idea."

Sunflower, who appeared to be the youngest sister, took a tin cup of water and sprinkled it over the hot stones. With a loud sizzle, steam shot into the air. No one talked during the rest of the solemn ceremony.

Several minutes later May sprinkled more water over the stones. Pearl wiped her hands in the rising steam and waved her hands around her body. The other sisters followed her example; Minnie and I mirrored the gesture.

The temperature in the lodge rose and my skin tingled, beads of sweat forming on my skin. Star produced a sage stick and swept it across her skin. May handed me a stick, and I did the same. The clean fragrance lifted from my skin.

With a loud sputter, water was poured over the stones and another cloud of steam erupted. Two sisters chanted in the Dakota language. I closed my eyes and prayed silently, thanking God for all my blessings: for my mother, for Sweetie, my friends, and for life itself. I was aware of how much I took for granted every day.

At the conclusion of the sweat, Star opened the door flap, and we exited one by one. The sun shone brightly, and a slight breeze cooled my hot body. Life was new again.

Minnie beamed, her face flush, her eyes wide in delight. The sisters' chatter broke the stillness, and we were invited in for breakfast.

Minnie drove back home. "Ray's daughters are so kind. They're lovely women, aren't they?"

"They were great." I had detected no animosity among them. In fact, I had never encountered such gracious people. "The sweat lodge was relaxing, wasn't it? Makes all your worries disappear."

"It was freeing," Minnie said. After a moment, she glanced over. "You and Star share some resemblance."

I couldn't see it. Star had such beautiful dark skin and was petite where I was tall. "I don't think so."

"Oh, yes," Minnie said. "You share the same eyes and mouth."

Once in town, Minnie waited in the vehicle while I knocked on Julie's door. Sweetie came running when she heard my voice, her eyes swollen, and her bottom lip quivering. I snatched her up into my arms, and she clutched my neck for dear life.

"I'm afraid it didn't go so well," Julie said. "She's always been fine when I've watched her during the day. The kids all get along so well. But when it came time for bed, she became anxious. I got up twice with her in the night when I heard her crying."

"I'm sorry that she was a problem."

Julie hugged me. "I've gone without sleep before; it's part of being a mother."

"Thanks for watching her. I'll make it up to you."

Sweetie whimpered as I carried her to Minnie's van. It was only a few blocks to home, so I forewent the car seat and held her.

"Didn't go so good, I take it." Minnie said.

A tear escaped down my cheek. "She must have thought I wasn't coming back."

"Poor thing," Minnie said. "I'm sure she has some dreadful abandonment issues. Hey, Sweetie, we're back now." Minnie stroked her cheek, but Sweetie turned her face and nestled into my neck. I fought against outright crying.

"Give her time," Minnie said. "She needs time and a lot of love."

Quirky Traditions

I didn't leave Sweetie's sight all day Sunday. I wanted her to feel safe and secure before I left for work the next day.

Usually I packed a sandwich and spent my thirty-minute lunch break at work, so I could leave by five, but on Monday, I skipped lunch and raced home to check on her.

"How's she been?" I asked Minnie.

Sweetie spotted me and came running, her little eyes rimmed in red. "Lia. Lia home."

"I have to go back to work, honey, but I wanted to see you." I glanced at my mother. This wasn't good.

"She's been a little upset since you left." Minnie laid down a feather duster. "But I'm glad you touched base with her. She's had lunch. I'll let you put her down for a nap."

Sweetie's eyes were puffy. She must have cried more than Minnie let on. I snuck away after she dropped off to sleep and returned to work with lingering anxiety. Despite Minnie's reassurance she'd be okay, I feared Sweetie's sense of abandonment had been reopened like a fresh scab.

The next morning, Sweetie cried when I left for work: clenched fists, snot-running, hysterical sobs. Guilt hung over me all day like a London fog. When I returned from work, Sweetie clung to me. She wouldn't let me out of her sight, petrified that I would leave her again. The next day, I snuck out while Minnie diverted Sweetie's attention.

I arrived home to find Sweetie crying. Minnie shook her head.

"I'm going to talk to Kent about bringing Sweetie with me to work."

"Oh, Liza. You can't exp—"

"Just for the morning," I continued. "Then I'll run her home for a nap."

"I don't know…"

"Do you have a better idea?"

My mother shook her head. This was not a normal situation. Sweetie had serious abandonment issues.

Summer passed slowly. My mother felt terrible that she couldn't comfort Sweetie in my absence. Both of us felt helpless at times. Weeks passed before Sweetie became more content to stay with Minnie, and I could go to work without worry constricting my chest and winding around my neck like a noose.

Autumn stalked in like a wild cat. Life finally became more normal for Sweetie, but there was no way I'd leave her with Julie anytime soon. I wouldn't risk putting Sweetie through more trauma.

I now measured time in new ways. September reminded me that in a few years, Sweetie would go to preschool. But fear crept in. Would I still be in her life? Would I be there to watch her grow? The thought never left me that someone could still appear and claim Sweetie. One night I watched a show about adoption.

314

One poor couple walked away without a child the day the adoption was to be finalized due to a technicality.

In October I diverted my worry with preparations for Halloween. I threw myself into planning everything from a spider-web cake to a special witch's brew punch to window decorations. Browsing costumes at the mall, Sweetie chose the good fairy from *The Wizard of Oz*. We had watched the movie several times, fast forwarding through the parts that scared her, mainly the wicked witch and those freaky flying monkeys. On All Hallows Eve, Minnie and I took her door to door, Sweetie waving her wand as each homeowner appeared. I think she thought that made the candy magically materialize. She stared at the other costumed kids, mesmerized by children turned fairy, witch, soldier, Batman, and Teenage Mutant Ninja Turtle.

Temperatures dropped and cold winds warned of changing seasons. Most people think of carving turkey in November, but at the Murphy household, Thanksgiving brought pumpkin carving. Minnie started the strange tradition when I was a child. My mother believed Thanksgiving deserved a special kid activity. I can guarantee we were the only people in town who stored October pumpkins in the cold stockroom to preserve them for the following month. Behind the front counter, Sweetie sat on the floor and drew features on the pumpkins. Minnie and I took turns carving. I was in the middle of creating a strange one-eyed smiling pumpkin that Sweetie designed when Beau entered the store.

"Thought I might catch you here," he said. "Hello, Mrs. Murphy."

"How are you, Beau?"

"Say, that's a crazy pumpkin you've got going there," he said. "Isn't it a little late for Halloween?"

"This was created by Miss Sweetie here. One thing you have to know about the Murphys," I rolled my eyes, "we have our own little world going on here."

"Hey, if it works for you, go for it," Beau said.

"If you don't have anything going on," Minnie said. "Why don't you join us for Thanksgiving dinner tomorrow?"

"He probably has plans, Mother," I said, my face warming.

"I'd love to join you," Beau said too quickly.

"We eat at noon," Minnie said, "at Liza's new apartment." She proceeded to give directions.

"Great, see you tomorrow, Liza." The bell chimed on his way out.

He left in a rush as if the invitation might be rescinded. Notably by me. I sighed and looked at Minnie. "Why did you go and do that, Mother?"

"Do what?" She turned on her heels and sashayed down the aisle. I had enough on my mind. Ray had announced the final adoption proceedings were scheduled for December 23rd. Minnie called me a nervous Nelly, but I couldn't relax until the adoption was all finished, signed on the dotted line, and paperwork processed. In the back of my mind, a chance that a relative would surface and claim Sweetie haunted me.

On a strange whim and a sudden desire to become domesticated, I had offered to make Thanksgiving dinner at my place. I'd never been interested in cooking, but the looming adoption had me reconsidering my priorities. Unfortunately, I'd never cooked a turkey. I had purchased the bird, potatoes, and stuffing mix, but that's where my expertise ended. I was relieved when Minnie said she'd be over bright and early with cinnamon rolls and coffee. Loose translation: she would teach me how to cook a Thanksgiving meal.

I dreaded what Beau would think when he saw my apartment. The sofa with its worn spots on the armrests. The steer-horn rocker. The mish-mashed decorating. Oh well, it was what it was. With Minnie's help, hopefully the food would make up for what class the apartment lacked.

True to her word, Minnie arrived at eight the next morning. We had breakfast and promptly got to work. She showed me how to sauté chopped onions and celery in melted butter before mixing it into the stuffing mix. Getting that mess into the turkey's cavity proved no small task. With that chore completed, I slid the turkey into the oven, and we sat down for a second cup of coffee. I had cheated on the pumpkin pie and bought one from the grocery. We made a trip back to Minnie's for two more chairs for the kitchen table since I had only two. Then we peeled potatoes, my least favorite activity of the day, cut them in half, and placed them in a pot of salted water. We would turn the burner on an hour before the turkey finished roasting. Next on the agenda was a green-bean casserole, which turned out simple enough to make.

Amid the hearty smell of roasting turkey, Beau arrived at quarter to noon. I was relieved to see he wore jeans.

"Afraid my apartment isn't too stylish." Darn. I'd promised myself not to apologize. Couldn't take my words back now. I had swept the floor and dusted. That would have to be good enough.

"I like the hardwood floors and the transom windows," he said, glancing around. "It's cozy."

"Make yourself comfortable," Minnie said, "while we finish up in the kitchen." She winked at me. "Liza will be right with you."

Sweetie looked up from her toys, assessed Beau, and turned back to playing.

"She's shy," I said over my shoulder as I followed Minnie into the kitchen. She showed me how to mash potatoes with a little butter and milk, while she made gravy from the turkey drippings.

Beau appeared in the doorway. "I can carve the turkey for you ladies, if you like."

"That would be nice." Minnie handed him the carving knife.

I glanced at Beau in his denim shirt, carving turkey in my apartment. How strange—this cute guy making himself useful in my kitchen. At last, we all sat down at the round table, our knees nearly knocking against each other. Minnie said a blessing. Sweetie kept eyeing the token man at our table. The jury was still out.

"Everything tastes so good," Minnie said. "Isn't Liza a good cook, Beau?"

That was going too far. "Mother helped with most of it."

"I didn't do much," Minnie said. "Just gave a few tips."

"My kind of food—meat and potatoes," Beau said. "Delicious, Liza."

"Thanks." I didn't feel right about Beau knowing where I lived. I wanted to keep a distance between Sweetie and any man in my life, including friends like Beau. It wasn't fair for children to get attached to someone who might not be around for long.

Full from turkey and all the side dishes, we retired to the living room and allowed our food to digest before tackling dessert. Minnie had brought a homemade lemon meringue to go with my store-bought pumpkin. With droopy eyes, we all watched a disappointing football game with the Chicago Bears when a knock came at the door.

Kent stood in the hall holding a double-layer chocolate cake. "Sorry to interrupt but my folks are visiting, and we ended up with too much food. Thought you might take some dessert off my hands."

"Come in, Kent." Amber and Kent had helped me move into the apartment, so he knew my address. Behind me, Beau said something to Minnie. This was going to be uncomfortable.

Kent's eyes widened at the sight of a man lounging on my sofa.

"You've met my mother," I said, "and this is Beau Bartlett. He teaches art at SDSU."

Beau stood and extended a hand. "Glad to meet you. You're Liza's boss, right?"

Kent nodded and shifted slightly toward the door. Before I could invite him to join us, another knock sounded. Was the television too loud? I hoped it wasn't the renter beneath me.

Julie stood in the hall, holding a Tupperware pie carrier.

"I thought you were having dinner with your folks." I waved her in. "Come, sit down."

"Hi, all. We had an early dinner, but with all the relatives at my mother's house we ended up with counters full of dessert. Ma said she'd end up as big as a house if I didn't take some over to Liza."

"Julie, this is Kent Swenson, my boss.

"Glad to meet you," Kent said.

"And this is Beau Bartlett. Remember my adult-ed painting classes? Beau was the instructor."

Julie flashed me a knowing smile. "Nice to meet you, Beau."

"Isn't this nice?" Minnie took the cake and pie from our unexpected guests. "Liza, bring in a couple of chairs from the kitchen."

The situation grew painful. I hated to hurt Kent's feelings. He would think I dumped him for Beau. But was it dumping if we never really dated? My mother didn't think about these fine nuances. To Minnie, it was one big party. I steeled myself against the coming lag in conversation but saw Kent busy talking to Julie. Did I see a sparkle in his eye?

"What do you do?" He sat next to Julie on one of the kitchen chairs.

Julie laughed. "Taking care of two little ones takes up my days now. I was an elementary school teacher before I had my children."

"Oh, you're married," Kent looked slightly deflated. "Anyone I know?"

"My ex-husband is a police officer. But obviously, we're not together anymore."

"That's too bad. Will you go back to teaching?"

"I'll wait until the kids are both in school. I want to enjoy my children while they're little."

"I don't blame you."

"I'm going to put some coffee on," Minnie said. "Then we'll have dessert." She rushed off to the kitchen.

Beau smiled over at me. "That was a great dinner, Liza."

"Thanks." My gaze flew back to Kent and Julie. I was trying to hear their conversation.

"What did you put in that dressing?" Beau asked. "It was really good."

Julie asked Kent about his practice. Something about pulling teeth. They both smiled.

"Liza?" Beau asked. "It was homemade, wasn't it?"

I glanced back at Julie. "Yes, of course the turkey was homemade."

Beau looked at me strangely. "I was talking about the dressing, but if you raised the turkey yourself, that's quite a feat."

"Of course, I didn't raise the turkey, silly. Where would I have room to keep a turkey?"

Minnie called from the kitchen. "Liza, come help me slice these pies."

Sweetie showed Beau her bears, the famous Bear Country souvenirs she slept with every night. This act was monumental. She was warming to a stranger.

"Is this the Mama bear?" Beau asked. Sweetie nodded.

I joined Minnie in the kitchen where she handed me a knife. She whispered, "I think Julie likes your boss."

"No way." I leaned around the doorway. They were laughing about something. "Julie's just being polite. He's definitely not her type."

Minnie shrugged and sliced the pecan pie Julie had brought. "There's some Cool Whip in the fridge," she said.

I peered around the refrigerator door as Kent leaned in towards Julie, listening intently to her story. There was no way those two had anything in common. I glanced at Beau slumped on the sofa. A dozen dolls and stuffed animals surrounded him, at least three on his lap. He pretended to snore, and Sweetie giggled as the dolls fell from his chest. My heart skipped a beat.

"Dessert and coffee," Minnie called. "Come help yourself. We'll take it back into the living room, so we can all talk."

Light flickered from three jack o' lanterns positioned around the living room. Julie was hanging on Kent's arm laughing, Sweetie was giggling, and Beau pretended the stuffed bear was attacking him as he slipped to the floor like an eel. Minnie hummed the tune to *The Sound of Music*. I looked down at my feet—I never wore shoes around the house. One sock was black and the other blue. And so the untraditional Murphy Thanksgiving turned out even more unconventional than usual.

Dark Spirits

Sweetie dumped her bowl of oatmeal over her head, effectively plastering her shirt and hair. A bath, shampoo, and fresh clothes were in order. We arrived at the antique store an hour later than usual that Saturday morning.

"Sorry, we're late. Sweetie had a run in with her breakfast this morning."

Minnie's face was solemn. "Someone was here asking for you."

"Asking for me?"

"Asking for the young Indian woman who works here." Minnie braced her hands on the counter. "She was a Native American in her late teens or early twenties."

My stomach twisted. I whispered, "What did you say?"

"I told her to come back this afternoon," Minnie said. "I figured that would give you time to make a decision."

"What do you mean?"

"I know you, Liza, better than you think I do. The missing supplies, your new van." She threw her hands in the air. "I'd probably do the same thing."

I plopped down on the stool. "Did you see a car?"

Minnie nodded. "Older Buick. Blue."

I slumped and buried my head in my hands. We were so close. One more month and the adoption would have been final. Though the VW van remained stocked, I had finally come to believe my backup plan wouldn't be necessary. I straightened and glanced at Sweetie, who played with stuffed animals Minnie kept behind the counter. My stomach flipped. What if the teen came back early?

I picked up Sweetie. It was time I faced the truth. "I'm going to talk with the girl. Would you take Sweetie to my apartment? I don't want her around when the girl comes back."

"Of course, I can do that," Minnie said. "I think you're doing the right thing. You need to find out more before you make an irrevocable decision." She rounded the counter and hugged me.

"Please take Sweetie *now*." I lowered Sweetie to her feet, but in revolt, she plunked her bottom on the floor.

"I told the girl this afternoon."

"I can't risk it. She might return early."

"If it'll make you feel better, we'll leave now." Minnie knelt down to Sweetie's level. "Pick an animal to take to our tea party."

Sweetie threw the teddy bear to the floor. "No! Stay with Lia."

I stooped to Sweetie's level. "I need you to go with Minnie. Be a good girl for me."

Minnie grabbed Sweetie's coat. Sweetie shook her head and crossed her arms. Where had she learned that? I picked her up and balanced her on one hip. With much maneuvering, I managed to slip her arms in the sleeves and zip the parka. I kissed her. "See you later. You go with Minnie." A bout of crying rose to a level I'd never heard from Sweetie.

"She'll be fine." Minnie took her from my arms and hurried to the door. The bells rang behind them.

Outside the window, Sweetie's arms flailed over my mother's shoulders. If people claimed dogs could pick up on their owners' emotions, surely a child could sense tension. Tears formed as I realized Sweetie had picked up on my fear and was probably terrified of being abandoned again.

An unearthly silence overtook Minnie's Antique and Curiosity Shoppe. Behind the counter, the pendulum on the clock swung ominously, marking every minute with a convicting tick. Tock. I prayed for a few customers to arrive and keep me preoccupied, anything to free me from my fears. The wind howled out the front window, lifting a paper sack into the air. I looked around. It might be a very long time before I stood in this store again. Minnie would be heartbroken if we left. For that matter, so would I.

I scrambled for the box of tissues Minnie kept in the mess behind the counter. The next several hours would pass like dripping molasses. I lifted a box of estate sale items to the counter and worked to keep my mind occupied by pricing them.

The bells over the door rang, and I flinched. Agnes Peterson caught my eye and smiled. She set two cartons of eggs on the counter.

"I think I'll take a look around," she said.

"Thanks for the eggs, Agnes."

I sorted through the estate box. The only things of value were a chevron Bakelite spoon; a wooden hand mirror with the black paint worn off at the handle, the bare wood varnished from years of use; and a midcentury Ekco red and white handled ice-cream scoop in excellent condition. With a sigh, I set the box on the floor. I couldn't dispel the sick feeling that wound around my heart.

The bells chimed again and I couldn't believe it—Holly Jones. I didn't think she'd ever set foot in the shop again after my refusal to sell her a typewriter. She avoided eye contact and headed down the aisle at the opposite side of the store. Apparently, her compulsion for vintage typewriters overpowered the sting of our last conversation. Fifteen minutes later, she exited the store without a word. We hadn't received any new typewriters in since the last time she'd visited. I couldn't help but remember her comment that she couldn't see me as a mother. Maybe her remark served as a portent. Maybe I wasn't meant to be Sweetie's mother.

Once the store emptied, I hurried back to the kitchen and made a ham sandwich. I brought the sandwich and a glass of milk to the counter. The clock read twelve-thirty. I nibbled at the sandwich and hoped the milk would settle my stomach.

The warm room was stifling. I tried reading an old *Time* magazine but couldn't concentrate on the words. I flipped through some back issues of *National Geographic*, content to browse through the pictures.

Promptly at one o'clock, the teenager strolled through the front door.

She wore a blue tufted parka over jeans. Our eyes met and my stomach plunged. She approached the counter, and we sized each other up for a few minutes without speaking. The girl glanced around, apparently searching for Sweetie.

"The little girl," she said. "She's not here?"

"No." I gripped the edge of the counter.

She appeared alarmed. "A foster home?"

My jaw clenched. "No. She's with my mother." I took a deep breath. "Is she...is she your sister?"

"No." The girl looked around as if I wasn't telling the truth about Sweetie's absence.

"Who is she to you?" Maybe Sweetie was this girl's child as Julie had suggested.

She clasped her hands and looked down. "She's not a relative."

"Who is she then?" My stomach sank. Someone out there could be looking for Sweetie. "Why did you leave her here?" I had to know the truth.

"That day I sold you jewelry. You had kind eyes. I thought because you're Native American, you'd take the child in."

"So if she's not related to you, who is she?"

"I found her on the streets the day I planned to travel to Seattle." The girl glanced side to side, although there was no one in the store. "I'm from the East Coast." She studied me, her brows creasing. "She was dirty and crying in an alley, her mother strung out on meth. You could see they were homeless. The woman begged us for money, said she'd feed the child." She shook her head. "She didn't fool me. She just wanted more drugs. My friends and I started to walk away. That was when the little girl began crying, and the woman slapped her to the ground. I couldn't leave her there. That baby was Indian like me. Without thinking, I grabbed her and ran to our car. My friends thought I was crazy."

The girl looked at me with sad eyes. "I have a scholarship. It's my first year of college, but I couldn't leave that child on the streets. My friends questioned what I would do with her. I told them, just drive.

"They thought the kid should go to social services. I know about foster care. I was in one once." Her eyes narrowed. "We debated across several state lines about what to do, and still I didn't have an answer. I wondered if I should forget college and raise the child myself. Maybe it was meant to be. But how could

327

I afford to take care of a child? Then we stopped in your store, so I could sell beadwork for some gas money.

"I figured you were older than me and you had a job. You spoke kindly to the child. I came back to check a few weeks later but you were gone."

I spoke quietly, "You had to know if she was okay."

She nodded, tears in her eyes.

"The child is fine. She's happy and healthy. I'm trying to adopt her, but if you know who her mother is…"

The girl shook her head. "I don't even know what tribe the woman is."

"Where did you find the child?"

The girl glanced down and shook her head. She was smart. She was cutting all connections, not even revealing the city where they'd found Sweetie.

I blurted, "I love the child. I love her with all my heart."

The girl glanced up and smiled.

"You did a good thing," I said. The young woman's face wavered from behind my tears. I came around the counter and hugged her. "Thank you for saving her."

The girl nodded shyly.

"Do well in school. Make a good life for yourself."

"Thank you." She started for the door.

I called after her. "Do you want to see her?"

"Could I?"

I locked the store. A young man and another girl waited in the Buick, staring at us. Worry enveloped their faces. "Would your friends like to come?"

"Let me ask them." The slim girl rushed to the car, and the window rolled down. They talked for a minute. Car doors opened and slammed.

"I'm Liza," I said.

"This is Matt and Marie," the girl said. "I'm Shawna."

I pointed down the street. "I live just a few blocks away."

Minnie gaped when she saw three strangers enter the apartment. She grabbed Sweetie and clung to her.

"It's okay, Mother. We have company." I glanced back.

Shawna smiled at Sweetie. "She probably doesn't remember me."

After a few moments, Sweetie left Minnie's lap and showed Shawna her Bear Country bears. "Maybe she does remember you," I said.

"She looks good," Matt said. "You wouldn't believe how dirty and tattered she was when we picked her up. A regular little rag doll."

"Aw," Marie cooed. "She looks so happy,"

"She looks loved," Shawna said. "I can sleep better now."

Before they left, Minnie gave the students traveling money. They were all headed home on Christmas break.

I followed them into the hall. "Shawna, you said you've been in foster homes. Do you have any family to stay with?"

"My father died a long time ago. My mother finally quit drinking," she said. "She's a different woman without the dark spirits in her."

"That's good," I said.

After they left, I replayed the conversation with Shawna.

"Thank heaven," Minnie said. "I was about to run away with you two."

"We'd probably need both vans then," I said glibly.

Minnie's eyes sparkled. "That would be quite an adventure, wouldn't it?"

I smirked. "Let's save it for a vacation."

End of the Rainbow

Christmas Eve Minnie was abuzz with holiday preparations, but my gift had arrived early. Sweetie was officially mine in the eyes of the state and the tribe. Minnie came up with the idea to celebrate the adoption on New Year's Eve.

"What better way to celebrate your new life than ringing in the new year?" Minnie hung an ornament on the tree in my apartment. "Besides, everyone is so busy at Christmas."

The road to adoption had been a long, hard journey, but the papers were signed—earlier than expected. The event called for a celebration.

"Let's keep the party small," I said. The faces of Minnie's bridge partners surfaced in my mind and, heaven forbid, her long list of eligible bachelors, the Ladies Aid group from church, and her Saturday night bar buddies.

"The invitation list is up to you," she said, "but I think we should invite Ray, don't you agree?"

"Definitely." If he hadn't admitted he was my father, the adoption would not have happened. He had his own family; he could have chosen not to get involved.

The formal adoption papers showed Sweetie's official name: Michante Murphy-Standing Rock. We were slowly acclimating her to her new name. Sweetie would probably always be my nickname for her, but her new name held special meaning. In Sioux, Michante means "my heart." She stole my heart from the beginning, and it will always belong to her.

That Christmas turned into my best holiday ever. We celebrated the day with just the three of us—Minnie, Sweetie, and I—in my apartment. I baked the ham, and Minnie made the suet pudding, a recipe handed down from her grandmother. Who would guess that a pudding made from ground fat, raisins, flour, and spices would be delicious? Minnie served it warm, topped with cream and nutmeg.

Anyone with children can testify that watching a child open her presents beats any gift a person could receive. Sweetie squealed upon opening each gift. It didn't matter if it was clothes or toys, she picked up each item, hugged it, and moved on to the next gift.

I tried to explain to Sweetie she was officially mine now, but how much can a two-and-a-half-year-old comprehend?

"I'm your Mama now," I said. Minnie helped out and started calling me Mama Lia.

I didn't care what Sweetie called me. She knew I loved her.

For our New Year's Eve adoption celebration, I invited Julie and her kids, Amber, Kent, Ray, Beau, and needless to say, Minnie. Those were the people who had stood by me—and put up with me—during the past year.

Minnie had ordered a cake with Liza and Sweetie written inside a big pink heart. Painted in frosting, a mama bear and her cub each held one side of the heart. I almost cried when I saw that cake. I had requested no gifts, but Julie brought a beautiful photo album to fill, Minnie gave me a scrapbook that recorded a child's life year by year and grade by grade, Kent brought Sweetie a stuffed hippo, and Beau delivered a stack of coloring books and crayons for Sweetie and blank canvases for me. Ray presented Sweetie with a buckskin dress with a beaded yoke and gave me a beaded choker.

Julie and I had planned ahead. Her kids would stay the night, Sweetie's first slumber party at the apartment. That way we could put the kids to bed and proceed with our adult party. Kent never strayed far from Julie's side. As I looked across the living room, he grinned like the smitten bowl of Jell-O he'd become around her. She had confided in me after the Thanksgiving event that she thought he was sweet.

"Are you going to go out with him?" I had asked.

"Is that all right with you? I didn't think you were interested."

"I'm not."

"Take that worried look off your face," she said. "I'm not jumping into anything."

"He comes on pretty strong," I warned.

"We've already talked about that, and we're taking it slow."

"Kent's a good guy," I had told her. And I meant it.

I relied on Minnie to babysit on those times I caught a movie with Beau or we went out to dinner. With the adoption party, I made another exception to my belief that Sweetie shouldn't be around any men that may or may not be in our life long-term.

At midnight, we rang in the New Year.

"To Liza," Minnie held up her champagne glass, "whose heart is bigger than Mount Rushmore and Sweetie, my new granddaughter. May they have many years of happiness and laughter."

"Hear, hear!" Beau said.

Everyone clinked glasses and toasted to the adoption.

Tapping her glass with a spoon, Minnie diverted our attention. "I have an announcement to make." She reached for Ray's hand, and he smiled. "Ray and I are getting married." It was so like Minnie to upstage me at my own party, but I was thrilled. Minnie deserved to be happy.

Congratulations spilled out for the couple while I freeze-framed like the popular song I liked in high school. First, I'd discovered the identity of my biological father after years of not knowing, and the next thing I know, my parents are getting married. That on its own would have been enough to deal with, but Minnie was a big part of our life now. How would Sweetie—Michante—react to not having Minnie around all the time?

How would I?

The irony of the situation hit. How desperate I had been years ago to escape my mother's influence. Now I worried over losing her. Life had an annoying way of playing the devil's advocate.

"I'm happy for you." I kissed my mother's cheek and hugged Ray. We all toasted to their upcoming marriage.

Minnie caught me in the kitchen while I was putting out more cheese and crackers, chips and dip. She wrapped her arm around me.

"Oh, honey. Lose that sad face. I'm still going to run the store and take care of Sweetie. Ray and I agreed I'd spend weekends at his place."

"He's okay with that?" I whispered.

"We're not young kids anymore. We each have our own lives. He said if he gets lonely, he'll drive down in the middle of the week and see me."

"Our family's growing, isn't it?" I said.

Minnie winked. "It's a good thing, huh?"

I nodded.

Beau stood in the doorway. "Can I help you ladies with anything?"

Minnie waved him over and handed him a bowl. "Would you fill that with ice? We need to change the drinks to soda at this hour." She abandoned the kitchen as if it was on fire.

"So, lots of changes for you," he said.

"Good changes. Definitely good changes."

Beau stepped up and leaned in close. I closed my eyes, his cologne swirling around me, and we kissed for the first time. My face flushed as he withdrew. He winked and returned to the living room.

The new year had only arrived, and I wondered what lay ahead in the coming year. I joined everyone in the living room and approached Ray with a question about the Agency Pow Wow that summer. So many new experiences awaited me.

Later that week, I invited Minnie for dinner. I had an ulterior motive. Over spaghetti and meatballs, I asked, "So where did you go on that mysterious trip you took?"

"I saw the Great Lakes and came back through Wisconsin and Iowa."

I gave her a pointed look.

"Oh, you want to know why." Minnie gazed at the floor. "After Ray's wife passed, he was lonely. He wanted to spend time together, and I knew it was too soon. He needed to grieve, and I would only delay that process. And there were his children to think about." She glanced up at me. "How would they have taken our being together so soon after their mother's death?"

"Was there another reason?" I asked.

"I've always been in love with Ray. I had to get away or I might have given in to him. And there was you to think about. I worried it wouldn't be easy for you to deal with the truth after all these years."

"So the dating marathon, that was about avoiding Ray?"

"Mm hmm." She shrugged. "What can I say? You know me."

"One more thing. Were you seeing Ray when .I was young? You know, the man at the movie."

"Ray wanted to see you. You were his child, after all. But I was torn. Was it fair to his wife and children?" Minnie lowered her head. "I still loved him. I didn't want our relationship to go somewhere it shouldn't." She swallowed and fought back tears. "After a few visits, I told him it wasn't a good idea. Even now, I don't know if I did the right thing."

I reached for her hand. "You didn't want to risk coming between Ray and his wife."

"I was the one who ran away and left him. I didn't tell him I was pregnant. It was because of my actions that he started a new life."

"We do what we think is best," I said. Sweetie was a prime example of that. "It doesn't mean it's always the right thing."

Minnie's eyebrow lifted. "Isn't that the truth?" She squeezed my hand. "I'm glad you didn't become a fugitive from justice."

"Me, too."

So what have I learned in the last few years?

That love is imperfect and oftentimes disappointing, which was why I became a regular at St. Martin's Church. There's only one love that's perfect. The rest of us have to forgive others and oftentimes ourselves.

I learned a young Indian woman rose from the ashes of her dysfunctional family and was working toward a counseling degree with an emphasis on drug and alcohol abuse. Shawna saw a little life in jeopardy and acted without thought of what it might cost her.

I learned a child can steal your heart and change your life forever.

I learned that a first love doesn't have to be the last.

I learned that Minnie would always be her peculiar, mysterious, unique self. She would definitely not be your traditional grandmother and for that I was glad.

I've gained new respect for my mother. She made mistakes and could have lived in regret, remained despondent and unhappy, but she chose to see the rainbow after the storm and in doing so, filled her life—and mine—with a myriad of color.

About the Author

Lucinda Stein was born in Minneapolis to parents who had grown up sixty miles apart in South Dakota but met in the Twin Cities. Raised in Watertown, South Dakota, she later moved to Wyoming and eventually to western Colorado where she now resides. A school librarian for twenty-one years, she enjoyed sharing her love of reading with students. Her books have been finalists for the Colorado Book Award and the WILLA Literary Award. Her short story, "Sulfur Springs," won the 2011 LAURA Short Fiction Award judged by Pam Houston.

Minnie's Antique & Curiosity Shoppe is an outcome of the author's love for anything vintage and her fond memories of her hometown. In her spare time, she stalks antique stores for treasures and enjoys hiking with her husband, Rob, and their shelter-rescue dog, Opie.

Follow the author at:

www.lucindastein.com
www.Instagram.com/lucindastein/
www.twitter.com/lucindakstein

If you liked this book (4 to 5 stars), please leave a review on Amazon or Barnes & Noble, so others will be persuaded to read this book and the author encouraged to write more stories.

Made in the USA
Columbia, SC
31 July 2018